Also by Daniel Klein

Viva Las Vengeance

Kill Me Tender

Blue Suede Clues

Where's Elvis? (with Hans Teesma)

Beauty Sleep

Embryo

Wavelengths

Magic Time

Such Vicious Minds

A Mystery
Featuring Elvis Presley

Daniel Klein

St. Martin's Minotaur
New York

www.minotaurbooks.com

Library of Congress Cataloging-in-Publication Data

Klein, Daniel M.
    Such vicious minds / Daniel Klein.—1st ed.
        p. cm.
    ISBN 0-312-31940-1
    EAN 978-0312-31940-3
        1. Presley, Elvis, 1935–1977—Fiction. 2. Photographers—Crimes against—Fiction. 3. Teenage girls—Crimes against—Fiction. 4. Impostors and imposture—Fiction. 5. Rock musicians—Fiction. 6. Memphis (Tenn.)—Fiction. I. Title.

PS3561.L344S83 2004
813'.54—dc22

                                                                      2004042757

First Edition: August 2004

10 9 8 7 6 5 4 3 2 1

For Danny B,
my doppelgänger in Taiwan

Acknowledgments

Thanks to my wife, Freke, my daughter, Samara, and my old buddy, Tom, for their incisive critiques of my early drafts. Also, to Joe Cleemann, my editor, whose help with later drafts was invaluable.

Thanks, too, to Tanya van Breevort, for her generous supply of Elvis lore, and to Roy Blount, Jr., for sharing his awe-inspiring collection of food songs with me.

As always, I am deeply indebted to the work of Peter Guralnick, whose sensitive and thoughtful biographies of Elvis, *Last Train from Memphis* and *Careless Love*, I reread constantly.

Finally, a special thanks to Kim and Bev Kimball, who so graciously preside over the Third Floor Art Colony on Main Street in Great Barrington.

DMK
deeklein_1@hotmail.com

Such
Vicious
Minds

7

Background Music

r. Strangelove was wrestling with his evil hand again, but Evil was getting the upper hand—it shot up in a Nazi salute.

"It would not be difficult, *Mein Führer* . . . heh, heh, I'm sorry, I mean, *Mr. President*," Peter Sellers as Dr. Strangelove said to Peter Sellers as the president of the United States.

Elvis howled. Man, that Sellers was one heck of an actor. Not only did he play three totally different roles in this movie, but the Strangelove character was two powerful personalities locked in one body, each fighting the other for supremacy. Now *that* was acting.

"The man's a genius!" Elvis said out loud, but if anybody heard him, it was only the projectionist. For the second night in a row, Elvis had rented the Memphian Movie Theater after regular hours for his own private use, bringing most of the gang with him. After the first screening of *Dr. Strangelove or: How I Learned to Stop Worrying and Love the Bomb*, a couple of the guys had slipped out to go to the fairgrounds and ride bumper cars, and after the second screening, only Jerry remained, sitting a few rows behind Elvis. But after the third run of the picture, when Elvis asked the projectionist to rerun the last reel again, and again, and again, even loyal Jerry had drifted off into a noisy sleep. Never mind, this flick was too complex for any of them to grasp anyhow. For them, a movie was either scary *or* it was funny—it couldn't possibly be both.

1

Elvis had heard that the script of *Strangelove* was written by a New York writer named Terry Southern who was supposed to be one wild and peculiar fella. Southern had spent most of his twenties living in Paris, supporting himself by writing dirty books, and generally doing every shameless thing he could think of. That was the sort of life that genuine writers led in preparation for writing their deepest stuff. Good thing it wasn't a requirement for becoming a rock-and-roll singer.

Or was it?

Elvis was past thirty now, and there surely wasn't anything deep about what was coming out of him lately. Not when your last film was *Roustabout* and they were pushing a rerelease of "Wooden Heart" as your next hit single. Those were about as deep as a bayou graveyard. Maybe if instead of spending his own twenties becoming the Colonel's prize canary, Elvis had done some real rousting about—say, on a ranch or on a police force— now he'd be singing from the soul instead of from the sound track.

> *"We'll meet again, don't know where, don't know when,*
> *But I know we'll meet again, some sunny day."*

That was Vera Lynn singing sweetly off screen while H-bombs were making mushroom clouds in *Dr. Strangelove*'s finale. The end of the world accompanied by a romantic ballad. There was a word for that—overlaying something deadly serious with something trifling. It made you want to grit your teeth and laugh out loud at the same time. It set up a fight inside yourself between the part that says, "This world is in one sorry pile of trouble," and the part that says, "So what? Life is just a big joke anyhow."

"Irony"—*that* was the word. It was one of Regis Clifford's favorites; he used it to describe just about everything in his life, although you had to wonder what it meant to him if he applied it to everything. Still, it was not a word that Colonel Parker or his film producer, Hal Wallis, could even begin to understand. They understood gold, not irony.

"What do you say, Mr. Presley? One more time?" the young man in the projection booth called down. The screen had gone white and Elvis could hear the snap-snap of the filled reel still spinning up there.

"I imagine you've got something better to do than watching the same darned movie over and over again, don't you, son?" Elvis called back.

"I don't know, Mr. Presley," the projectionist said. "This flick catches me different every time."

By God, this kid understood the movie, and he was just a high school boy.

"Me too, but let's call it a night," Elvis said. He dug into his pocket, pulled out a roll of twenties, peeled off five of them, and set the bills on the seat next to him. "Thank you, son. Left a little something down here for your time."

Jerry woke up just enough to stumble out to the car, then instantly fell asleep again as Elvis started her up. It was almost three in the morning, but Elvis did not feel all that tired. Like most times after he'd been sitting in a movie theater for hours, the whole outside world felt movielike, like he was just an actor in the movie of his life. He considered going out to the fairgrounds—he'd rented that out for his personal use until daybreak too. But after *Strangelove,* slot-car racing and playing tag with dabs of cotton candy didn't appeal much. Elvis decided to take the long route back home to Graceland.

Man, why couldn't he make a movie like *Strangelove*? A genuine thinker instead of a genuine time-waster? The thing to do was just forget about the Colonel and Wallis, and get ahold of that Terry Southern fella himself. Maybe Peter Sellers too. Just call them up and tell them that he'd like to make a movie with them. A *real* movie. Maybe one in which he played two or three roles himself. Sure, he'd done that in *Kissin' Cousins,* played a straitlaced army guy and a country bumpkin in the same flick, but in the end, the biggest difference between those two characters was their haircuts. Yup, just get ahold of that Terry Southern writer-fella on his own.

At the gate, Elvis saw a pair of cars parked right in front of the portico; one was the Colonel's Cadillac coup, the other a Ford pickup that Elvis had never seen before. All the lights were on in the front sitting room. This sure was out of character for the Colonel—he was usually tucked in by ten o'clock sharp for what he called his "beauty sleep." "I keep waiting for it to work," he always joked.

Elvis waited a minute for the gates to open, then tapped a shave and a haircut on the horn. Jackson came wobbling out from behind a rosebush, tugging at his fly.

"Sorry, Mr. Presley," Jackson said, unlatching the gate. "Nature called."

"We're going to have ourselves some sorrowful-looking roses next spring," Elvis said. "What's going on in the house, Jack?"

"Got me," Jackson said. "But whatever it is, they been goin' at it for the better part of an hour."

Elvis parked in the driveway a good fifty feet from the house. Jerry was still asleep, snoring louder than a duck call, and having himself some sweet dream that put a smile on his boyish face, so Elvis decided to leave him be in the car. Elvis was just stepping under the portico when he heard Colonel Parker's voice through an open window. "Now what's supposed to make me trust you, Mr. Crampton?" he was saying.

Familiar question, that. The Colonel was always wondering why he should trust anyone. No big mystery about that—Parker figured everybody was as wily as he was.

"For one thing, my Carol-Sue don't want to embarrass herself any more than she has to," another man's voice said. "She got her own reputation to think about, you know, even if she ain't no movie star."

"That sounds reason enough to just leave things be then," Parker answered.

"Yup, that and five thousand dollars," the other man snapped back.

Elvis quietly let himself in the front door, headed for the sitting room, and then pushed that door wide open with both his hands.

"That's him!" a young woman cried, pointing at him. "He's the one who done me!"

The gal pointing her finger was a big-chested thing with her hair up in a beehive, the way Priscilla said she wanted hers, and with a sloppy-lipped mouth that looked like it could hold its own in a Louisiana gin joint. She was dressed sort of Sunday-like in a flowery dress that buttoned all the way up to her chin, but the way she shifted her hip as she pointed at Elvis didn't much look like she was on her way to church.

"Done what to who?" Elvis snarled back at her.

"You know what," the young woman said, more softly this time. For a second, it looked like she was going to wink at him, but she caught herself before she went through with it.

"Some things decent folk don't name out loud," the man next to her said.

This had to be Mr. Crampton, the man the Colonel was unsure about trusting. And the girl would be Miss Carol-Sue, Crampton's young wife or girlfriend. She looked to be about twenty-five, and Crampton couldn't have been more than forty. The Colonel stood on the other side of Crampton, an unlit cigar in his mouth. He was wearing his let's-all-just-be-friends expression, the one he wore to contract negotiations at RCA.

"I don't know what anybody could be thinking here," Elvis said, steady as he could. "But I have never seen this lady before in my entire life."

"Now that ain't so, Elvis," Miss Carol-Sue said. This time a wink escaped before she could stop it. "I mean, your eyes were wide open the whole danged time. Seemed pretty well pleased with what they saw too."

At this, Crampton gave Carol-Sue a quick slap on the backside. Yup, she had to be his wife—his cheating wife, no doubt. And for some godforsaken reason, Crampton had gotten it into his head that she was cheating with Elvis. Well, he wouldn't be the first man to have that particular fantasy. More than once, some seething cowboy had charged up to Elvis in Memphis or Hollywood or Vegas and accused him of having seduced the man's wife or girlfriend. One of them had even spit in Elvis's face before his cohorts could wrangle him away. Elvis figured that their women had probably swooned at one of his movies, or written his name all over their address books, or even, possibly, murmured, "Elvis," at what you wouldn't call the appropriate moment, and the fantasy infidelity had just taken off from there.

Of course, there was always the possibility that one or two of the women who *had* ended up in bed with Elvis—say, that long tall Sally he discovered under the covers when he came back to his hotel room in Vegas that time—might have had a husband at home. Well, how was Elvis to know? At moments like that, a man doesn't exactly feel like conducting an in-depth interview about the obliging young woman's marital status.

Men get more jealous than women. Elvis's mama had once told him that, and as he got older, he knew what she meant. When a woman gets jealous, like the way 'Cilla did about Ann-Margret, she gets all pouty and weepy and hurt. But when a man gets jealous, he feels like a freshly gelded stallion, and about the only relief he can think of is kicking the teeth out of whoever is responsible for that unkindest cut of them all.

But apparently Mr. Crampton had a better idea. He'd kick some cash out of Elvis.

"Now, listen here, Mr. Crampton," Elvis began. "Marriage can be a real trial, I'm sure. But whatever problems you and your missus are—"

"She's his daughter," Parker said, not taking the cigar from his mouth. They were the first words he'd uttered since Elvis banged in there.

"That a fact?" Elvis said. Crampton must have been a teenager himself when he knocked up this child's mama.

"I'm sixteen," Carol-Sue said earnestly to Elvis. "And I was a virgin until you had your way with me in the backseat of that pink Cadillac car of your'n."

It was all Elvis could do to keep from bursting out laughing. He didn't know which was more unbelievable: that this busty tart was only sixteen or that until quite recently she'd been a virgin. It was all one big, outrageous comedy. Yes, what this scene needed was some ironic music on the sound track, like the Supremes singing "Baby Love." He could just hear it in the background. Elvis grinned.

"That's statutory rape in this state, mister," Crampton said. He withdrew a stiff piece of paper from inside his shirt and held it out in front of Elvis. It was the birth certificate for one Carol-Sue Bobbie-May Crampton, born at Blount Memorial Hospital in Decaturville in 1948. Elvis's grin vanished.

"Little lady," Elvis said, looking seriously into Carol-Sue's eyes, "I am mighty sorry if some misguided individual took advantage of you. But that individual was not me."

"But there's only one Elvis," the girl replied. The way she said it, it sounded like a small-town deejay introducing Elvis's latest record.

"That's true, ma'am. And this here Elvis never laid eyes on you before tonight."

"Did too. And laid more than just eyes on me at that."

"Did not!"

"Did too!"

No, "Baby Love" wouldn't quite do it. How about Billy J. Kramer singing "Little Children"?

"Now let's be serious," Elvis said. "I swear on my mama's grave that I never—*never*—had any kind of relations with this young lady, and that's the end of it. I'd be happy to give you some gas money to get yourselves back to Decaturville, but that's it."

"It's her word against yours then," Crampton said, a smug look on his foolish face. White trash, that's all these folks were. Whenever Elvis used that expression, he remembered Selma saying that you never heard anyone saying "colored trash," because, she said, they thought it would be a redundancy. It took a sensitive colored person like Selma to notice something like that.

"That's right, her word against mine," Elvis said.

"And we just wait and see who the judge and jury believes," Crampton said. Oh yes, Crampton had the whole scenario worked out, probably right down to Carol-Sue's Sunday-school wardrobe for the trial. Or maybe he would get her up in a nun's habit.

Colonel Parker suddenly pulled his wallet from his back pocket. It was packed tight with hundred-dollar bills, and now he counted out fifty of them on top of the TV set. He then handed Crampton a blank piece of paper and a ballpoint pen. "Make out a receipt for 'services rendered,' " he said, then turned to Elvis and murmured, "This way, at least we can take it off your taxes."

Elvis abruptly snatched the bills off of the TV, but several got away from his grasp and floated like peach blossoms to the floor. Carol-Sue immediately got on her hands and knees, gathering them up. In the process, the top two buttons of her modest frock popped open, revealing a cleavage deep enough to bury all the gold in Fort Knox. Elvis wrenched his eyes away from this spectacle as fast as he could, but not fast enough. Crampton had taken in Elvis's downward glance and now shook his head back and forth, like a scolding preacher.

"Damn it! This is wrong, Colonel!" Elvis barked. "It's blackmail. And it's blackmail for something that never did happen. I'm not giving these people a cent of my money."

"Let me have it," Parker said. He took the money from Elvis, then made a quick half turn and handed it to Crampton. "Now get your sorry asses out of here," he said to the pair from Decaturville.

Crampton and Carol-Sue made a beeline for the door.

"You should be ashamed of yourselves!" Elvis shouted after them.

At the door, Carol-Sue suddenly stopped and looked back at Elvis with her saucy baby-blue eyes. "Of course, if you wanted to make an honest woman of me—"

"Get out of here!" Elvis bellowed.

2

Meat Loaf Blues

*S*on, there's no difference between true publicity and false publicity," the Colonel explained in his most sickly sweet tone of voice after they heard the pickup leave. "There's only good publicity and bad publicity. And what we had right here was a bona fide case of potentially very bad publicity. So let's just forget about it, okay?"

But Elvis couldn't forget about it. Paying off those two con artists amounted to buying their lie. It was like dealing with them in stolen goods, and that gave Elvis a slimy feeling inside.

"Sometimes a man's honor is worth more than any kind of publicity," Elvis said.

"Yup, that's just about what Jerry Lee said right before his career took a nosedive," the Colonel replied.

Elvis blanched. It was just like Parker to bring up Jerry Lee Lewis at a time like this. Not that Jerry Lee was ever that far from Elvis's mind. Both Elvis and Jerry Lee were graduates of Sun Studios in Memphis, and both were credited with forging rock and roll into the biggest musical force of the century. But lately, there were some people who said that Elvis should be handing over his crown as the King of Rock and Roll to Jerry Lee because Jerry remained the real McCoy, while Elvis had turned into just another pop warbler. Of course, in terms of record sales, there was no question about who was king; Elvis had heard that these days Jerry Lee needed to take gigs in Delta roadhouses just to make ends meet. But maybe that was just the point: in a genuine Delta roadhouse, nobody would sit still for one verse of "Wooden Heart."

But it was only Jerry Lee Lewis's nosedive that was on the Colonel's money-obsessed mind. That happened just seven years back: Jerry Lee was on a triumphant tour of England when his thirteen-year-old cousin, Myra, innocently informed a reporter that she and Jerry Lee were man and wife. The press went crazy: this wasn't just a child bride, this was an *incestuous* child bride. Yes, indeed, those rock and rollers were just as sick and depraved as decent folk had been saying all along. That turned out to be the last big tour of Jerry Lee Lewis's life. Fact was, some people said that if Jerry Lee hadn't taken that nosedive, Elvis would be begging *him* for the crown today.

"There's a big difference between me and Jerry Lee," Elvis muttered.

"Not all that big," Parker replied, gesturing with his head toward Elvis's bedroom above them. It was in that bedroom where Priscilla Beaulieu, age nineteen, was sleeping right this minute, and God knows, she had been sleeping there most every night since she wasn't much more than fifteen. Hardly a day went by when Parker didn't remind Elvis how hard he had to work—how many strings he had to pull—to keep the tabloids from turning Priscilla into the next Myra Lewis.

Elvis was just about to remind Parker, for the umpteenth time, that the difference was that *his* relationship with Priscilla was chaste—technically speaking, that is—and Priscilla would remain a virgin until the day he married her, the way a man's bride should be. But what was the use of going over all that with the Colonel again? The Colonel would just say—again—that if Elvis's fans knew he was sleeping in the same bed with a pretty young girl and *not* doing the natural manly thing with her, that would be bad publicity too. Maybe even worse publicity. So Elvis left it at that and wandered into the kitchen.

Cook had left a fresh meat loaf on the counter, the baking pan still warm. Next to it was his mother's old tin gravy boat filled up with mushroom gravy, but that had jelled into a pathetic gray paste. Elvis considered heating the gravy on the stove, but instead went to the fridge, took out a bottle of ketchup, and squirted half the contents onto the meat loaf. He took the whole pan into the den, sat down, and dug in.

If you were honest about it, a man spent more of his time thinking about food than he did about sex. Both are just animal appetites, and fact is, the only one of the two you can live without is sex. Yet sex was the only one they wrote songs about, that is, if sex and love were more or less the same thing, which seemed to be the case most of the time. Did anybody ever write a song called "My Lips Are Just Dripping with Barbecue Sauce?" Or how about "I'd Go to the Ends of the Earth to Eat Your Meat Loaf?" Now wouldn't that be one catchy number?

Elvis could just reach the neck of his old Gibson behind his chair. He swung it around in front of him, catching a gob of ketchup on its waist, plunked a G major chord, and sang.

> *"I'd go to the ends of the earth to eat your meat loaf,*
> *But I wouldn't cross the street just to say hello to you."*

Grinning, Elvis shifted down to a bluesy minor fifth.

> *"Woman, you always leave me feelin' so empty,*
> *But your meat loaf leaves me feelin' so sa-tis-fied . . ."*

Hey, why not? "The Meat Loaf Blues." A song that told the plain truth for a change: When a man gets *really* hungry, he goes into the kitchen, not into the bedroom. Now that would be a genuine revolution in rock and roll, wouldn't it? That Beatle fella, John Lennon, was always getting snippity in his interviews about how the time had arrived to see through all the lies of the world. But then he goes and sings "I Wanna Hold Your Hand," not "I Wanna Hold Your Fork."

Elvis laughed out loud. Now *there* was an original idea for a motion picture. This big-time rock-and-roll star decides he wants to sing about the truly important things in his life—food, and sleeping late, and reading on the john. And, of course, everybody tells him he's crazy, that it will ruin his career. But he follows his dream and records "The Meat Loaf Blues" and "One Flush for History," and lo and behold, his fans love it. The truth sets them free. Sure, this character would find the girl of his dreams too, but she wouldn't be some empty-headed ding-dong with a turned-up nose and a girly giggle, she'd be this tall French lady who could cook a six-course gourmet supper while discussing the Normandy landing.

Hot dog! Man, if he wasn't thinking just the way that Terry Southern did! That *Strangelove* movie was about the lies we tell ourselves about war, so why not a movie about the lies we tell ourselves about love? And about music? And about food, for that matter.

Elvis reached out for the telephone, punched in his private line, and dialed the operator.

"Operator."

"Morning. I want to reach a fella up in New York City, but I don't know his number," Elvis said.

"Is this . . . Is this Mr. Presley?"

"Yes, it is, ma'am."

"Oh my! I wondered if this would ever happen, you being in Memphis, and me being a Memphis operator. Nighttime operator, which there aren't that many of, you know, because not so many people call long-distance at four in the morning as they do during the daytime when they're not asleep. And there being a lot fewer of us nighttime operators means there's a better chance that someday I'd have Elvis Presley on the other end, unless you were asleep too, of course."

"Ma'am, his name is Terry Southern, and I do believe he lives in Manhattan up there."

"I'll see what I can do, Mr. Presley. First, I'll have to call information up there, and that can be a hassle, you know. They don't do things plain and simple up in New York City. No sirree, it's a whole song and dance just to get a telephone number from one of those New York operators who acts like it's some kind of privilege to be talking to her at all."

"S-O-U-T-H-E-R-N. First name, Terry. Although I suppose it could be Terence in the directory."

"I'll ring you back just as soon as I get him on the line, Mr. Presley. And listen, in case you ever need to get ahold of me—direct, you know—just ask for Lizzy, Lizzy Griswold. Or Grizzy. Some folks call me, Grizzy. So it's Lizzy or Grizzy."

"Okay, Lizzy. I'll be waiting by the phone here."

Elvis set down the phone and picked up his guitar again.

"Lizzy, Grizzy, Mizzy I-don't-care," Elvis sang. "I just want some peace of mind."

The phone rang. Elvis grabbed it. "Hello, Mr. Southern, sir?"

"It's me, Elvis. Carol-Sue Crampton."

Elvis cringed. "Damnation. What do you want now, woman?"

"I'm at a pay phone. Snuck out of my house with my piggy bank and walked a mile to call you."

"Yeh, well, that piggy bank must be pretty full after that number you and your daddy pulled out here."

"Weren't my idea, that business. I just wanted you to know that, Elvis."

"You went along with it, so it's your doing too. But you're having second thoughts about it now, aren't you, child?"

"That's true. But I am not a child, Elvis."

"I figured as much."

"I mean, I *am* only sixteen. And I was a virgin until you and I—"

"That's it! I'm hanging up now, girl!"

"But I just shouldn'ta told Daddy about it. That was the mistake I made. Shoulda just kept it 'tween you and me. Our sweet little secret."

Elvis shook his head incredulously, then hunched over the receiver and spoke more quietly. "Listen, little girl, I won't tell your daddy, but have you been smoking that marijuana stuff that makes you see things that aren't there?"

"I have not," Carol-Sue replied indignantly. "It's the devil's own weed, you know."

"Well, then, how do you account for the fact that you believe that I—you know—that I took advantage of you in the backseat of my car, when I know sure as there's a God in heaven that I never even saw your face before tonight?"

"I . . . I don't rightly know, Elvis," Carol-Sue stammered. "But I'll tell you this—it breaks my heart that you can't even remember the most beautiful night of my young life."

"You tell me exactly what you think happened, Carol-Sue," Elvis said.

"All right. I was out walking with my dog, Fluffers, round about nine o'clock, when your pink Cadillac convertible comes driving up Tinker Street and—oh, Jesus! Here comes Papa now! Out lookin' for me in the truck. I gotta run, Elvis!"

"I need to hear this, girl."

"Pappy will kill me. Meet me after Sunday school, Elvis. Out behind the statue." And with that, Carol-Sue Crampton hung up.

Elvis set down the phone and picked up his guitar again, but whatever inspiration he had been feeling before was now gone. He didn't feel the urge to sing about meat loaf *or* love. And he sure as heck did not feel like singing a song about a trumped-up statutory rape. The phone rang again and Elvis immediately snatched it up.

"You must've been hallucinating, child!" Elvis barked into the receiver.

"That's a distinct possibility," the voice on the other end said. It was a man's voice, and either the phone line or that voice had a whiskey rasp to it.

"Mr. Terry Southern?" Elvis said.

"Last time I looked, although I try not to look too often," the man said. "And are you Elvis Presley?"

"I am, sir," Elvis said.

"Elvis the Pelvis?" the man tittered.

"That's not a label I'm proud of," Elvis said.

"Hell, I'd be proud of it," Southern said. "It's not a bone that women take much note of in my anatomy."

Elvis had to smile. The man talked like a writer. "What bone do they take note of, Mr. Southern?"

"The one between my ears," Southern said. "Listen, Presley, did you ever consider that most people tend to be asleep at five in the morning?"

"Afraid I didn't think about it one way or the other," Elvis said. "I'm sorry if I woke you."

"As it happens, I was just going to bed." Elvis could hear Southern light a match, then take a deep inhale. "But I assume you didn't call to inquire about my sleeping habits."

"No, sir. I'm calling because I want you to write a movie for me. And maybe for Mr. Peter Sellers too. Something like *Dr. Strangelove*. Only different, of course."

"The same but different, eh?" Southern said, chortling. It was not a pleasant laugh. "You sound just like a Hollywood producer, Presley. Same, but different. Tall, yet short. A formula film, but totally new."

"That's not what I'm saying," Elvis replied testily. "I'm just saying I want something with the same kind of irony you put in *Strangelove,* if you follow my meaning."

Elvis heard Southern take another long draw on his cigarette.

"Well, I must admit, that's not what I expected to hear you say," Southern said. He sounded impressed, and for a moment, that pissed Elvis off. Why does everybody always assume that my own mind is just as undeveloped as those of the characters I play in my movies? he wondered. One reason, he figured, is because these northerners have the idea that everybody south of Roanoke is several bricks short of a full load. They think the reason we talk slower than they do is because there is a speed limit on our thought processes. It would never occur to them that we linger over our words because they feel so succulent in our mouths.

"I'm serious," Elvis said.

17

"I'm expensive," Southern replied.

"We can work something out."

"I suppose you have an idea for this script."

"I do."

"And what would that be, Presley?"

"Meat loaf," Elvis said.

Southern's laugh was so loud and scratchy that Elvis had to hold the phone away from his ear.

"That's the best idea for a movie I have heard in a long time," Southern said, finally. "Tell you what, Elvis. You send me a plane ticket and I'll come down there so we can talk. I've been needing a little change of scene anyhow."

Elvis left a note on Jerry's desk to wire a plane ticket for Memphis up to Mr. Terry Southern, and then, as the sun rose, Elvis went to bed.

3

Doomsday Ditty

I see you found my meat loaf," Cook Mary said as Elvis ambled into the kitchen in his silk pj's.

"Found it and finished it," Elvis said, gingerly picking a strip of bacon off a hot skillet on the stove. "As good as my mama's and then some."

"Secret's in the bread crumbs," Cook said. She was rinsing collards under the spigot and only turned her round black face to his for a second for his good-morning smile. "Soak 'em for a day in knuckle fat. That's where all the bass notes in the flavor come from."

Elvis beamed. Priscilla sometimes said that the reason he was in no hurry to marry her was because he was already married to Cook Mary. More than an ounce of truth in that. On the cover of Mama's one and only cookbook, *The Settlement Cookbook,* it said: "The way to a man's heart is through his stomach."

"How come they don't write songs about food, Mary?" Elvis said, sitting down at the counter.

"Where have you been at, Mr. P?" Cook said. "Ain't you never heard Ella Mae Morse's 'Solid Potato Salad'? Or Junior Walker sing 'Home Cookin'?"

"Sure, but—" Cook slid a plate of piping hot biscuits covered with redeye gravy in front of Elvis. Man, how did she always have them ready just as he stumbled down the stairs, sometimes as late as two in the afternoon? She sensed when he was going to wake up before he did.

"Or how about Jelly Roll's 'Big Fat Ham'? Or Junior Brown's 'Peelin' Taters'?" Mary went on.

"I'm talking about songs that go to the top of the charts," Elvis said, stuffing an entire slippery biscuit into his mouth.

"Like 'Wooden Heart' is gonna be," Mary said, fussing with the greens again.

Was there just a bass note of sarcasm in the way she named his new single? Elvis chewed hard on his biscuit. Of all the people working at Graceland, Cook Mary was the only one he could count on to say what she truly believed, no gravy added to make it go down easier.

"Not my best, is it, Mary?" Elvis said.

"Not your worst, either," she said. "But I gotta admit that any song that starts off by rhyming 'heart in two' with 'hard to do' has a long way to travel before it sets my heart on fire. Not to mention all that German double-talk in the middle."

Elvis felt a ripple of rancor. If anybody else had said something like that about a song he'd recorded, Elvis would have snapped his head off. And in this case the main reason for that would have been because he was dead right. It was German double-talk, all right.

"They don't write truly good songs about sleeping late either," Elvis said. "Or about reading in the bathroom or watching TV or picking your nose."

Cook issued a big booming laugh. "You got some imagination, Mr. P," she said.

"I'm talking about songs that see life like it is, not life in some fairy tale," Elvis said.

"Hallelujah to that," Cook said. "But you know, Mr. P, folks want a song to take them to a better life than the one they're stuck with. To give their dreams a melody."

"But what if a song gave their own true life a melody? Gave it wings? Made them see the glory in what's right in front of them?"

"Now that would be one fine song," Cook laughed. "A gospel number dedicated to the glory of washing a bushel of collard greens!"

"Now that's an idea who's time has come!" Elvis laughed back.

Cook wiped her hands on her apron, then reached into one of its pockets. "A letter came for you this mornin', Mr. P. Special delivery, signed for it myself. I didn't think they delivered on Sundays." She put an envelope on the counter next to Elvis's plate.

It was covered with high-priced stamps and a half dozen cancellation marks, and in the left-hand corner it said, "Sheriff Timothy 'Tip' Oliphant, 3 Main Street, Waynesboro, Tennessee." Hot digitty! Another deputy badge for his collection. Ever since the *Commercial Appeal* had run that article about Elvis liking to be sworn in as deputy sheriff anywhere he could, he received a phone call or a letter with an offer at least once a week. Elvis ripped open the envelope and flattened the letter in front of him.

Dear Mr. Elvis Presley,
You've got yourself one heck of a problem out here and I hope I can be of assistance in solving it for you. But it's going to take some doing.

You'd best call me soon as you get this, Waynesboro 846, or there's no telling what this young girl's going to do. I think you know what I'm talking about.

Your fan,
Sheriff Tip

Holy moley, that Carol-Sue child and her daddy sure were busy. And, darn it, the Colonel *had* been wrong: if you pay folks blackmail, they don't go away—they just come back for more! But why were the Cramptons grousing to the law over in Waynesboro when they came from Decaturville? Carol-Sue claimed that her backseat ruination had transpired when she was out walking her dog, but she sure as heck wouldn't be dog-walking a whole county away from home.

Elvis lifted the plate of biscuits in one hand, the letter in the other, and strode to the den, where he kicked the door closed behind him. One way or the other, it seemed like women were always kicking up some kind of a calamity in his life. And they surely took up far too much space in his mind. No wonder he wanted to sing about meat loaf. He dialed up Waynesboro.

"Sheriff Tip, at your service."

"Elvis Presley here."

The man at the other end let out a 'Whoopee!' worthy of a rodeo.

"It's an honor, Elvis," he said finally. "I am your number one fan in all of Tennessee."

"Glad to hear that, Sheriff."

"And I am glad to hear *you* whenever I can. Which is just about most of the time. Why just this minute, I had 'Wooden Heart' on the turntable right here on my desk. That's a song for the ages, I'll tell you."

For just an instant, Elvis considered quizzing the man about what he thought about that German verse, but then thought better of it.

"You wrote that I got some kind of problem over there in Waynesboro," Elvis said.

"Afraid so," Sheriff Tip said, lowering his voice. "More like a catastrophe than a problem."

"Miss Carol-Sue Crampton?" Elvis murmured.

"Who?"

"I thought—"

"It's the Kent girl, Elvis. Jeffrey and Mary-Lou's eldest. The one that's got 'jailbait' written all over her fifteen-year-old bosom. You shoulda read the fine print."

"I never saw the girl in my life, Sheriff. In fact, I haven't been near Waynesboro for a good three years."

"That's not the way Muffy Kent tells it," Oliphant said. "Of course, she's a melungeon, you know—you can see it in her lips. Got those from her nigra granddaddy."

"What the hell does that have to do with anything?" Elvis snapped back, then immediately regretted it. It sounded like something that a guilty man would say.

"I figure we should talk in person, Elvis," Oliphant went on. "Maybe we can do a little honest horse trading, if you gather my drift. I could come down to your place right about now, actually."

"I'll come there," Elvis said.

"Just trying to be accommodating," Oliphant said, sounding disappointed. He obviously had been hoping to get a personal tour of Graceland along with his other horse trades. "We'll be waiting for ya."

To keep folks from rubbernecking, Elvis borrowed Jerry's Chevy pickup for the trip. For the same reason, he dug out his race car driver jumpsuit from *Viva Las Vegas* and put it on, although it felt a little snugger in the waist than the last time around the track. He figured it made him look more like a gas station attendant than whatever the heck he was supposed to look like these days. Half the time when he got all dressed up in a flowing silk shirt and skintight trousers, he felt like a bad actor playing a movie star.

When Elvis flipped on the truck radio, out came the stentorian voice of a hellfire preacher who was running through the most exhaustive litany of sins Elvis ever did hear. Not just the sin of lust in general, nor lusting after thy neighbor's wife in particular, but lusting after your sister-in-law *or* your second cousin *or* your dentist's receptionist *or* that fine-looking woman visiting your wife from Alabama. The man went on and on until Elvis found himself cackling. Strange that Jerry should have his radio dial set to this station; he never struck Elvis as the religious type. Maybe Jerry just listened to get personal tips; this preacher surely had one expansive imagination when it came to objects of desire.

Come to think of it, how about a song about lusting after a whole catalog of women instead of one more ditty about undying love for just *one* woman? Now there was an honest sentiment for you. Of course, women might not take too kindly to a song like that. Unless they had the same lustful desires for a whole regiment of men. Could that be possible? The Bible didn't even say a thing about lusting after thy neighbor's *husband.*

Elvis turned off of Route 385 onto U.S. 72 and headed east. How could two underage girls get it into their heads that he had seduced them? Maybe it was just a fantasy along the same lines as those men who had convinced themselves that Elvis had made cuckolds of them. Instead of a nightmare becoming so powerful that it seemed real, it was a dream of passion that became so powerful that these youngsters actually believed it had happened. Digby Ferguson—may his soul rest in peace—once said that the movie screen is a bridge between your conscious and your unconscious. When somebody sees you up there in the movie theater, bigger than life, your image sneaks right into their brains along with their wishes and their genuine memories, and they can't tell the difference anymore. Truth was, perfect strangers were always coming up to Elvis and acting like they knew him like a neighbor.

But two young girls with the same fantasy not more than fifty miles apart from each other? Could be some sort of mass hysteria, but that did not seem likely. More likely that somebody was orchestrating this, some con man who'd come up with yet another scheme for bilking bucks out of the rich and famous. He'd probably started out by asking himself what was Elvis Presley's most vulnerable point—his Achilles' heel, as Digby would say. From there, the con's mind went straight to Priscilla, and from there it was just a hop, skip, and a jump to underage girls. It probably wasn't hard to recruit a girl like Carol-Sue Crampton to tell a juicy fib in exchange for a one-way ticket to New York City so she could finally get her genuine life started. And then he'd thrown in this Muffy Kent child for good measure, just to show he meant business. Big business.

The con man could very well be Carol-Sue's pappy. Crampton looked like he had less going on upstairs than a one-story house, but he certainly was well organized with that birth certificate he produced so smartly. Maybe Crampton figured that he cashed in for five thousand dollars with one night's work, so how about doubling his money in two nights? That would account for the two girls living so close to each other; it would keep down Crampton's traveling expenses. But then why would he include Sheriff Tip in his scheme?

Or maybe it was something else altogether. Like an impostor. Some twisted bastard who calculated that investing in a pink Cadillac and growing a pair of sideburns would pay off in all the sweet young flesh he could dream of. Heaven knows, just about any man will tell a lie to enlist a woman's sexual cooperation, so how about the ultimate lie of who you really are? Still, just how gullible could a young girl be—even a young girl with a host of movie dreams in her head? Would she be fooled enough by a pink car and some sideburns and maybe a Brylcreemed pompadour to make the biggest sacrifice of her young life? For one thing, when those girls looked up at his six-foot face on a movie screen, they could see every crease of his smile, every pore on his cheeks, every lash on his eyelids. They were probably experts on what he really looked like, so you wouldn't think they could be taken in by a crude imitation.

A road sign said, "Cantrell, Tennessee, Home of Vanderbilt Law School," followed ten feet later by a sign that said, "Cantrell, Tennessee, Home of 1956 Okra Queen, Miss Annie Gipson." They surely had a lot to be proud of in Cantrell. Elvis wondered if Miss Annie Gipson had capitalized on her notoriety and opened up a dress shop or maybe a beauty salon with a neon sign in the shape of a crown. Or of an okra. Heaven knows, if she'd had the Colonel running her career, she'd be starring in a whole string of movies with her dancing through fields of okra in a peasant blouse that showed off her lily white shoulders. You're better off with a beauty salon, Miss Annie, he thought.

The most distressing part of the impostor scenario was the notion that a young girl would give up her virginity, just like that, if she thought her deflowerer really was Elvis Aron Presley. It put a bad taste in Elvis's mouth. It was not just unhealthy for those youngsters, there was something unhealthy in it for him too. There had to be something ungodly in having that kind of power, whether or not you exercised it.

But, damn it, he had *not* exercised it. One thing about being a star is that you don't *have* to trade on your renown to seduce young women; the young women do all the seducing for you. The honest truth was he turned down their offers nine times out of ten, especially if he thought they should know better.

But just a minute—how big was the difference between seducing a woman by telling her that it was her chance of a lifetime to bed down a star, and her seducing *you* because she's thinking the very same thing? Did a man have the same responsibility to refuse himself a little sexual recreation in that case too?

Way deep down in Elvis's mind was one last suspicion: that he actually *had* seduced these young girls without knowing it. Like a sleepwalker. Or somebody with a split personality. The mind was a mysterious thing. A few years back, when he saw that based-on-a-true-story movie, *The Three Faces of Eve,* he'd had a distressing feeling of recognition that he never told a soul about: just like Eve, Elvis sensed another, different person stirring inside himself. Actually, he'd had hints of that ever since he was ten years old, when he would occasionally find himself arguing out loud with an unruly fella inside him. This second Elvis had a lot in common with Eve's second face; the Elvis inside didn't care a rat's ass for Bible teachings or personal ambition or even for close harmony. No, the Elvis inside just wanted one thing: *action.* If it feels good, do it. He just wanted to satisfy his appetites and satisfy them fast. No regrets, end of story. If the second Elvis ever got the upper hand like that Nazi inside Dr. Strangelove sometimes did, all hell could break loose in Decaturville or Waynesboro or just about anywhere else within driving distance of wherever the first Elvis was.

Elvis didn't know how to calculate the possibility of this theory being true. It surely did not seem likely, but then again, it probably hadn't seemed very likely to Eve either. But even deeper down was Elvis's fear that if there was a second Elvis, he was none other than Jesse Garon Presley, his identical twin who had never got himself born. Maybe Jesse Garon had slipped inside him at the last minute. And maybe Jesse Garon was still trying to break out.

Waynesboro seemed to have nothing to brag about, so the sign advertising its city limits just added a simple four-line poem:

LIFE IS SHORT
DEATH IS SURE
SIN THE CURSE
CHRIST THE CURE

It sure made you wish that Waynesboro had its own Okra Queen.

Elvis parked directly in front of the sheriff's office. He clamped on his motorcycle cap, pulling the visor down to his eyebrows by way of camouflage, then strode to the door and walked in without knocking.

Five people stood and applauded. The fat one with the star on his chest that looked like an oversize pasty was obviously Sheriff Tip. But Elvis hadn't any idea who the others could be: neither the frail-looking woman with braided hair wearing a choir robe, nor the three teenage boys of three different heights, but of equal distribution of pimples.

"This, here, is a historical moment," Sheriff Tip said, striding up to Elvis with his hand outstretched. But instead of grasping Elvis's extended hand, the sheriff made a fist and thumped it against Elvis's breastbone. Maybe it was some kind of local greeting.

"Brought out the seat of honor for you, Elvis," Tip said. The man had a natural volume level to rival that of the lust-obsessed preacher. Tip abruptly pulled an Indian blanket from off a protrusion in the middle of the office; under it appeared a leather-upholstered La-Z-Boy, same model Elvis had bought for his mama.

"Last man to sit in this got so comfortable he confessed to half a dozen murders his neighbor committed." Tip laughed with his mouth wide open. His breath smelled of a brand of mouthwash that was probably local too.

Elvis took his seat, and damn if all five of them didn't applaud again.

"Wanted you all cozy like before the show began," the choir lady said.

"Thank you, ma'am, but I've come up here on personal business," Elvis said.

"Oh, this is personal, Mr. Elvis," the choir lady replied. "About as personal as Judgment Day."

Elvis could not help wondering if the choir lady also happened to be the author of Waynesboro's very own road-sign doomsday ditty.

"Sheriff Oliphant, sir," Elvis said to the sheriff. "You understand, I drove all the way up from—"

"This won't take but a minute or two," Tip said. He picked up his desk chair and brought it around next to Elvis's. "Up here in Waynesboro, we like to loosen up some before we talk business. It takes the business out of business, if you know what I'm saying."

Elvis did not have much idea what Tip was saying, but he decided it would probably take up less time to go through whatever kind of chitchat loosened folks up in Waynesboro than to try to argue with this fellow.

Suddenly, the choir lady brought her chair next to Elvis's too, and then the three speckle-faced boys yanked guitars from the under the sheriff's desk, lined up side by side, plunked their instruments, and began to sing:

> *"Love is like love*
> *Even more like love*
> *Than love is*
> *Ya, ya, ya*
> *Even more like love*
> *Than love is . . ."*

Elvis realized as soon as the boys opened their mouths that the most important thing was not to laugh. Even a smile could be taken in the wrong way—which is to say, the *true* way. For starters, the lyric itself was half-baked Beatles with none of Lennon's smarts. In fact, it didn't make any sense whatsoever. And the tune—Elvis was pretty sure he detected something like a tune in the groans that issued from the boys' throats—was worse by far than any written by the hacks who composed the songs for his *Kissin' Cousins* movie. Actually, there was something personally reassuring about that comparison.

Elvis sat perfectly still until the trio wound up with the song's final, heartbreaking "Love is like love is like *you!*" and then, following Sheriff Tip and the choir lady's lead, burst into applause.

"Sweet," Elvis murmured, almost hoping he couldn't be heard.

"Just about ten times better than anything I ever heard on the radio," Tip said, then tapped Elvis on the chest again and said, "Present company excluded, of course."

Elvis nodded as noncommittally as he could manage.

"We call ourselves the Waynesboro Five Minus Two," the shortest and heftiest of the three boys said.

"You don't think that's too hard for ordinary folks, do ya?" Tip asked Elvis in a confidential tone.

"No, sir," Elvis said.

"That, there, is our very own Jarvis," the choir lady said, pointing at the boy who had spoken. Apparently she and Tip were the proud parents. "And then there's Will Wilkensen over there, and Will Jones over there."

"We were thinking of calling ourselves Two Wills and One Way," their very own Jarvis said.

"You got a way with numbers," Elvis said.

This elicited a laugh that equaled that from the midnight crowd at Howie Pickles's act at the Sahara. Elvis decided it was either time to get immediately on with his business with the sheriff or to get the heck out of Waynesboro as fast as he could.

"We need to speak alone right now," Elvis said to Tip.

"All these boys need is a break," Tip replied, putting his hand over Elvis's arm on the La-Z-Boy's armrest. "I figure the rest will take care of itself. You know, once the right people hear what the boys can do. But it's always that first break that makes or breaks you, isn't it?"

"Sheriff, I only came up here to talk about some made-up allegation that—," Elvis began again, scooting up to the edge of his seat.

"Listen, you give my boys a break, I give you a break," Tip said. "You understand what I'm saying, Elvis?"

"Can we talk about this privately, Sheriff?" Elvis said, standing.

"Man to man?" Tip said, standing also, and putting his arm on Elvis's shoulder. He turned to the others and told them to wait outside. Then, as soon as they'd left, he said, "Let's talk turkey, Elvis."

"Okay, shoot," Elvis said, even though his instincts were screaming at him that he didn't really want to hear a word of Tip's turkey talk.

"It's pretty simple," Tip said. "If you get my boys an audition with that Colonel Parker what's made you so famous, I can make this whole Muffy Kent predicament disappear faster than a minnow can swim a dipper."

Actually, there was one part of the sheriff's proposition that did appeal: Elvis would get a real kick out of forcing Parker to sit through the Waynesboro Five Minus Two's entire repertoire. Especially the part when the Colonel would take his cigar out of his mouth and bark, "How about the Waynesboro Five Minus *Five*? Take a hike, boys!"

"Just an audition," Elvis murmured.

"Right," Tip said, slapping Elvis on the back. "That Parker's a Jewish fella, right? They control all of that show-business business, don't they?"

Elvis grimaced. No, the Colonel didn't happen to be Jewish— he was Dutch or something like that—but that was none of this narrow-minded cur's never-you-mind.

"And how do you get rid of the Muffy Kent problem?" Elvis said.

"Easy," Tip said, grinning. "I get my boys to come forward and say they've had their way with that jezebel too. Put it down in writin'. If you get a whole posse saying they done the same gal, it switches from statutory rape to soliciting, quicker than sweat."

Elvis's pulse ratcheted up to double time.

"And would that be true, Sheriff?" Elvis said, keeping his voice as neutral as possible.

"What part?"

"The part about all those boys doing the Kent girl," Elvis said.

Tip shrugged, grinning. "Could be, for all I know. Them boys are real heartbreakers up here in Waynesboro. Local heroes, don't you know. Around here, they get more pussy than Elvis Presley—if you'll pardon the expression."

"But you don't know it as a fact," Elvis said.

"I'm telling you, they'll put it in writin', Elvis. That's all you need to know."

"In exchange for an audition with the Colonel."

"We understand each other."

For a few seconds, Elvis had been eying the turntable on the sheriff's desk. Now he walked over to it and lifted up the top. The 45 of "Wooden Heart" was sitting there just as Tip had said it was when he phoned. Elvis picked up the record, studied it for a second, and then flung it across the room like a boomerang, catching Sheriff Timothy "Tip" Oliphant's neck with its edge.

Stunned, Tip tripped backward, grasping at his neck. A thin line of blood had appeared there.

"What . . . the . . . fuck!" Tip stammered.

"You'd sully that girl's reputation just to—" Elvis now saw a letter opener on the desk. He grabbed it, spun around, and sank the blade into the backrest of the La-Z-Boy. It wasn't leather after all, just some kind of flimsy brown plastic that ripped open easier than a paper bag to reveal cotton wadding. Elvis took a couple more stabs for good measure. The La-Z-Boy now looked more like a cotton field after a hailstorm than a seat of comfort.

"That's . . . that's government property!" the sheriff managed to say, but it was clear that he was not going to make one move in Elvis's direction. No surprise there. The fat man with the big mouth had no more spine than a catfish.

"And you're a government disgrace!" Elvis retorted, starting for the door.

"Who the hell do you think you are?" Tip croaked.

"Elvis Presley," Elvis said, and he swung out the door.

Out on the sidewalk, Mrs. Oliphant and the three boys looked at Elvis expectantly.

"You got the job, boys," Elvis said, making his way to the pickup. "A job worthy of your talents."

"Really?" Jarvis said.

"But you're going to need a dustbin to do it properly," Elvis said.

He got into the truck and sped away.

4

Statuary Rape

Elvis kept his foot on the accelerator and his eyes straight ahead until his blood simmered down to a slow boil. Then, to ease that boil down to a low fever, he occupied his mind by thinking up songs to put on the sound track behind his encounter with Sheriff Tip. How about, "It's a Lazy Afternoon," while he was stabbing up that La-Z-Boy? Probably too obvious. Maybe Kate Smith singing "God Bless America" as the camera panned to the flag on the wall behind the sheriff's desk. But that seemed to cross the line from ironic to just plain mean-spirited. Ah, now he had it: Little Anthony and the Imperials singing "Going Out of My Head" while Elvis just stood there quietly listening to all that trash coming out of Sheriff Tip's mouth. That'd do it.

There was one question that Elvis had not been able to keep at bay all this while: What was Sheriff Tip going to do now? Clearly, the man was not feeling amiably disposed toward Elvis at this particular moment. And the sheriff had at his disposal a case of statutory rape to throw at Elvis by way of retribution.

Statutory rape! God almighty, that wasn't just a speeding ticket. Last night, Elvis had reflexively discounted the ominousness of the charge simply because the Colonel had made such a to-do about it. But it was ominous and then some. Not just because of the Jerry Lee Lewis implications for his career, but for the shame it would bring upon everyone around him—Priscilla, his daddy, and worst of all, his mama's spirit that hovered just over his left shoulder every minute of the day. Never mind that the charge wasn't true; it could stick to him like flypaper.

The ugly truth was, a whole lot of people were just dying to believe something loathsome about Elvis. That was plain human nature. They see somebody riding high, getting all the breaks and all the girls, and they start praying for disaster to strike him down. They justified it to themselves by saying the man needs humbling, but it's the envy in their hearts that makes them feel it. Yes, indeed, there would be folks throwing all-night parties if Elvis Presley got convicted of statutory rape.

Elvis glanced up at a street sign: Billy Nance Boulevard. Stringtown was ten miles to his left, Decaturville ten miles straight ahead.

No, there was no brushing this whole thing aside with some ironic background music. Elvis gunned it for Decaturville.

Carol-Sue Crampton had said to meet her behind the statue, but Elvis crisscrossed Decaturville a half dozen times without seeing anything that began to resemble a statue except for one granite angel on a pole out in the cemetery, and there was nobody visible anywhere near that. Of course, it was getting toward five o'clock, and Sunday school probably got out at two at the latest, so Carol-Sue could have come and gone already. Elvis considered asking somebody in the street where they had a statue in this town, but he didn't want to take the chance of being recognized in Decaturville. Not today.

He started heading out of town for the last time, passing the high school on his left and the holy-roller church on his right, when he saw a street sign that said Tinker Street. Carol-Sue had mentioned that one; it was where she walked her dog that night. Elvis turned onto it.

There was that statue, except it wasn't man-made—God had sculpted this one. At the far end of Tinker Street in front of what looked to be a glacier-scooped pond, a massive hunk of limestone shot up from the ground a good fifteen feet. It was roundish all the way up to near the top, where it then got sort of scraggly, like a poorly made curtain hanging around its curved tip. It looked like nothing so much as a grown man's organ standing at attention. So this is what they memorialized in Decaturville. Under the circumstances, it seemed sort of fitting. Statuary rape.

And there was Carol-Sue Crampton lolling on the ground with her back up against the statue, a lollipop in her mouth. If you didn't take into account what that statue seemed to stand for, you might take her for the innocent child her daddy painted her out to be. That is, until you got a little closer and saw that with the way she was lounging there and what she was wearing—one of those new London, England, miniskirts—she was showing more underwear than a Memphis clothesline.

Elvis slowed the truck to a crawl, then stopped where the road ended, no more than twenty feet from where Carol-Sue was sitting. Leaving the motor running, he cranked down the window.

"Miss Carol-Sue?" he called softly.

The girl looked up and smiled at him demurely, like she was a college coed waiting on the steps of her sorority house for her date to show up. Then she placed her lollipop on a rock, languorously stood, tugged her sleeveless pink V-neck blouse down, and wagged her hips as she dusted off the bum of her panties like she was dancing the samba. Elvis tried to look away, without success. This little girl had more tantalizing moves than a Las Vegas fan dancer. But Elvis was thankful for one thing: she hadn't shouted out his name. If she had, he would have hightailed it out of there in a heartbeat.

"You *do* keep a girl waiting," she said, walking slowly toward the pickup. Today, her voice was pure southern belle by way of *Gone with the Wind*. No doubt Carol-Sue Crampton had show business aspirations of her own, just like the Waynesboro boys. Did Elvis sniff another blackmail audition request in the wings?

When she reached the truck, Carol-Sue grasped the lip of the window and bent forward so that her face was right next to Elvis's. In the process, she flashed more plump white bosom than any child that age had the natural right to possess. By God, if Muffy Kent was anything like this girl, maybe Sheriff Tip had been on to something: a sixteen-year-old female with that much endowment probably should be locked up for *everybody's* protection.

"Take a good look at me, child," Elvis said to her.

"Now that would be a delight for any woman," Carol-Sue cooed. Half of her head was through the window now. Elvis could practically feel the heat wafting off of her. He squirmed in his seat.

"So you tell me, Miss Carol-Sue, now that you have a good look, this is not the same person who did that business to you, is it?"

"Seemed more like pleasure than business," Carol-Sue tittered. "But I'm kinda nearsighted, you know, Elvis. I'd better come around in there with you, if I'm going to perform a satisfying job."

"Beg pardon?"

"Of inspecting your face," Carol-Sue said.

"You seem close enough."

"Not really."

From the start, Elvis's plan had been to keep the girl out of the cab and one foot on the accelerator. Things were chancy enough that way.

"Just take a good look from there," Elvis said. "And tell me the exact differences between me and this other fella."

"I know how important this is to you, Elvis," Carol-Sue said, all innocent like again. "That's why I want to do this just right."

Elvis hesitated just a second, but that was long enough for Carol-Sue to scoot around the truck, yank open the passenger door, and plunk herself next to him with her bare young legs straddling the floor shift. Quicker than sweat, as Sheriff Tip would say, and that is exactly what was dripping from Elvis's brow.

"The eyelashes are exactly the same," Carol-Sue said. Her own wispy eyelashes weren't more than three inches away from the ones she was inspecting.

"You sure, child?"

"Surer than sure."

Surer than sure? More like love than love is? No wonder Elvis didn't reach number one on the hit parade anymore; he didn't speak the same language these young people did. He didn't even subscribe to the same brand of logic.

"Mouth is the same," Carol-Sue was saying, reaching out her fingers to touch his lower lip. "Feels the same too, though it's hard to tell for certain this way. Guess we'll have to do the taste test."

Carol-Sue puckered up. Elvis twisted his face away. And in that instant, he saw a flash in his side mirror—a Ford pickup heading down Tinker Street straight for them. *Lordy!* Daddy Crampton out on patrol and Elvis with the man's daughter practically sitting on top of him.

Elvis revved the engine, then reached for the shift stick between Miss Carol-Sue's legs. He popped the clutch and hung a hard left. The truck bounced over the curb onto the damp loam at the edge of the pond, its wheels squealing, slipping in the mud. Abruptly, it caught traction, then lurched forward toward the massive stone erection. Elvis yanked on the steering wheel, then pulled his head back as the side mirror whacked against the statue, sending shards of glass flying past his face. One moment later he was racing up Tinker Street, flying past Daddy Crampton's Ford coming the other way.

"Hee-haw!" Carol-Sue yodeled. She had shimmied up her miniskirt so it bunched around her waist like a fluffy garter belt, and every time Elvis shifted, she clamped his hand between her thighs and giggled. *Satan, get thee behind me!* Yes, indeed, Sheriff Tip, lock these girls up and throw away the key—otherwise the entire social fabric of this country could unravel in a week's time.

In his rearview mirror, Elvis saw Crampton's pickup swing around the statue just the way he had. And now Crampton was burning rubber no more than a hundred yards behind him. Elvis took a hard right where the county road met Tinker Street. He pressed the accelerator to the floor.

"Of course, I always remember a man's chest better than his face," the girl who claimed to have lost her virginity just last week chirped in Elvis's ear. With that, she reached out, snagged the pull tab on the zipper of his jumpsuit, and yanked it down to his belly.

"Woman, you are a shameless thing!" Elvis hollered, trying to brush her hand away. But the Ford was gaining on him and the road had narrowed, so he kept both hands on the wheel.

Carol-Sue slipped her hand under the fabric and touched Elvis's right nipple, teasing it with her fingertips. *Lord help me!* He should have thrown her out of the truck and *then* skedaddled. That way her daddy would have stopped to tend to her, and Elvis could have gotten away. Too late now. With one hand, he grabbed the youngster's wrist so hard she let out a little yelp.

Straight ahead was a culvert with no more than a half dozen rotting planks balanced on a drainpipe by way of a bridge. Elvis brought his hand back to the steering wheel, but by then his front right tire had already caught the edge of a plank, jolting it sharply to the left. Elvis slammed the brakes. The pickup teetered to the left, then to the right. And then it kept *on* teetering to the right. Jerry's Chevy pickup truck just perched there balanced on its two right tires.

It probably hung there for no longer than a minute, but it felt like ten at least. It felt like that slow-motion sequence in *Rashomon* that filled Elvis with dread every time he saw that film. With the tempo slowed down, Elvis had time for a half dozen scenarios to pass through his head. But it wasn't his life up to now that played on the screen of his mind, it was his life to come: In a courtroom. On the television news. Behind bars. In the poorhouse. In purgatory. Rotting in hell.

Finally, the Chevy tumbled over completely, coming to rest on the roof of the truck's cab in the bottom of the culvert.

Carol-Sue Crampton was giggling upside down, the top of her head pressed against the truck's roof, her body in a somersault crouch just above it. No harm seemed done to her, thank God.

Elvis's position was more complicated. His head was lodged between the spokes of the steering wheel. The right side of his body was sprawled out, his right arm cradled around Carol-Sue's waist where he had tried to catch her in midtumble, while the left side of his body was crushed so hard against the door and all the hardware on it that the numbness began only where the pain left off.

Above him, Elvis heard a car door slam shut. Then a man cursing and beseeching God in alternating breaths. Then the man's feet skittering down the culvert toward him.

No, Elvis's near-death scenarios didn't begin to do justice to his fate. This here was no mere statutory rape. It was abduction on top of that. Not to mention endangering the life of a minor. Heck, why not throw in attempted murder while you're at it. Yep, forget all about that poorhouse episode; Elvis was going to spend the rest of his natural life in jail.

"Elvis, if you ain't dead already, I'll kill ya!" Carol-Sue's daddy was cursing as he approached the upturned truck.

"Guess the only thing to do is marry me, Elvis," upside-down Carol-Sue said.

Under the circumstances, Elvis did what any rational human being would do: he passed out.

5

Doin' the Contusion

*M*eat loaf?"

"No! *Please,* no!"

"I'll IV it, Elvis. That way you won't have to chew."

"Not for my last meal."

"Your *last,* is it?"

"Before they hang me."

"Oh, that's good. Terrific, in fact. Let me get my notebook, I should be taking this down."

Elvis batted one crusted eyelid open, then the other. Everything was white: the walls, the ceiling, the overhead lamp, the window curtains. The sheets in the bed where he lay. The taut straps across his chest and legs. This must be purgatory, that celestial waiting room between heaven and hell—a white promise of heaven, but you can't even get yourself out of bed.

A man's head slid into view at the foot of Elvis's bed. Big face, three-day stubble, hair shooting off in ten different directions, thick glasses with flesh-toned plastic rims. *An ironic smile.*

"Mr. Southern, sir?" Elvis said.

"In the flesh—and loads of it. I didn't have any trouble finding you. All I had to do was read the headline of the local rag at the airport newsstand."

"What'd it say ?"

"It says you're not dead yet, you just look that way," Southern said.

Elvis smiled, and that made his face hurt like crazy.

"The spoke marks are particularly fetching," Southern went on. "Looks like a full-face tattoo of the peace symbol."

"Red?"

"In a purplish sort of way," Southern said. "But you've got a fat lip that's red. And two round red blotches on your cheekbones that bear a cute resemblance to Raggedy Ann's."

"What time is it?"

"Suppertime. And it's Tuesday, by the way, Elvis. You've been out cold for thirty-six hours and counting."

"Holy moley!" Elvis tried to raise his head, but the muscles in his neck nixed it. "The girl okay?"

"On top of the world," Southern replied. "I think she's out shopping for a wedding gown as we speak."

"Be better off if I had died."

"I wouldn't say that," Southern said, simpering. "She looks like a healthy specimen. A first-class baby-maker. And that's exactly what a man should look for in a wife."

Seemed like Mr. Terry Southern was of the Regis Clifford school of mockery—*everything* was ironic to him.

"For one thing, I'm already promised to another woman," Elvis said.

"You mean that *older* woman, Priscilla?" Southern drawled.

"You shouldn't be making fun of a man when he's down," Elvis said.

"You're right, I'm sorry," Southern said. "I always forget that some people still take their lives seriously."

"And you don't?"

"Elvis, I wouldn't know how to," Southern said, sounding serious. "Especially considering that it all seems like a dream to me."

"A bad dream?"

"Nope, just a senseless one."

"Then why do you even bother writing movies and books?"

"Somebody has to record the dream."

"What for?"

"Now that you mention it, I can't think of any good reason," Southern said. "So I guess I'll stop writing. It takes too much out of me anyhow."

Elvis tried to bring his right hand up to scratch his forehead. It did a little twitchy thing first, but then the hand responded as he had instructed it.

"How much damage did I do myself?" Elvis asked.

Southern picked a clipboard off of the foot of the bed and studied it. "For starters, you have an entire page's worth of contusions," Southern said.

"Sounds like one of them new twitchy dances they're doin'."

"Oh yes, everybody's doin' the contusion," Southern laughed, then flipped the page. "Here we go, Elvis—a hairline fracture in the pelvis, of all places. We might have to change your tagline. And some indeterminate trauma to the brain."

"That don't sound good."

"It might be a blessing. A man's brain needs some nudging now and then just to keep it from repeating itself," Southern said. "Who knows? Maybe it's just what you needed to get in touch with the Inner Elvis."

The Inner Elvis. That's the one who might have gotten him into this mess in the first place.

"Listen, partner," Southern went on, "you just get yourself better. No hurry to get started on our script. I've made myself comfortable in your guest room. Fabulous cook you've got there, by the way. We could write fourteen movies about her meat loaf. But in the meantime, you've got a small army camped out in the hospital waiting room. Mostly press, but also Mr. Parker, Miss Priscilla, a couple of your pals, a lawman named Tip, and a Mr. Morgan Crampton."

"I feel sick."

"I thought you might say that," Southern said. "Why don't I tell them you're still out cold?"

"I'd be much obliged."

Southern came up the side of the bed and patted Elvis on the top of his indeterminately traumatized head.

"Remember, Elvis, it's all just a dream," he said.

Dead of night. Sweet scent of orange blossoms coming through the open hospital window. Tree frogs hitting the off beat of the cicadas' triplets. Peaceful, this, whether it was dream *or* reality. A troubled man could do worse than lying in a county hospital in the middle of Tennessee while the rest of the world got on with its business of making bad decisions.

Good Lord! What was that? Off to the left, near the billowing curtains, Elvis saw a face. At least, he *thought* it was a face. It was just on the cusp of his peripheral vision, and it slipped in and out of view with each flutter of the curtains. No, it *was* a face. *It was his own face!*

"Dream!" Elvis said out loud, hoping to wake himself up.

"If you say so," the face answered back.

"Who are you?"

"Elvis. Elvis Aron Presley," the face said. The voice even sounded like his own, though maybe a couple tones higher. Now it took a few steps toward him, stopping at the foot of the bed. The body looked the same too—maybe a tad slimmer, more the way Elvis had looked when he got out of the army. And that rayon black shirt with a kerchief around the neck was straight out of Elvis's closet.

Elvis squeezed his eyes tightly shut. *Dream! Dream! Dream!* he repeated inside his brain. He tentatively opened one eye, then the other. *Still there!*

"You're the Inner Elvis, right?" he said.

"No, the *Outer* Elvis," his doppelganger replied, smiling. Man, even the smile was like his own, with just a hint of a snarl on the upper lip. That snarl was probably the Inner Elvis trying to twist the innocence out of his mouth.

"You're scaring the bejesus out of me, you know," Elvis said.

"Didn't mean to. Actually, I came here to offer my services. Three in the morning seemed like an opportune time."

Now Elvis knew what was happening here. This was that Dickens *Christmas Carol,* except it wasn't Christmas. And it was happening to him, not to Scrooge. This thing at the foot of his bed was the Ghost of Christmas Past or Future or whatever. A moral lesson was on the way. Well, good. Elvis was definitely in the market for a moral lesson.

"Thank you," Elvis said. "What kind of services do you have to offer?"

"Well, it seems you'll be needing all kinds of help with the scrapes you've got yourself into lately."

Since he'd woken up, the exact nature of those scrapes had not obtruded on Elvis's consciousness. Now he *really* wished he could go back to sleep. That is, if he *was* awake. If you wake up in a dream, can you go back to sleep?

"What do you figure you can do for me?" Elvis said.

"Your number one problem right now is the Crampton girl," the ghost said. "She appears to be a very determined person. Which in some cases is an admirable quality. But not in this one."

"What can you do with her?"

"Take her off your hands," the ghost replied, smiling. "In fact, if it comes to that, I can even walk down the aisle with her."

"You certainly are an obliging ghost," Elvis said, smiling back.

"That's what I'm here for."

And then it hit Elvis! No, by golly, this was not a dream! And that was not a ghost hovering at the foot of his bed. No, that was flesh and blood. It was the impostor who had turned Elvis's life into a nightmare in just a few days' time. The impostor who haunted him worse than any ghost possibly could.

"I could kill you!" Elvis tried to holler, but it came out of his mouth soft as a bleating lamb. Nonetheless, the effort of it made his face throb.

"Wouldn't that be suicide? Or fratricide? Or something like that?" the impostor said, grinning.

"It would be justice," Elvis said.

"I never did you any harm."

"Maybe not to your twisted way of thinking. But you've been a menace. How could you do that to those two young girls?"

"I never did a thing to any young girls," the impostor said. "You must be mistaking me for somebody else."

"I know who you are!" Elvis said. "You are the one that's been trying to pass yourself off as me."

"You got that part right. But I am *not* the one who assaulted those girls. Or *submitted* to them, as the case may very well be."

"The hell you aren't!"

The impostor stepped around the corner of the bed and up to Elvis's right side. "I am not that awful person, Elvis. I want you to believe me."

"You're worse than awful!" Elvis said as vehemently as his condition would allow.

With that, the imposter quickly removed the kerchief and began unbuttoning the black rayon shirt. Underneath the shirt was some kind of a chest bandage that the imposter twirled off in a good dozen swing-arounds. It was all Elvis could do to keep his already-traumatized brain from losing consciousness right then and there. No more than one foot in front of Elvis's face, on full display, was a pair of small but shapely breasts. And they were sitting on the appropriate spots on the impostor's chest.

For one dizzying moment, a singular, appalling thought passed through Elvis's indeterminately traumatized brain: *Jesse Garon was a girl!* And then the thought was gone.

"It wasn't me who did those little girls, Elvis," the impostor said, now buttoning up her shirt again.

"Guess not," Elvis said. God knows, Carol-Sue claimed she always remembered a man's chest better than his face. "But who are you?"

"I was born Sarah Whipple," she said. "Part Cherokee on one side and part Jewish on the other, with a whole lot of Anglo-Saxon in between. Just like you."

Elvis managed a painful nod.

"I mean, when I heard we shared the exact same mongrel pedigree, that confirmed everything for me," she went on. "Same mix of blood coursing through our veins, same mixed message tapping out from our genes."

"You surely do look a whole lot like me," Elvis said.

"I could say the same about you," Sarah replied.

"It's kind of creepy, actually."

"Tell me about it."

"But you just make it worse by dressing up like me. And doing your hair up in the same way. And where did you get those sideburns from, Miss Sarah?"

"Got the glue from the hardware store. The little hairs are my own, plucked from someplace you don't want to know about."

"What do you go through all that trouble for, Miss Sarah?" Elvis said. "You seem a fine-enough-looking woman just the way God made you."

"But I'm *not* a woman, Elvis. Not inside."

"Excuse me, ma'am, I hit my head pretty bad, so I'm not following you that good."

"It's simple. On the outside, I'm all woman, but inside—you know, my *inner* self—is all man. And that man keeps banging on the walls of my insides day and night, just trying to get out."

It didn't sound that simple to Elvis, unless she was talking about something like that *Goodbye, Charlie* movie, where this tough guy gets murdered, comes back from the dead as Debbie Reynolds, and then has one devil of a time trying to figure out if he feels more like a girl or a boy. But that was just a movie. Still, Elvis did have a feel for what it was like to have an inner self who was contrary to your everyday self.

"So you try to accommodate this inside fella by dressing up like a man and all," he said.

"That's it exactly."

"But why like me? Why not his own self? Or doesn't this inner fella have much of an imagination?"

"Listen to me, Elvis," Miss Sarah said, sitting down on the edge of the bed. "Being like I am is not exactly a picnic. Especially if you've got two Bible-thumping parents and three redneck brothers. If they knew what was really going on inside of me, they'd either hustle me off to an exorcist or burn me at the stake. In their eyes, I'd be nothing but a pervert."

"I can see how'd they think that. It *is* a peculiar thing, if you don't mind my saying so."

"Except to me it ain't peculiar, it's just the way I am," Miss Sarah said. Her voice still sounded an awful lot like Elvis's own, and now knowing that she was a girl made that fact even more disturbing. "Anyway, you can see that this is no ordinary pickle for a person to be in. I couldn't just come down for breakfast one morning with my hair cut short and my titties bound up, wearing a cowboy shirt and jeans. My mama is a hysterical woman and my daddy is a violent man. He'd as soon kill me as look across the table and see his one and only daughter done up like that."

"But your hair *is* short and your—"

"That's what I'm trying to tell you. They *love* you, Elvis. They've got every record you ever made. They spend their butter and egg money to see every movie you make two or three times. Your picture's on the wall of every room of our house. You are the *king* at my house. And starting when I was about twelve or so, my brother, Ralphie, started to see the resemblance I had to you. Teased me about it. But my daddy kinda cottoned to it. He liked to say I must be your secret sister."

Or my secret twin. "Go on," Elvis said.

"Well, when I was about thirteen—that was when you were in the army over there—folks around here started dressing up like you, sideburns, pompadour, and all. At first, I think it was just their way of saying that they missed you so awful they needed some kind of substitute Elvis to get them through the duration, you know? But then it started to get wheels of its own. Elvis look-alike parties and dances. Elvis look-alike concerts. Elvis look-alike contests."

"I've heard about that foolishness," Elvis said.

"Well, that's when it all clicked together for me," Miss Sarah said.

"That you could walk around as a man if that man was me," Elvis said.

"Bingo!" Miss Sarah said. "Once folks get their minds around the notion of dressing up as somebody else—that somebody being you—then the whole sex matter doesn't make a never-you-mind. Truth is, people thought it was sort of cute, kinda like dressing up a pussycat to look like Elvis."

The image of his cat look-alike flashed in Elvis's mind. It did not look the least bit cute to him.

"And once I started winning one Elvis contest after another—I mean, I can sing 'Love Me Tender' so you'd think there was a Victrola in my throat—once that happened, my daddy and mama were about as proud of me as if I'd won the swimsuit competition at the county fair."

Suddenly, Elvis heard footsteps in the hospital corridor coming in their direction. Miss Sarah stood up; she looked scared. Elvis could not help but wonder if that was the way *he* looked when he was frightened.

"Oh God, I'm not supposed to be in here," Miss Sarah whispered. "Should I hide under the bed?"

Too late. A stooped figure appeared at the door. Mr. Terry Southern.

"Couldn't sleep worth a damn," he said, stepping into the room. "So I decided to buzz on over and see how my partner in crime was doing."

Southern adjusted his glasses on his nose as his eyes went from Elvis strapped down in the hospital bed to the Elvis standing upright next to it.

"Jesus, Elvis, this friggin' movie is writing itself," Southern said.

6

A Herring Doesn't Whistle

*I*f you want to kill yourself, why don't you just jump out the window, son. Probably be less painful than twisting in the wind, the way you're doing now." Colonel Parker was standing at the foot of Elvis's bed, his Stetson in hand in front of his chest like he was standing at the foot of a grave.

There had been no fooling the nurses this morning that Elvis was still unconscious, and anyway, he was way too hungry for that ruse. An IV might give you all the nutrients a body needs, but it leaves your stomach howling. His first visitor had been Priscilla, who had tried her best to act concerned about Elvis's health, but there was no disguising the fact that all she was really thinking about was her fiancé's alleged sexcapades, not to mention his rumored upcoming shotgun wedding to that hussy he was cruising with when his truck flipped over. You couldn't rightly blame Priscilla. The way Elvis had handled her was by acting as dazed and bewildered as a man with indeterminate brain trauma might actually be, rolling his eyes up into his head every now and then, and murmuring strings of words that sounded like a Waynesboro Five Minus Two lyric.

The Colonel was Elvis's second visitor.

"I've been working around the clock to keep this monster in the box," Parker was saying. "First off, I'm stringing along those three Waynesboro yodelers with some pie-in-the-sky fantasies. I told them they could open for you at your next concert. Right this minute, they're rehearsing. Of course, I wouldn't put those pimply kids on stage if they were Hank Snow's long lost brothers, but it gives us a whole lot of stall time."

"And Sheriff Tip will take care of that Kent girl who says I did her," Elvis said.

"He seems a resourceful fella," Parker said.

Oh, he was resourceful, all right, if that meant about the same as crafty. But lying broken boned and broken spirited in a hospital bed, Elvis wasn't quite up to disparaging Sheriff Tip's methods at this particular moment.

"Miss Carol-Sue is a different kettle of sharks," Parker continued. "I'm stalling her and her daddy by helping out with the wedding plans."

"Not going to happen, Colonel!" Elvis said, loud as he could. He tried to sit up as he said it, but the straps snapped him back down. That morning, Elvis had pleaded with the nurses to unstrap him, but they had insisted that if they did, his pelvis wouldn't set right.

"I'll stall the Cramptons long as I can," Parker said. "Meantime, they've promised to keep quiet to the press about the nuptials. The press has set up a regular Hooverville out on the hospital lawn, in case you haven't heard. Keeping them pacified is a full-time job in itself."

About now, it would probably be the right thing to thank Parker for *his* resourcefulness, but Elvis couldn't get himself to do it.

"I could handle all that, son," Parker said, shaking his head back and forth, "but then you had to go and hand-feed the shit to the fan."

"What are you talking about?"

Parker removed an envelope from his jacket pocket and tossed it onto the bed beside Elvis. Two black-and-white Polaroid photographs jutted out from the open envelope. Elvis picked one up.

It was pornography. Pure, ugly pornography. A naked young

woman with her legs spread wide sitting on top of a car trunk.
And a grown man with his trousers down around his ankles standing in front of her giving her the business. You only saw the man
from the back: slicked-back hair, silky-looking shirt. But the girl's
face was in full view. She looked on the young side. The *very*
young side. Elvis flung the photograph back at Parker.

"You should burn this filth, Colonel!" Elvis snapped. "Pollutes
the mind just looking at it."

"It's not your mind I'm concerned about, son. It's your neck.
Look at that other photo."

Elvis brought the other Polaroid up to his eyes. It was virtually
the same picture, except taken from a yard or two farther back.
The girl's face was harder to see, but the rear of the car easier. It
was a Cadillac convertible. And its fully visible license plate was
Memphis 23. The license plate on Elvis's pink Cadillac convertible. Elvis flung this photograph at Parker too.

"Same filth!" he snarled.

"Incriminating filth," Parker replied.

"Lying filth!"

"Admissible-in-court filth," Parker said.

"When the heck was this supposed to have happened?" Elvis
said.

"Last night," Parker said. "Wee hours."

Elvis brightened. "Well, damnation, it's easy to prove that's a
lie. A whopper! Everybody knows I've been strapped in this bed
for the last three days."

"Like Houdini in a straitjacket," Parker said.

"What's that supposed to mean?"

"The night receptionist here, a Miss Daisy Ambrose, swears
she saw you come bopping in the front door around about two
thirty in the a.m. Chased you to the stairwell, then lost you. She
says by the time she got up to your room, you were strapped back
in your bed and snoring. Or *pretending* to snore, as she put it."

"That wasn't me. That was Miss Sarah!" Elvis said.

Parker looked back at Elvis with a raised-eyebrow expression which insinuated that Elvis's brain damage was much worse than the resident neurologist had diagnosed.

"She's one of those impersonators," Elvis explained. "Looks more like me than I do." *Now there was a Waynesboro Five Minus Two lyric for you.*

"A woman," Parker murmured.

"Uncanny, isn't it?"

"Right up to where 'uncanny' meets 'unbelievable,'" Parker said.

"Wait until you see her," Elvis said. "Most amazing thing I ever did see, but I saw it with my own eyes. With her shirt buttoned up, she coulda fooled my mama."

"How about with her pants down? Like in this picture here? I don't think she could have fooled anybody's mama ass naked. Or anybody's fifteen-year-old daughter, for that matter."

"Must have been another one."

"Another Elvis?"

"Another impersonator."

"Oh, *that* one," Parker intoned sarcastically. "The one who mints licence plates identical to yours."

"It's possible," Elvis said.

"I'll tell you what's possible, Elvis," Parker said. "Putting a rocket ship on the moon is possible. Going to happen any day, I hear. But some guy who drives a pink Cadillac car with your licence plate on it and who looks so much like you that high school girls from good southern families are willing to do the deed with him out in the open air—well, the word for that is improbable."

"For heaven's sake, you don't think I'd do a thing like that, do you?"

"It's not my opinion that counts, son."

"Well, *do you?*"

Colonel Parker looked down at his shoes, and he was not a man who gave up on eye-to-eye contact easily.

Good Lord, could the Colonel possibly be right? Could the In-

54

ner Elvis have mobilized himself last night, unstrapped his broken body, gotten himself back to Graceland where he picked up his pink Cadillac car, gone off and found a willing teenager, done the deed, then brought the car back, returned to the hospital, strapped himself back in, and then awakened without remembering anything of it? Elvis would have to be completely out of his mind for something like that to happen, and there was a big difference between being confused and being plumb crazy. Heck, all that running around was even more than the second face of Eve could handle in one night. And just one minute: one thing that Elvis and the Inner Elvis shared was a fractured pelvis. Surely one job requirement of a statutory rapist is an intact pelvis.

"The young woman in question even described that spanking new purple crisscross motif on your face," Parker said, still not looking up. "And *nobody* knows about that. I've made sure of that. Your people don't even want to imagine that pretty face of yours with a scratch on it."

"Well, *some* people know about it. Like every nurse and doctor in this hospital. And it can't be that hard to paint your face purple," Elvis said.

"Listen, son, they've got a joke in Holland that goes like this. Lex says to Kees, 'What's green, hangs on the wall, and whistles?' And Kees says he doesn't know, so Lex says, 'A herring.' Kees says, 'A herring isn't green.' And Lex says, 'Put some paint on it, it's green.' And Kees says, 'But a herring doesn't hang on the wall.' And Lex says, 'Put a nail through it, it's on the wall.' 'Well, damn it,' Kees says, "A herring doesn't whistle.' And Lex says, 'So, it doesn't whistle. Why are you so picky?' "

"This ain't a herring, Colonel—it's a pickle," Elvis said. "Who the heck took those pictures anyhow?"

"A man named Anonymous," Parker said. "A man who says he's got ten more Polaroids where those came from. Plus a sworn affidavit by one Amy Coulter, age seventeen, from near Jackson up in Madison County. Which happens to lie about halfway between here and Memphis, in case you were wondering."

"What does he want?"

"Twenty thousand dollars."

Elvis felt his blood pressure pump up; it made his brain hurt.

"I won't pay it, Colonel!" he growled. "And it ain't the money either. That wouldn't stop this craziness anyhow, and you know it. Tomorrow it'll just be somebody else, some poor child who gets herself ruined for married life by this madman. It's a setup, a criminal setup, plain as day. I mean, what's some photographer doing out on a country road in the middle of the night? Think about it. They're in cahoots—the impostor and this photographer."

"Somehow I don't think that'll make any difference to the photo editor of the *National Enquirer*," Parker said. "Think about *that!*"

"Mr. Presley?" A nurse said, sticking her head inside the door. "Time for your medication, darlin'."

Parker placed his Stetson back on his bald head. "Listen, son, I found a specialist over at Vanderbilt who's going to pay you a visit one of these days. A Dr. Helga Volk. She's very interested in your case."

"What's her specialty?"

"Head shrinking," Parker said. He tipped his hat to the incoming nurse and strolled out the door.

"Don't you pay that photographer son of a gun one cent!" Elvis called after him, but Parker was gone.

Elvis had no idea what was in the cup of pills the nurse gave to him, but one of them—the long red capsule, he figured—gave his brain a jolt of gladness. *And* confidence. By God, he wasn't going to take this plot against him lying down. One way or another, he had to get himself out of this hospital bed and on the trail of this fella who was trying to do him in. That is just what Elvis was thinking when the nurse stuck her head inside the door again and said, "Your cousin is here, Mr. Elvis. She says she's come a long way. You up to seeing her?"

"My cousin?"

"Miss Sarah Presley."

"I don't have any cousin named—" But then Elvis caught himself and said, "Oh? *Sarah* Presley? Show her in."

One minute later, in three-inch high heels, an A-line pink felt skirt, and a V-neck pink angora sweater, a statuesque—if broad-shouldered—blonde came sashaying into Elvis's hospital room and up to the side of his bed.

"She surely is a Presley," the nurse tittered from the door.

"I'm in disguise," Sarah Whipple whispered to Elvis, sitting down on the bed.

"As what?"

"A woman," she murmured.

Gladdened as Elvis's brain was, it still had to execute a couple of trapeze flips to gather in all the levels of personae perched next to him. First off, Miss Sarah looked just plain sexy sitting there—sex-kitten sexy. Especially that sly simper on her fleshy lips . . . *God help me!* Elvis flipped to the next level, where now he saw his own face framed by long blond hair, wearing pink lipstick and more mascara than he'd even think of putting on for a stadium concert. But the contour of the face, the shape and flash of the eyes, and yes, that delicate-but-naughty smile on the full lips—those were his very own. It was a shocking thing to behold.

"I can't tell you how bad it stung yanking off those sideburns hair by hair," Miss Sarah said. And there was Elvis's own voice again, just a few notes higher.

Yikes, here comes the third level—the inner man who was trapped inside Sarah Whipple's body. Elvis's mind went somersaulting up near the peak of the big top. He wondered if he could pry another one of those long red capsules from the nurse.

"Figured this was the only way I could get in here, at least during daylight," Sarah was saying. "That manager of yours has enforced a relatives-only policy out in the waiting room. Himself excepted, of course. And Miss Priscilla and Mr. Southern."

"I'd be proud to call you cousin, Miss Sarah," Elvis said. "You sure look nice and pretty. Maybe you should think about dressing up like this more often."

"Elvis, I thought I explained all that to you!" Sarah responded indignantly.

"I do understand, ma'am," Elvis said. "It's just that you look so much more attractive as a woman than you do as me, and—"

"What? Don't you like your own looks?" Sarah interrupted him. "Now listen, I've got a bunch to tell you."

"I'm listening."

"Well, first, I just spent the most poetic morning of my life. Heaven on earth. Picnic out by the golf course. Strolling hand in hand by the riverside, stopping here and there for some smooching. And I am here to tell you, that little girl sure can pucker."

Maybe *two* of those long red pills. "You talking about Miss Carol-Sue?"

Sarah blushed. "She is a sweet young thing, Elvis," she said. "I wouldn't blame any man for—"

"Why?" Elvis did the interrupting this time. There were still some details he did not need to know about. "Why'd you take her out picnicking?"

"A dry run, so to speak," Miss Sarah said, flashing that all-too-familiar smile again. "Had to make sure I could pass the test with her. And I passed with flying colors. She sure does love her Elvis, Elvis. We are one lucky man."

"*Two!*" Elvis snapped vehemently, although he wasn't exactly sure why. "We are two different people, Miss Sarah. And you can't be passing yourself off as me just to . . . you know."

"Hey, I'm doing this for you, my friend," Sarah said. "The fact that I enjoyed it is just a bonus. That Carol-Sue needs some serious controlling and that Colonel of yours isn't entirely up to the job. She's just bursting to tell every reporter on the lawn that you and she are getting married. At the Red Walnut Church of Christ, in case you were wondering. You can just about see the steeple from the window here. It took me some intense sweet-talking to get her to promise to keep our little secret."

Elvis found himself wondering how Miss Sarah handled it when Carol-Sue made her inevitable grab for the buttons on her shirt, but he couldn't get himself to inquire.

"Didn't she wonder what I was doing out of the hospital?" he asked instead.

"I told her I snuck out because I couldn't take another day without her sweet lips."

A disquieting answer, but it would have to do.

"But I saved the big news for last," Miss Sarah went on excitedly. "There's a grapevine out there called the 'Elvis Look-alike Grapevine,' and it was buzzing like a sawmill all last night about this young fella named Kevin Cote. I know him. He came in second to me out at the Blossom Festival Elvis Contest last April. The boy has the pipes, but he's seriously lacking in the locomotion. Prances around the stage like he's got St. Vitus' dance. Anyway, the word was that Kevin was telling anyone who'd listen that he knows the boy who compromised a young girl named Muffy up in Waynesboro. The boy who had seduced her by telling her that he was actually you."

"Unstrap that belt," Elvis said. "The one around my chest. I need to sit up for this."

After Sarah did as he asked, Elvis pressed his hands down on the mattress on either side of himself and propped his trunk upright. A sharp pain shot from his pelvis all the way up his spine before subsiding.

"So I went out to Kevin's place, out there in Dogwood Heights. Lives with his mother in one of those trailers that look like oversize lawn ornaments," Sarah continued. "Tapped on his window to wake him up."

"What did he say?"

"He says he knows enough to write a book, but he won't tell anyone but you."

"So bring him in here. I'll tell the nurses he's a cousin too."

"Won't do it. Kevin says he needs to show you something, and whatever it is, it ain't portable."

"But they aren't letting me out of here for another couple days, and this can't wait."

"I already figured that," Sarah said. "So I said you'd meet him tonight. One o'clock in the a.m. You figure you could get yourself ambulatory with a pair of crutches? I've got a driver for you."

"You certainly are something, Miss Sarah, but you're forgetting that they keep a close eye on me in here. Checking in on me all the time—patting my pillow and tucking my sheets. You'd think they had more important things to do."

"No doubt they do," Sarah said, "but I've got that all figured too. Which means I best get busy. Putting on my sideburns is a laborious process, Elvis. It ain't gluing on the hairs that's hard. It's the fetchin' 'em."

7

Pudding in a Perambulator

*M*iss Sarah had the whole thing planned out better than a Brinks robbery. She snuck into the hospital at midnight, more or less the same as the night before, but this time she covered up her silk shirt and black pants—both a lot roomier-looking than last time—with a green surgical gown, topping it off with one of those paper hats surgeons wear. Then, zippity-dip, she is stripping down right in front of Elvis, first the gown, then the shirt and pants— man, it *was* a crime that such a sweet-looking body should be so vexed with itself—and next, she sits Elvis up and pulls off his smock. Presto change-o, Miss Sarah is lying under the sheets, all strapped in, complete with that purple peace-signish thing artfully drawn on her face, and Elvis is teetering by the side of the bed, wearing the silk shirt and pants, topped with the hospital gown and cap.

Getting himself out of that hospital bed had been more uplifting and less painful than Elvis had anticipated. Sure, every time he took a step on those wooden crutches, his pelvis answered back with an insult. But being unstrapped, and up and about on his own, was thrilling, like playing hooky on a day that just begged for fishing.

Elvis's white Caddy was idling outside the service door in the rear of the hospital. Off to his right, Elvis could see a good dozen pup tents on the hospital lawn, most with hurricane lanterns hung

61

by their entrance flaps. A literal press encampment. One journalist seemed to be looking in Elvis's direction, but took no notice; to him, Elvis must have seemed just another green-gowned surgeon rushing home to see his wife before she gave up on him and went to bed.

The driver who Miss Sarah had drafted was none other than Mr. Terry Southern, who came dressed for the occasion in chauffeur's livery, rented from Elvis's old friends the Lansky brothers. According to Mr. Southern, he and Miss Sarah had become fast friends virtually overnight. He had even pretty much promised her a part in their upcoming screenplay. That Miss Sarah certainly had packed in a lot of socializing in the past twenty-four hours.

"Sarah's an amazing person," Mr. Southern said. "I haven't had such an enlightening conversation with a transvestite since that little mix-up in a Paris brothel ten years ago."

"What kind of mix-up?" Elvis asked from the backseat.

"Complicated story," Mr. Southern said. "At the time, I was too young and horny to see the humor in it."

"Where are we going, Mr. Southern?"

"I'd rather you called me Throckmorton," Southern replied. He appeared to have trouble figuring out how to put the car in forward gear, but he finally lurched off at a fast clip. "It's my nom de goof. This is all very hush-hush, you know."

No, it was probably no exaggeration that Southern did not have an inkling of how to take his life seriously. And that was not a promising quality for a man chauffeuring a broken-boned crash victim.

"So where are we headed, Throckmorton?"

"Hardin County, Sir. Crump, Tennessee." Southern suddenly swiveled around in the driver's seat, his moon-shaped, unshaven face grinning under his chauffeur's cap. "Who makes up these names, Elvis? *Crump?* Sounds like a bowel ailment."

"Gol-dang it! Would you keep your eyes on the road, Mr. Southern?"

Elvis braced his hands against the armrest. Southern swiveled back around and turned the wheel just in time to miss the first poetic line on a series of Burma Shave road signs.

"Should be there at exactly nineteen hundred, sir," he said.

There was Mildred's Come-And-Get-It, something between a truck stop and a gin joint on the outskirts of Crump. A backlit frosted-glass sign in front of Mildred's advertised Elvis look-alike contests every night of the week, twice on Saturdays and holidays. Judging by the parking lot in back, where Southern brought the Caddy to a pelvis-jolting stop, Mildred did an impressive business for a Wednesday night in a town of only a few hundred souls. Also judging by the parking lot, everybody in Hardin County drove either a pickup truck or a Cadillac convertible, and most of the Caddies—it was hard to tell for certain in the dim light out there—appeared to be pink. From where they were parked, Elvis scanned as many of the Caddy licence plates as he could. None came close to Memphis 23.

A rap on the side window. Hovering on the other side of the glass was a young man's face: wide-set eyes, slicked-back black hair with a ski-jump flip in front and a few hairs curled down on the forehead, smooth skin, sly smile. He looked a whole lot like Elvis, except not at all. All the pieces were close enough, but somehow they didn't fit together to look even half as much like Elvis as Miss Sarah did.

"Kevin Cote," the face said.

Elvis opened the window. "Elvis Presley," he said.

"I've been expecting you. She said you weren't looking yourself these days," Kevin said. "I'll tell you, Elvis, I'm going to treasure this moment for the rest of my natural life."

"Good to hear," Elvis said, then added hopefully, "Hope I will too."

From inside Mildred's Come-And-Get-It came a burst of raucous cheers, followed by catcalls and applause.

"It'll be starting any minute now," Kevin said. "We'd best get you set up out here so you can see everything."

"See what?"

"You'll see. Seein' is believin'."

"*Believe* what?"

"Believe what you *see.*"

Was it Elvis's indeterminate head trauma, or had every young person in Tennessee taken to talking in circles lately?

"I'd rather stay put," Elvis said. "Not too steady on my feet just now."

"You're going to have to stand up to show me what you need to anyhow," the boy said.

"I'm not following you at all, son."

"Didn't Miss Elvisetta tell you?"

No doubt, "Elvisetta" was Miss Sarah's nom de goof on the Elvis look-alike circuit. But Elvis still didn't have a clue as to what the boy was talking about.

"Listen, I understand the information I've got is very valuable to you, if you follow my meaning, Mr. Presley," smiling young Kevin Cote said.

Man, the whole darned country had turned into a bunch of wheeler-dealers. Nobody made a gift of anything, and everything was up for sale. It surely was a sad commentary on the state of the world today. It was as if the Colonel had set up a national franchise of Carny-Man Schools, like those Arthur Murray Dance Studios. Jeez, in order to capture the cynicism in *Dr. Strangelove,* all Mr. Southern had to do was open his eyes.

"What's your price, boy?" Elvis muttered.

"Personal instruction," the boy said, the simper never leaving his lips. "Straight from the horse's mouth, in a manner of speaking."

"What kind of instruction?"

"Your *moves,*" Kevin said. "That thing with your hips. That skipping right leg. The neck thing."

"The neck thing?"

Kevin strummed some air guitar while gyrating his head from

64

one side to the other. Actually, the move looked more like Howdy Doody than St. Vitus' dance.

"You see?" the boy said when he'd finished. "It needs some smoothing out, you think?"

"I give you a lesson, and you tell me who seduced Muffy Kent by saying that he was me," Elvis said.

"More than tell you, Elvis," the boy said. "I'm going to point him out to you in the flesh!"

"Help me out of here, Throckmorton," Elvis said to his chauffeur. "And then help me out of this danged surgeon's doohickey."

A few minutes later, at exactly one o'clock in the morning, his crutches stabbing his armpits, Elvis Presley demonstrated "the neck thing" under the flashing neon lights of Mildred's Come-And-Get-It in Crump, Tennessee. It was a humbling experience.

"You got to loosen up, boy," Elvis explained. "Like your head and the rest of your body are barely on speaking terms. Fact is, they are listening to different parts of the music—the body's dancing to the melody, but the head's bouncing with the bass notes."

Kevin Cote tried again. Howdy Doody was under no threat of replacement.

"Got it this time, didn't I, Elvis?" the boy said.

"You surely did," Elvis replied.

Another rowdy cheer erupted from Mildred's, this time closer and louder. Elvis looked up.

About two dozen young women, most of them teenagers, but a few looking like their teens were a bittersweet memory, had gathered in a semicircle at the rear of the roadhouse. They were the ones making that ruckus. A door swung open, and now, one at a time, a dozen young men strolled out into the center of that semicircle. Every one of the boys was dressed in a loose-fitting silk shirt and skintight pants. And every one of them had black, slicked-back hair. The contestants, taking their final curtain call.

"This is it. Come on," Kevin said, and he started toward the edge of the loop of young women.

Elvis limped after him, keeping his head hunched low and his collar turned up so that his face was covered on the sides all the way up to his eyeballs. Of course, with all those boys looking something like him, it wasn't all that difficult to blend in with the crowd. Mr. Terry Southern brought up the rear.

Closer up, Elvis could see the contestants' faces clearly. Ten of them looked a lot like Kevin Cote—all the Elvis parts, but not one *whole* Elvis between them. Peculiar thing, a man's face, Elvis mused. You didn't really have that many variables to play with— two eyes, a nose, mouth, cheeks, hair. Not that many pieces to the puzzle. And when you think about it, how different, say, can one person's mouth be from another's? A smidgen more flesh here, a one-degree different angle of smile there? Yet you can pick out your daddy's face in a crowd of hundreds. Even pick out his face at a family reunion. Maybe in order to be a prizewinning Elvis look-alike, like Miss Sarah, you needed more than just the facial features, you needed some Inner Elvis shining through to unite them.

Neither of the two remaining contestants looked much like Elvis at all. Both were overweight, one of them bordering on porky.

"Cattle call," Kevin whispered to Elvis.

"Which ones are the livestock?" Elvis said.

"This goes on every single night after the show," the boy said. "It's the main reason most of us got into this business. Heck, the prize Mildred gives the winners is worth no more than a pack of Wrigley's. These girls are the real prizes. Our groupies."

Next to Elvis, Southern had sidled up behind one of these young groupies and was now stealthily reaching for the hem of her kilt skirt. Elvis smacked Southern's hand with the tip of a crutch.

"Just doing research," Southern murmured. "The secret of any great film is verisimilitude."

Elvis leaned toward Kevin. "But obviously these girls know that they're actually going home with a, uh—"

"An imitation?" Kevin offered.

"Well, at least not with me," Elvis said.

"Ninety-nine percent do," the boy answered. "They figure that if they can't have the real McCoy, they'll make do with a duplicate. Of course, some of them—mostly the real pretty ones—make a fella work real hard for the prize. Got to put on a private show for them, sometimes in just your briefs, which can be kind of mortifying. And, of course, you got to let them call you Elvis the whole time, which isn't really much of a problem."

The entire idea made Elvis feel disgusted and giddy, in fairly equal parts.

"What about that other one percent?" Elvis said.

"That would be your Miss Muffy Kent," Kevin said, smirking. "She had never been to any of these shows until that one time a couple of weeks ago. Her friends brought her down from Waynesboro—that is, if you call malicious bitches 'friends.' They told Muffy that they were going to fix her up with Elvis Presley himself. Said they had given Elvis a photo of her and he was just dying to make her acquaintance. Muffy bought the whole package."

Elvis gestured toward the contestants. "But that child would have to be blind to believe—"

"Not completely blind, Elvis, but about as nearsighted as a mute bat," Kevin said. "That's why she wears glasses thicker than hubcaps, otherwise all she can see is the outlines of things—kinda like a fuzzy cartoon. Except, of course, she wasn't wearing her glasses that night. Not when she wanted to look so alluring for the King of Rock and Roll."

"Which one? Which one did she go with?" Elvis said.

"That's your man," Kevin said, pointing at the real porker skulking behind one of the better-looking look-alikes.

Not only did the boy whom Kevin fingered look like a life-size Joe Palooka doll all dressed up as Elvis, but he had a walleye that was looking toward Mississippi while the rest of him was facing Arkansas.

"Son, if this is your idea of a joke, getting me out of my hospital bed just so you could—"

"It's his voice, Elvis," Kevin said. "When he does your voice, it sounds more like yours than Miss Elvisetta's does, and that's saying plenty. Heck, some folks say his voice sounds more like yours than yours does."

Has Kevin been writing lyrics for the Waynesboro Five Minus Two?

"Truth is, Goodyear Bobby takes this whole deal a lot more serious than the rest of us do," Kevin went on. "He claims he is in possession of a rare gift, God given. He says he's not imitating your voice, he's *channeling* it."

"But you're only supposed to be able to do that with dead folks," Elvis said.

"Guess he's making an exception," Kevin said. "Anyway, using that voice, Bobby can fool just about anybody into thinking he is Elvis. He's always phoning up radio stations and saying he's you."

"He can only fool you if you can't see him," Elvis said. "*Or* feel him. Miss Muffy probably could barely get her arms around that fella, so how could she think it was me?"

"*Desire,* Elvis. With a heap of desire, a woman's reckoning powers can make incredible adjustments. Especially if she believes that the love of her life's very own voice is whispering sweet nothings in her ear. And most especially if she's never before had a man of *any* size lying on top of her by way of comparison."

"For a youngster, you sure seem to know a lot about women," Elvis said, genuinely impressed.

"Not enough," Kevin replied. "I usually come in last at these cattle calls. If I score at all, that is. It's my moves, you see. Most of these girls, when they see me dancing up there on Mildred's stage, it doesn't exactly turn their minds to thoughts of lovemaking. Like that night Miss Muffy came here, I was doing a pitch-perfect performance of 'Teddy Bear,' complete with your twitching-foot thing, when I tripped over myself and fell headfirst into the lap of Trudy Jessel—prettiest groupie of them all—right in the front row."

Elvis could not help smiling.

"I figured that would cause me to strike out again back here," Kevin went on, "but I thought I'd give it a try anyhow, so I stuck around, even after everybody else had pretty much paired off or gone home empty-handed. So that left just Bobby and me."

Elvis glanced to his right to see if Mr. Southern was taking all this in too, but the man was now chatting animatedly with one of the over-the-hill groupies. More research, no doubt.

"Now Bobby, he *never* scores," Kevin continued. "It's obvious why, but you've got to admire his persistence. And that night it paid off, all right. Just as I was heading for my car, I saw these three girls approach him—Muffy and her two so-called friends. I kinda slipped back behind that sign there and heard the whole thing. Goodyear Bobby got the setup in a heartbeat, talked just like you did in *Viva Las Vegas,* saying how much he'd heard about Miss Muffy and what a pleasure it was to meet her, and why didn't the little darlin' come out for a spin in his pink Cadillac car so they could get to know each other intimate like."

"Wasn't he worried that she was underage?"

"Bobby?" Kevin laughed. "Heck, most of these girls are under-age, Elvis. That's what makes them so sweet and willing."

"But it's statutory rape."

"They reserve that charge for movie stars," Mr. Southern chimed in. Apparently he had been listening after all.

Southern was probably right. If you put away every young man in Tennessee who'd had his way with a girl under the age of eighteen, farms all over the state would be filing for bankruptcy because of the labor shortage.

"Muffy never told a soul about it," Kevin said. "But her girl-friends sure did. That's how her daddy heard. He got madder than a wet hornet and charged off to tell the law that Elvis Presley himself had ruined his child in the backseat of a Cadillac car."

Elvis took a deep, rib-tingling breath and let it out slowly. So this was where all his life-deranging troubles had come from—nothing more than a fat boy who'd had the chance of a lifetime to have his first sexual experience. If Elvis's pelvis had not been aching so much, he would have done a little jig of relief right then and there.

"Tell Bobby I'd like to have a word with him," Elvis said to Kevin, then turned around and limped back toward his car.

A moment later, Kevin arrived with walleyed, blimp-shaped Goodyear Bobby huffing beside him.

"Are you *really* Elvis?" the boy greeted him in his adolescent voice.

"I am," Elvis said. "But don't shout it out, okay?"

"Jeez, Elvis, with that purple business on your face, you'd've come in behind me in the contest tonight," Bobby said, giggling.

"That's why I didn't enter," Elvis said. First impression, he liked this kid. He leaned down on his crutches, so his face was right in front of Bobby's. "I know all about your adventure with Miss Muffy Kent, son," he said softly.

Goodyear Bobby's rotund face burst into a hundred-watt beam.

"I guess I've got you to thank for that," Bobby said. Then, with an instantaneous switch of vocal gears, he added, "Thank you. Thank you very much."

Man, he did sound more like Elvis than Elvis did himself—*whatever* the heck that meant.

"Well, I'm glad you enjoyed yourself, Bobby, but—"

"We enjoyed *you*, Elvis," Bobby interjected, back in his own voice again. "I had to channel every inch of you to do that girl authentically."

Elvis blinked his eyes closed for a moment. Nope, just now he didn't have either the time or the energy to execute any more mental flips on the subject of personal identity.

"Son, I need a big favor from you," Elvis said. "I need you to tell Miss Muffy's daddy that it wasn't me who sampled his daughter, it was you."

Bobby's beam dimmed to a flicker.

"But . . . but what if he makes me, m-m-m-marry her?" the boy stammered.

"Well, you said you *enjoyed* her, boy, and that's all that counts." It was Mr. Southern speaking. He must have crept up behind Elvis without him noticing. "That's exactly what a man should look for in a wife."

"But I'm only seventeen!" Bobby protested. "Still in high school!"

"High school is a notorious waste of time," Southern said, coming around the rear of the Caddy with his antique groupie in tow. "You'd be better off in the army. That way, you can marry the girl and leave home in the same day. Truth is, that's the secret to a long, happy marriage."

"Please!" Goodyear Bobby was trembling, which, in turn, agitated his belly, making it slosh around under his shirt like pudding in a perambulator. If Kevin's theory was correct, Muffy Kent must have had an entire mountain of desire in order to fool her senses into thinking that was an Elvis-sized man bumping bellies with her.

"Let's get real, here," Kevin was now saying. "If Bobby confesses, old man Kent is going to bring his daughter out to identify him. *With her glasses on!* Now don't get me wrong, Bobby, but it just could be that on second look Muffy won't want to marry *you.*"

For one heartbreaking moment, Goodyear Bobby looked crestfallen. You couldn't help but feel for the youngster.

"It's worse than that," Mr. Southern said. "She'll insist that it wasn't even Bobby that she'd been with. She just won't believe it. Or admit to herself that it could've been him. Bobby's confession won't be accepted. They'll think he's one of those loonies who go around confessing to any crime that will get them some attention."

"But I *did* do her!" Bobby bellowed, his voice cracking. *"Twice,* in fact!"

By golly, the male of the species sure was a crazy beast. He'd rather hang by his neck than give up one ounce of sexual pride.

Daniel Klein

From the corner of his eye, Elvis saw two Studebaker sedans pull up in front of Mildred's. Out jumped six men in dark suits. Each one of them had a lean, uncharitable face that looked somewhere between a hellfire preacher's and a drill sergeant's. Instinctively, Elvis ducked down his head.

"The Legion of Decency," Kevin whispered. "Out on their nightly search."

"For what?" Elvis asked.

"Indecency," Kevin said. "Mostly in the form of sexual goings-on. But they missed the action here tonight. Mildred keeps changing her hours to keep them off balance."

The six men appeared to have just figured this out too, and returned to their cars. A couple of them looked like they were packing heavy artillery under their jackets. They slammed the car doors loudly and took off.

"There's something else I need to know, son," Elvis said to Bobby. "What can you tell me about Miss Carol-Sue Crampton over in Decaturville? And another one—Amy something—up in Madison County."

"Afraid I haven't had the pleasure, Elvis," Goodyear Bobby replied.

The pair of Studebakers had circled around the parking lot and now passed no more than ten feet away from where Elvis's group was standing. It was too late for Elvis to turn away. In that instant, Elvis caught his reflection in the rear side window of the second car.

Or was that somebody *inside* the car who looked more like Elvis than anybody Elvis had seen that night or any other night?

8

Willie the Wonder Worm

Elvis slipped into a half sleep for most of the ride back to the hospital, although every time Southern hit a bump, he was jerked awake with a sharp pain in his hip.

If Goodyear Bobby's story solved anything, it was only one-third of Elvis's predicament, and a weak third at that. Bobby might confess in front of a judge, but there would be Miss Muffy Kent with her glasses on, insisting that it was Elvis who had seduced her, not Bobby. "They're pretty easy to tell apart," she'd say, and the whole jury would laugh their heads off.

Sitting next to Southern in the front seat was the superannuated groupie he had picked up. Her name was Virginia, which seemed an irony in itself, and she talked in a high-pitched little-girl voice that only compounded that irony.

When they reached the rear of the hospital, Southern helped Elvis out, then on with his surgical smock and cap.

"I'm thinking of calling our movie *Moonlight in Vermont*," Southern said.

"What the heck for?"

"It's my favorite song."

Miss Virginia had rolled down her window and now looked out at Elvis.

"Are you really Elvis?" she asked.

"No, I just play him in the movies," Elvis answered.

"I thought so," she said.

Miss Sarah popped up in the bed as soon Elvis entered. "You won't believe what happened while you were gone!" she said.

"Try me."

While they switched clothes and places, Sarah Whipple told her story: She had drifted off to sleep shortly after Elvis left, only to be awakened at about one thirty by a strong odor. "Smelled like the dentist's office from hell," Sarah said. "And if there's one thing I hate, it's the dentist. Turns out my sniffer was right. Alginates, the stuff they make dental molds out of. A whole big pot of it sitting on the side of the bed."

"Nurse left it there?"

"No, Miss Krafty. Krafty Plaster, although that's not her real name."

Of course not. Nobody was who he said he was these days.

"I open my eyes, and there she is sitting right next to me, stirring her pot and grinning at me." Sarah paused to button up her silk shirt. "Did I mention that she was wearing a see-through blouse?"

"No," Elvis said. "Guess she wasn't a nurse, then. Unless the night shift dresses more casual."

"So she stops stirring and then starts to unstrap me," Sarah continued, "all the while fluttering that see-through right in front of my face. I'll tell you, Elvis, that man inside me was just beside himself with excitement."

"I can imagine," Elvis said, although he couldn't—not completely.

"And then she slips her hand under the sheet, heading down for my demilitarized zone, if you know what I'm saying," Sarah said. "It was one trying moment for me, Elvis. I knew Miss Krafty was going to be in for a big disappointment when she got there, but at the same time, her huntin' hand sure felt good to me."

Elvis didn't think he could take much more of this. He tried to shift the subject. "What was that dentist's pot all about?"

"She wanted to make a mold of it," Miss Sarah said. "A plaster cast. She's already got Little Richard's and a bunch of other rock-ers'. But she said her collection is worthless without yours. Which she thought was mine, of course."

"My *what*?"

"Your Wilbur, Elvis."

"Huh?"

"You know, your black root."

"Beg your pardon?"

"Your *wild thing,* Elvis. *Willie the wonder worm!*"

"Lordy, woman, make a plaster cast of it?"

"It's her hobby," Miss Sarah said. "Like collecting stamps, but more personal like."

"What the heck kind of hobby is that?" Elvis said.

"Some girl from England started it. She and her cohorts called themselves Plaster Casters. Krafty's group—they're kind of imi-tating them. Krafty says that in the Roman days, artists sculpted head statues of their most important men. Like Caesar, you know? But these days, what separates one powerful man from another isn't his face, it's his wherewithal. So Krafty's made it her mission to sculp that."

"There's not a museum from here to Australia that will display garbage like that."

"She's thinking more like New York City than Australia," Miss Sarah said. "Anyway, good as her huntin' hand felt, I pushed it away before she could find what I was lacking. Didn't want to blow our cover, you know."

Miss Sarah threaded the straps across Elvis's torso. Just now, those straps made him feel more secure than trapped. It sure was one unfathomable world out there.

"I told Miss Krafty that I wasn't in the mood," Sarah went on. "Said I'd rather we just talked this time."

"*This* time?"

"We had ourselves a good talk, too. She's an art student, the re-bellious type. Comes from the same kind of family as mine, only a whole lot richer and a whole lot worse. Her daddy's got Jesus and her mommy had more important things on her mind, so she took off when Miss Krafty was just a toddler. Miss Krafty is scared as hell of her daddy. The man would as soon pop her in the skull with his Bible as read it to her. To him, they're both just Bible lessons. So anyhow, Krafty left Daddy's manse too, and now she lives with her mama up near Jackson."

"So her daddy's probably not too pleased with his daughter's hobby," Elvis said.

"You said a mouthful," Miss Sarah said. "He's a corporal in the Legion of Decency."

"The Legion of—?" Elvis stopped. He could hear footsteps—two sets of them—coming down the hospital corridor toward them. Both sounded too light-stepped to be either Parker's or Southern's. Clearly, Miss Sarah had heard them too. She darted her head from side to side, then dashed toward the room's only closet and shut herself inside.

"Doctor here to see you, Mr. Elvis," a nurse said, sauntering in fresh as a daisy. Morning shift.

"Kinda early, ain't it?" Elvis said. "Haven't even had my breakfast yet."

"Forgive me, Mr. Presley," said the woman following the nurse into the room. She was tall, with luxuriant red hair piled up in little waves on top of her head, like a stack of pancakes. She wore a doctor's coat over a smart print dress, a stethoscope dangling from her long neck, and she spoke with some kind of accent that had a lot of mucus in it. "I have grand rounds up in Nashville at exactly seven a.m. This was the only time I could see you."

"You the head doctor?" Elvis asked.

"I'm a neurological psychiatrist," the woman said. She bowed her head stiffly in a sort of military gesture. "Permit me to introduce myself. Dr. Helga Volk."

"Elvis Presley," Elvis said. He felt it would be proper to shake her hand, but both of his were stuck under the straps. In any event,

Dr. Volk had already strolled to the foot of his bed, where she yanked up the sheet, revealing Elvis's feet.

"*Damnation!*" Elvis thundered. "What was that?"

"A mere pinprick," Volk said. "Your extremities appear to be sensate."

"I coulda told you that," Elvis said.

"What day is it, Mr. Presley?" the doctor said.

"Wednesday . . . No, it's Thursday, but it still feels like Wednesday."

"In what way, Mr. Presley? In what way does it *feel* like Wednesday?"

Elvis smiled. The lady was a headshrinker, all right.

"It feels like Wednesday because I haven't had enough sleep for Thursday yet," he said.

"And who is the president of the United States?" Volk asked. The way she said 'president,' with all that phlegm in the *s*, sounded just like Dr. Strangelove.

"Johnson," Elvis said, then added for good measure, "Lyndon, not Andrew. He was from around these parts, you know. Andrew, not Lyndon."

Volk loosened Elvis's chest strap.

"Grip my hand as tightly as you can," she commanded.

Elvis withdrew his right hand from under the sheets, then reached out and grasped the doctor's hand. It was surprisingly soft and smooth, almost like a young girl's. Elvis looked up at the doctor's face. The lady was wincing. Elvis immediately let go.

"Hope I didn't hurt you, ma'am," Elvis said.

"You have a very strong hand, Mr. Presley," the doctor said. If Elvis had not known that Dr. Volk was a professional, he would have thought he heard a trace of admiration in her voice.

"I play the guitar," Elvis explained.

"So I understand," the doctor said. "I also understand that when you perform in public, your hips twitch in an apparently uncontrollable manner, similar to St. Vitus' dance."

"That's a disease, isn't it?" Elvis said.

Dr. Volk issued a throaty laugh. "Yes, a neurological disease," she said. "Unless, of course, you believe in a divine puppeteer who pulls your strings. That is what St. Vitus himself thought."

"Well, he *was* a saint, wasn't he?" Elvis replied, winking at her.

The doctor responded by reaching up to her head and swiftly removing a half dozen bobby pins. Her rich red hair tumbled down to her shoulders, instantly transforming her severe countenance into that of a warm and wise European lady, kind of like the French lady Elvis had pictured as the love interest in his meat loaf movie. Volk then straightened up and immediately resumed her professional bearing.

"Tell me, Mr. Presley, do you ever experience any mental disturbances? Unwanted thoughts? Hear voices?"

For a reason that Elvis could not begin to understand, the question incited a small squall of emotion inside himself. So much so that he felt tears gather in the corners of his eyes. Volk signaled the nurse to leave the room, then sat down on the edge of the bed.

"What just happened, Mr. Presley?" she asked softly.

Elvis shrugged.

"I can assure you that anything you tell me will go no farther than this room," the doctor said.

How about as far as that closet? Elvis remained silent.

"Troubling thoughts have a way of festering inside us if they are never spoken," Volk went on in a subdued voice. "Perhaps I can help."

Elvis looked into the doctor's eyes. There was a kindness there that reminded him of his mother. Heaven knows, when Elvis was a boy and talked over worrisome things with his mother at the kitchen table, he always felt better afterward. Unburdened. And the fact of the matter was that nobody since then had ever wanted to know what he was really feeling—not his deepest, truest thoughts and emotions. Sure, the press would ask him how he *really* felt about, say, Ann-Margret and Priscilla, but they were just digging for copy; they didn't give a hoot if those true feelings were tying him in knots. And, yes, the Colonel often asked how Elvis was feeling, but obviously his real question was, *Are you feeling up to making me some more money today, boy?* Even when Priscilla asked Elvis to speak his mind, he knew it was not the absolute truth she wanted to hear. They both knew that would be too painful.

"What are you thinking right now?" Volk asked softly.

"Doctor, sometimes I feel another Elvis inside me," Elvis whispered. "And that he might be getting me into a heap of trouble."

"In what way?"

"He goes out in my car and seduces high school girls," Elvis said.

"And this other Elvis—he is not *you?*" the doctor said.

"Well, he is and he isn't, ma'am. I mean, I wouldn't do such a thing in my right mind."

"But in your right mind, do you ever *feel* like seducing high school girls?"

Elvis shrugged again. "I'm human, Doctor," he said. "And on top of that, I'm male. I feel like doing all kinds of things that I don't actually do. That's why God gave us willpower."

"God?" Dr. Volk looked down at Elvis with a quizzical smile. "Freud says that God is the invention of tyrants. That he is an efficient way to keep us satisfied with less than we deserve."

"I guess Dr. Freud never felt God's spirit moving inside him," Elvis said.

"If he had, he probably would have diagnosed it as ulcers. Or his mother." Volk leaned closer to Elvis's face. "Who is this Elvis inside you? Do you know him?"

Elvis felt that squall do an encore.

"Sometimes I think he might be my identical twin brother," he whispered, after a moment. "Jesse Garon. They say he died when we were born. But maybe he lives inside me. And he's angrier than hell."

"Fascinating," Dr. Volk murmured.

It was at that moment that they both heard a loud sneeze coming from the far end of the room. Actually, *three* loud sneezes in quick succession.

"What was that?" Volk said, rising.

"Must be that fellow in the next room," Elvis said. "He's got the influenza, I hear."

A fourth sneeze. Dr. Volk headed straight for the closet and opened its door. Standing inside with a handkerchief to her nose was Sarah Whipple, sideburns, silk shirt, tight pants, and all.

"Danged allergies," Miss Sarah said in her most pitch-perfect Elvis voice. "Tickles my nose hairs."

"Mein Gott in Himmel!" Volk blurted. She reached out for the windowsill to steady herself. Elvis understood just enough German from his army days—and from 'Wooden Heart'—to realize that Dr. Helga Volk did possess some notion of God, whether or not Dr. Freud approved.

Elvis was about to explain to the good doctor what, exactly, was going on here, when his inner giggle took over. And he was still giggling a moment later when another young woman came sashaying in the door of his room. It was Miss Carol-Sue Crampton, all done up in a high school cheerleader's outfit that wasn't even trying to cover her underthings. Instinctively, Elvis turned his head toward the wall.

"You stood me up!" Carol-Sue exclaimed to the room in general.

"Sorry, li'l darlin', I been kinda tied up," Miss Sarah Whipple answered, stepping out of the closet and up to Carol-Sue. "But I'll make it up to you, I promise."

With that, Miss Sarah took Miss Carol-Sue by the arm and led her out of the room into the hallway.

"I am not feeling so well," Dr. Volk murmured.

That Girly Hip Thing

Elvis managed to coax two long red capsules out of the nurse this time. He told her that the pills made his pelvis feel more like part of his own body and less like somebody else's. It probably would not have mattered what he told her; the nurse seemed to really like him. Before she left, she reminded him again that his hip would be X-rayed first thing tomorrow morning.

With the pills calming down the worrying part of his brain while pepping up the can-do part, Elvis worked on a plan. At least one thing the Goodyear Bobby episode proved was that there was very likely more than just one fella out there seducing teenage girls by saying he was Elvis. Heck, if those Elvis look-alike groupies liked to pretend that the look-alike was the genuine article while they were going at it in the backseat of a Cadillac car, how big a leap could it be from being fooled by someone else? More like a hop and a skip.

But, of course, no matter how much desire was inebriating a girl's brain, she would have to have eyesight as bad as Muffy Kent's to be fooled into thinking that Kevin Cote or any of those other contestants at Mildred's Come-And-Get-It actually were Elvis. Then again, Carol-Sue seemed to have pretty good eyesight, and *she* was apparently fooled by Miss Sarah. That Miss Krafty Plaster too. So far, that is; there was a built-in limit to that particular masquerade. But Miss Sarah—or Elvisetta, as she called herself on the circuit—was in a class by herself. Maybe Miss Sarah was so much better at impersonating Elvis because she had so much more at stake in the enterprise: it was the only way she could keep that Inner Man of hers from shredding up her insides.

Best thing to do at this point was to search the whole region for any young man who looked as much like Elvis as Miss Sarah did. And probably the best way to do that was to visit as many look-alike contests and dances or whatever as he possibly could. Elvis sure hoped Miss Sarah paid him another visit before nightfall so that they could execute their switcheroo again.

Colonel Parker walked in. If he had looked distressed at his last visit, he looked positively anguished this time. Elvis sure was glad he had two of those red pills under his belt.

"I've got good news and I've got bad news," Parker said.

"I'll take the good news first."

"The good news is that I didn't give that photographer a dime. Had it all ready in fresh one-hundred-dollar bills, straight from Fidelity National, but he never saw the color of it."

"I appreciate that, Tom," Elvis said. "If you do business with criminals, you turn into one yourself. That is a fact of life."

"The bad news is that I didn't give him the money because when I got to our meeting spot he was dead," Parker said. "A bullet between his eyes. Murdered. *Freshly* murdered, judging by the amount of blood still pulsing out the back of his head. What was left of it, that is."

Parker was always at his most eloquent when describing ugliness.

"Who did it?" Elvis said.

"That's what the police over in Bolivar would like to know," Parker said. "As things stand now, even *I* am a suspect."

Despite himself—and the present circumstances—Elvis found the idea of Colonel Tom Parker being a murder suspect fascinating. Even kind of entertaining, especially since Parker had seriously entertained the idea that Elvis was a rape suspect. But this feeling lasted for only a second, of course, before the gravity of Parker's situation set in.

"How can they suspect you, Tom?" Elvis asked.

"Because even though I reported the murder, I was the last known person to see the son of a bitch. Whose name turns out to be Manard Frew, incidentally," Parker said. "Plus there's the fact that when the chief of police searched me, he found two hundred one-hundred-dollar bills in my pocket. For reasons that make absolutely no sense to me, carrying twenty thousand dollars on your person means that your character is highly questionable. Not that you happen to be wealthy and a prodigious shopper, for God's sake, but a potential murderer. Since when is being well-heeled a federal offense? This would never happen in Las Vegas, I'll tell you."

For another fraction of a second, Elvis could see something comical—maybe even *ironically* comical—in Parker's predicament: the man who lived for money gets done in by money.

"But they aren't going to arrest you, are they?" Elvis said.

"Not unless I leave the state," Parker said. "They released me on my own recognizance."

Maybe it was that extra red pill, but the notion of being on your *own recognizance* struck Elvis as being comically absurd too. Those words had to mean that you recognized yourself. Well, that shouldn't be too hard a job. Or was it?

Abruptly, Elvis had a sobering thought. "Did they find those pornographic pictures on this Frew fella?" he asked. "You know, those Polaroids he was peddling."

"No!" Parker said, sounding piqued. "The son of a gun hadn't even brought them with him."

"Mighty good thing, under the circumstances."

"It was a bait and switch, Elvis," Parker grumbled. "By God, I was this close to falling for a bait and switch!"

Yes, indeed, professional pride was right up there with sexual pride when it came to male self-destructiveness. Parker, the king of carny conmen, reacted real badly to being outfoxed, even if his reaction dropped him down a foxhole of his own making.

"But if the police *had* found those photos, they'd have put two and two together and seen that you'd come there to pay him blackmail," Elvis said. "Or *not,* as the case may be. Inasmuch as murdering a man is a whole lot cheaper than paying him twenty grand. Now that would have made you into the *prime* suspect, Colonel, and you'd only be under *their* recognizance right this minute."

"That's ridiculous," Parker said.

"Well, they would at least have part of it right," Elvis said. "I mean, you *were* going to meet Frew to pay him blackmail. There is no denying that part."

Colonel Parker squinted his eyes so tight that he looked like an Eskimo, a wounded and exasperated Eskimo.

"Listen here, Elvis," Parker said, keeping his voice low. "You don't think I could actually do a thing like that, do you?"

Elvis let the question hang there for a long, delicious moment. Was it Elvis himself, or was it the Inner Elvis who was taking so much devilish pleasure in the Colonel's discomfort?

"Do a thing like what?" Elvis asked in an innocent voice.

"You know, son," Parker said, letting his voice trail off.

Elvis kept looking up at him like he didn't know.

"Kill a man," Parker said, finally.

"It's not my opinion that counts, Tom," Elvis replied. Man, how could behaving so mean-spiritedly feel so darned good?

Parker looked about as forlorn as a kid who has found coal in his Christmas stocking, and Elvis felt a stab of guilt. In fact, he was just about to assure the Colonel that he didn't doubt his innocence for one minute, when two men in police uniforms sauntered into the room. Both of them looked tall enough to play in the NBA.

"Thought we'd find you here, Parker," one of them said. He had a five-pointed gold star on his chest, the kind Elvis collected.

"Step back from the bed and put your hands straight out in front of you," the other officer said to the Colonel.

"Who the hell do you think you—?" Parker began.

"Shut up!" the first officer finished. With that, he yanked Parker around and grabbed both of his hands. The other policeman snapped a pair of handcuffs onto Parker's wrists.

"Thomas Parker, you are under arrest for the murder of Manard Frew," he said, enunciating each word so precisely you'd think he was talking on Voice of America overseas radio.

"You are making a terrible mistake, Officers," Elvis said.

Both policemen turned to face Elvis. It was the first time either of them had even acknowledged Elvis's presence. The gold-star cop raised his right hand and pointed a finger at Elvis.

"You should be ashamed of yourself, Mr. Presley," he said.

"Beg your pardon?"

"We found those sickening photographs when we searched Frew's room," the officer said. "Doing a high school girl out in the open air like that! Absolutely shameless. You'd think a man of your stature would have more Christian sense."

"The Legion of Decency has got your number, all right," the other officer chimed in. "The devil sent you here to corrupt our young people. And not just with that girly hip thing you do on-stage, either. You bring your debauchery right down here among us on the back roads of Madison County."

"Those photos are phony!" Elvis said. "That's not me. It's just somebody posing as me."

"We checked out the licence plate on the Caddy," the first officer said. "It's yours, all right."

"That's phony too!" Elvis said, raising his head off his pillow.

The first officer came up alongside the bed and looked down at Elvis with hellfire eyes.

"If it's all so damned phony, why'd you send out your gal Friday here to appropriate those photographs?" he growled. "And not just appropriate them either, but make sure the photographer had snapped his last picture."

"I never asked him to do any such thing!" Elvis snapped back. And then, without thinking, Elvis added something that he would immediately regret. "Anything Colonel Parker did was his own doing."

The forsaken look in Parker's eyes when Elvis said that made Elvis feel like the low-downest of sinners. He had betrayed Colonel Parker to save his own skin. Betrayal was a sin right up there with envy and wrath, head and shoulders above lust. Elvis was no better than Judas.

"But Parker didn't do anything!" Elvis cried out. But it was too late. The two police officers from Bolivar were already leading Tom Parker through the door and into the corridor.

Elvis's head dropped back onto the pillow. At that moment, he would have given anything in world to be someone else.

10

Moonlight Serenade

*Y*ou're starting to look like yourself again," Mr. Terry Southern said as they pulled out onto the highway. "Those spoke marks are just shadows now. Pink shadows. Even your lip has lost a little weight."

"My hip feels a whole lot better too," Elvis said.

"Time heals all wounds. Or is it the other way around?" Southern said. He reached down to a paper bag at his feet and withdrew a glass casserole dish of meat loaf. "Your Miss Mary thought you could use some genuine sustenance. She says the reason hospital food is so unsavory is they want you to get better as slowly as possible. Keeps their bed count up. I'm putting Mary in our motion picture too, by the way."

"Along with Miss Sarah," Elvis said.

"You have more natural talent down here than in all of Beverly Hills," Southern said.

The meat loaf was still warm. Southern had neglected to bring any utensils, so Elvis scooped up a ball of the stuff with his bare hand and brought it to his mouth. Man, only one bite and he could feel his insides firming up.

Just when Elvis had almost given up on her, Miss Sarah had come waltzing into his hospital room around midnight in full Elvis concert regalia. This time their switcheroo had been accomplished in a minute flat, but the rest of Elvis's plan had changed.

87

He would not be looking for look-alikes tonight. He needed to find out who, exactly, this Manard Frew fella had been, and what had been his connection to the man who seduced Amy Coulter as a photo opportunity out on that Madison County back road. What's more, did Frew have anything to do with Carol-Sue Crampton and her daddy? Or even Muffy Kent and Sheriff Tip? And, of course, the biggest question was why would somebody want Frew dead?

Right now, Elvis and Southern were headed for Deer Creek, north of Jackson, where Frew was listed in the telephone directory.

"Maybe we should be taking this opportunity to talk about our movie script," Southern said as Elvis continued hand-feeding himself.

"If things keep going as they are, about the only movie I'll be capable of shooting is a remake of *Jailhouse Rock,*" Elvis said between chews. "They're getting the location polished up as we speak."

"Don't worry, Elvis. Everything will work out in the end," Southern said.

"I thought you didn't believe in Hollywood endings."

"Only in real life." Sometimes Mr. Terry Southern piled on so many levels of irony that they seemed to cancel each other out.

Elvis decided now was as good a time as any to tell Southern his movie idea about the rock star who decides to sing about ordinary things like the joys of eating meat loaf and reading Civil War history books on the john and picking his nose. And how, despite what everybody around him predicts, his songs become huge hits. Southern nodded encouragingly throughout, but when Elvis had finished he said, "Interesting, Elvis, but the plain truth is, judging by the last few days, your ordinary life is anything but ordinary."

"But this movie is not about me," Elvis protested.

"That's right, you just play yourself in the movies," Southern said. "Speaking of which, I'm still worn out by my little pas de deux with that Virginia woman. She has more energy than any teenager, I'm here to tell you. More hunger too. I find myself liking Tennessee living more every day."

"Glad you're keeping yourself busy."

"Anyway, between bouts, Virginia told me her theory about what was going on with these teenagers who think you seduced them," Southern said. "Fascinating theory. The woman has a lively imagination in more ways than one."

Elvis had finished the meat loaf and now was trying to figure out how to loosen up the fat-soaked bread crumbs stuck in the corners of the casserole dish. The only viable option appeared to be putting his face right inside the dish and tonguing them. Why not? Mr. Southern did not strike him as a stickler for table manners.

"She thinks he's a hypnotist," Southern continued. "That he wears one of those medallions around his neck, just like yours, and he dangles it in front of their eyes, swings it back and forth in the moonlight, and one, two, three, they go under. Then the guy says, 'This is Elvis speaking. Let's rock and roll, sweetheart.' "

Elvis raised his head from the casserole. "But you can't be hypnotized unless you want to be," he said.

"That's what I told Virginia. And she said, 'Oh, they *want* to be, all right.' "

It was similar to Kevin Cote's theory about the power of desire to fog a woman's senses.

"Sounds possible, but not likely," Elvis said, diving into the dish again.

"Likely or not, it certainly is going to make one mesmerizing scene in our movie."

The late Manard Frew's address was listed at 3 Wilbur Street in the center of Deer Creek, although when they got there it appeared that all Deer Creek possessed was a center, and only a dozen houses of that. It also appeared that all of Deer Creek had turned in for the night. Not even a porch light was on. Hardly surprising for a small Tennessee town past midnight. Or even past 10 p.m., for that matter. Southern pulled up in front of 3 Wilbur.

From the size of the structure and the number of names listed on the mailbox in front, it was obviously a boardinghouse. For a good minute, the two of them just sat there in silence.

"I didn't think this part through," Elvis said finally. "Country folks get real surly if a person wakes them out of a sound sleep. Even if it's a fireman."

"How about if it's Elvis Presley?" Southern said.

"Hard to say," Elvis said. "I'm real popular in these parts, but sleep is more popular. That's actually the point of my movie idea, Mr. Southern. It's the natural, ordinary things that people value."

"Listen, you've got to get back to the hospital by sunrise," Southern said. "So if we're going to do anything, we have to do it now, Elvis. It's what they call in the motion picture business 'the ticking clock.' Or is it the other way around?"

Elvis led the way up the flagstone path to the front door of the boardinghouse. A dog barked a few houses down Wilbur Street and was answered by another dog a few houses up in the other direction. The moon seemed to shine brighter here than in Decaturville; Elvis could see his shadow sharply etched on the lawn, complete with the single crutch that he required now, under his left shoulder.

There were a half dozen doorbell buttons next to the door, each with a different name beside it. Manard Frew's was next to last. The top one, for a Mrs. Roger Rule, seemed most promising as the headmistress of the establishment. Elvis pressed it, waited, then pressed it again longer. He heard some rustling about inside, then some cursing, shuffling feet, more cursing, and the door opened. The tip of a shotgun jutted through the opening.

"If'n you didn't come here to tell me I inherited a million dollars, prepare to meet your maker," a woman's voice said.

"You inherited a million dollars, lady!" Mr. Terry Southern answered from behind Elvis.

"If'n you're pulling my leg, you can forget about ever walking again," the woman said.

"Sorry to wake you up, ma'am, but it's kind of an emergency,"

Elvis said, extending his hand inside the door just above the rifle barrel. "My name is Elvis Presley."

"Yeh, and my name's Tallulah Bankhead," the woman said.

"Pleased to meet you," Elvis said.

The tip of the shotgun pushed into Elvis's belly.

"I really am Elvis, ma'am," Elvis said. "I swear it on my mama's grave."

"If'n this is a prank, I really am going to wound you, boy. Nobody wakes up Agnes Rule in the middle of the night without leaving with a souvenir to prove it." With that, she withdrew from the door, snapped on the porch light from inside, and then came onto the porch with the gun still pointing at Elvis's midsection. She looked close to eighty and she was wearing a man's seersucker robe and open galoshes. "Stand under the lamp," she ordered.

Elvis did as he was told.

After a moment, the woman said, "You got a mask on?"

"No, ma'am."

"Then what's that pink cross doing on your face? It ain't Ash Wednesday. And that lower lip sure looks like it's made outta rubber."

"I had an accident, Mrs. Rule. Car accident."

"Yeah, guess I heard about that on the radio, didn't I? But what's that goop around your mouth?"

"Meat loaf, ma'am. Eatin' on the run."

Mrs. Rule paused a moment, then, "I still ain't convinced one hundred percent. Sing me somethin'."

"Beg pardon?"

"Sing me a song, you know, like only Elvis himself can do it. That'll prove it one way or t'other."

Elvis considered explaining to the woman that singing would not prove anything, not with the likes of Goodyear Bobby around. Or Miss Sarah Whipple, for that matter. But with that rifle again pressing into his belly, Elvis decided that a couple of verses of a song was probably a better alternative. In a world of imitations, the genuine article has to work overtime.

"Any song in particular?" Elvis asked.

"I like that new one, 'Wooden Heart,' " Mrs. Rule said.

Elvis leaned his crutch against the porch railing, spread his legs wide, took a long breath, and began to sing.

> *"Can't you see I love you.*
> *Please don't break my heart in two."*

"Louder," Mrs. Rule interrupted. "You sound more like Whispering Jack Smith than Elvis Presley."

"Don't want to wake your tenants up, ma'am," Elvis said.

"And I don't want to shoot your gizzards out," Mrs. Rule replied.

Elvis started from the top again, doubling his volume, but Mrs. Rule stopped him again.

"Can't barely hear ya," she said. "You're singing like you're ashamed of your song."

Mrs. Rule had at least part of that right.

"It's an old folk song, ma'am," Elvis said. "Not a screamer."

"So think like you're singing this folk thing to a pretty young thing way in the back row. And if'n you sing so it touches her heart, she's goin' to wait for you after the show and make your pecker happy to be alive."

Elvis blushed, which probably made his face a uniform pink for a brief moment. He had forgotten how earthy folks deep in the countryside could be. Behind him, Southern murmured, "Cock's tickling. Or is it the other way around?"

Elvis began again, this time at full volume.

> *"That's not hard to do.*
> *. . . 'Cause I don't have a wooden heart."*

Next door, at number 2 Wilbur Street, the porch light flashed on. Then the porch light at 4 Wilbur. Meanwhile, right behind Elvis, inside number 3, the sounds of a whole lot of feet moving around. Mrs. Rule butted the gun against Elvis's hip by way of encouragement. Elvis kept singing.

"Muss i den, muss i den,
Zum Stadtele hinaus."

Actually, singing it at full throttle like this, the song wasn't half bad after all. Sure, the lyric was lame and clumsy, but the *beseechingness* of it came through loud and clear. That kind of yearning needed some volume. Elvis spread his arms wide and launched into the second verse, the one about there being no strings on his love.

From the corner of his eye, Elvis saw a troop of folks in robes and pajamas come traipsing across Mrs. Rule's lawn from next door. A couple of them carried flashlights, which they began to train on him as he sang. And now, right at the bottom of the porch stairs, two couples started dancing something between the twist and the Charleston. Elvis turned to face them, executing his neck thing as he swiveled around. The couples, bright-eyed teenagers in all-season flannel pj's, smiled up at him. Elvis smiled back.

Man, he felt good. Better than he'd felt in a long time. Even if he was being prodded by a shotgun, singing *live* for folks—no mike, no studio, no band, no playback in an MGM sound booth—made his spirits soar. By God, he'd almost forgotten what it felt like to be so much a part of a song that it did your breathing for you.

He took the German verse up a third, just for the thrill of it, like he was harmonizing with the sonic memory of the last verse he sang. Every porch light in all of Deer Creek was on now, and people were streaming from every direction toward Agnes Rule's boardinghouse, some with candles in their hands, looking for all the world like a church processional. The boardinghouse itself had emptied out, including an elderly couple in wheelchairs who stopped on the porch right next to Elvis and began clapping their hands on the offbeat. And now, at the far end of Wilbur Street, Elvis saw an open window on the top floor of a ramshackle Victorian house, and smiling out was a entire family of colored folks. Elvis saluted them, and sang out:

> " *'Cause I'm not made of wood*
> *"And I don't have a wooden heart.'*

When the song was finished, the citizens of Deer Creek cheered and applauded so long and loud that it sounded like every rooster in Madison County woke up and joined in. A few people called for encores, and actually Elvis was all ready with one— Hank Snow's "Kentucky Moon"—but Mrs. Agnes Rule stepped right in front of him and called out to her neighbors, "Go back to sleep, you good-for-nothin's! Elvis and me got to talk."

Many other events would come to pass in that town before the twentieth century would finish up, but from that night onward, the fourteenth of October would be celebrated in Deer Creek, Tennessee, as the Day Elvis Gave Us a Moonlight Serenade.

Manard Frew's second-floor room was a sight to behold. Elvis did not know quite what he was expecting, but a few open bottles of Kentucky bourbon would not have been out of place. But no, the late Mr. Frew's room was as tidy as a cat's backside, not frilly, just neat and artful like, with framed photographs lined up on the walls and two floor-to-ceiling bookcases filled up with hardbound books. Mrs. Rule kept them at the threshold, looking in.

"I already had the Bolivar police force messin' around in here," Mrs. Rule said. "Not to mention those two Klansmen with hoods on their heads who turned the place upside down afterward. Didn't find what they were lookin' for either. You ever hear a Klansman curse? It's enough to make a turtle blush, I'll tell you."

"What were they looking for?" Elvis asked.

"Some kind of photographs. And that's just about all Manard has in here, so it took a lot of lookin'."

Southern had taken a single step inside the room and was studying one of the black-and-white photographs on the near wall.

94

"By George, the man was a certified intellectual," Southern said.

Mrs. Rule grabbed him by the sleeve and yanked him back into the hallway.

"Certifiable nutcase is more like it," she said. "And slower with the rent than a Gypsy. He went over to the other side owing me for two months."

"How much is that, Mrs. Rule?" Elvis asked.

Agnes Rule paused, clearly trying to think up the biggest number she could. "Fifteen bucks," she said.

Elvis reached into his pants pockets. Fortunately, Miss Sarah had left some spending money in there. He peeled off fifteen ones for the landlady.

"St. Peter's kinda picky about his tenants," Elvis said. "Can't get into heaven with unpaid rent."

Mrs. Rule nodded a little thank-you and let the two enter the room. Southern went straight to the photograph he had been scrutinizing.

"I can't believe it," he said. "A numbered print by Cartier-Bresson. And right here next to it, a signed Halsman. The rest are Frew's apparently, and some of them hold their own with the big boys. Look at this one, Elvis."

He pointed at a photograph of a young dwarf fishing off the side of a bridge. It was the expression in the young man's eyes that made the photo so compelling: he looked as if he were momentarily transported to a place where his deformity did not matter.

"Manard had an eye for freaks," Mrs. Rule said.

"A merciful eye," Elvis said. "How did he make his living?"

"He didn't," Rule said. "For a bit, he tried advertising himself as a wedding photographer, but that didn't last long. Nobody wants wedding photographs where folks look like they're at a funeral. But Manard would just say, '*I* didn't pose them that way,' and give the folks their money back. After that, he took odd jobs. Some, very odd. He invested in one of them mimeograph machines over there—musta cost him a small fortune—and set up a business doing newsletters for folks over in Jackson. Spent a lot of time on them. Said nobody could write a decent sentence anymore, so he had to rewrite every newsletter hisself. Not that his clients could tell the difference."

Southern began nosing around the mimeograph machine in the corner of Frew's room.

"What kind of folks need newsletters?" Elvis asked Mrs. Rule.

"Small businesses and Rotary Clubs and like that," she said. "I think Manard did his biggest business with that veterinary clinic in Jackson. Monthly thing about dog ticks and cat cancer and any other damned thing those hucksters could think up to scare you into bringing in your pet for a five-dollar checkup. Manard would try to spice it up with dog jokes and little cartoons he drew himself of dogs sniffing each other's hindquarters, but they made him take those out."

"The man was an artist, through and through," Southern said, now poking through a file he had withdrawn from a drawer in the table that held the mimeograph machine.

"One reason that newsletter enterprise didn't do so well is all of Manard's clients had to drive down to Deer Creek to do business with him,'cause he didn't own a car hisself," Agnes Rule continued. "And most folks can think of a whole lot of reasons for not driving to Deer Creek. You know how snooty city folks can be."

"City folks from Jackson."

"And a few other fancy places."

"So you saw all of Mr. Frew's clients come and go," Elvis said.

"Hard to miss a stranger in Deer Creek," Rule said.

"Were any driving pink Cadillacs?" Elvis asked.

Mrs. Rule smiled. "Mr. Presley," she said, "that coupe of your'n outside is the only Cadillac car I ever seen in the flesh. Mostly pickups, as I recall. Except for them girls what drove up from Medon. They rode up in some kind of English sports car with the top down like they was movie stars. Actually, one of them kinda looked like a movie star."

"They were customers of Manard's?" Elvis said.

"Yes indeedle-doody."

"What were they sellin'?"

"Don't rightly know," Mrs. Rule said. "But I wouldn't be surprised if they were selling their own sweet selves. You gotta wonder what this world is coming to when bitches advertise just like veterinarians."

"Bingo!" Southern called out.

He sidled up to Elvis with a mimeographed newsletter in his hands. Its masthead read SWEPT!, which made you think it was for a housecleaning concern, but when you looked just below it, you saw that SWEPT was an acronym which spelled out the organization's true mission: "Sleep With Elvis Presley Tonight!" Paper-clipped to the top sheet was a strip of photographs from one of those automatic photo machines you find in bus stations. Five smiling young women with their faces jostled together stared out from the photos, two in midwink. And one of those winkers looked for all the world like Ann-Margret.

"Dang it!" Elvis said.

"Yup, she's the one," Mrs. Rule said.

11

Roll Along, Roll Along

There's gotta be a connection to Frew's killer here somewhere," Elvis said after leafing through the latest issue of *SWEPT* while Mr. Terry Southern tore along the county road toward the interstate. It was a dismaying periodical: earnest, polished, and thoroughly smutty.

"I'll tell you, it gives a man hope when young Tennessee girls put out their own literary journal," Southern replied. He had loaded up a paper bag with all of Manard Frew's newsletters, files, notebooks, and correspondence. Old Miss Agnes, of course, had required a deposit for carting these off. After a long calculation, she had come up with the number of seven dollars and twenty-five cents. The woman had imagination.

"Well, it makes me sick," Elvis said.

"Oh, come on, Elvis, I'd give my left nut to have a newspaper totally devoted to having sex with me."

"*Fantasy* sex," Elvis corrected.

"Even better," Southern said. "Saves on the wear and tear. One thing about fantasy sex is you can't get any diseases from it."

"Except if they *think* it's real. Then you get something worse than disease, like blackmail and career-ending press and a busty young thing who's planning our wedding day."

"It could be worse," Southern said. "She could have been flat-chested."

Maybe he was the most intelligent screenwriter in America, but it sure was difficult to have a meaningful conversation with Mr. Terry Southern. Elvis turned back to the first page of *SWEPT*. In the upper-right-hand corner was an old-fashioned woodcutty line drawing of a giant Elvis being brushed up by a bevy of young women with brooms, one of which was brushing perilously close to the giant's crotch. Apparently *SWEPT*'s editors were more welcoming to Manard Frew's artwork than the veterinarians were. And in a box in the upper-left-hand corner was the club pledge, which was apparently to be intoned with one's right hand over the left breast:

> I, {name}, being of ripe body and passionate heart, do solemnly swear to do everything in my power to get the King to make me Queen for a night.

In another box just below that was the club motto:

> Virginity a Burden, Elvis the Cure.

It sounded distressingly like the doomsday ditty on that sign outside of Waynesboro.

The lead story in the newsletter was headlined "Close, but No Cigar!" and was about that girl who had been in Elvis's room at the hospital—the one imitating those Plaster Casters. It began, "Miss Krafty Plaster came within inches of her prize at Blount Memorial Hospital in Decaturville last Wednesday night." In the next-to-last paragraph, Miss Plaster was quoted as saying, "Sure, having a statue of Elvis's manhood on my mantel would make me proud, but just imagine what I'd go through to get it fit for molding." The story ended with the commentary: "Better luck next time, Krafty!" You'd think they were cheering on the local girls' softball team.

The second page was a long, surprisingly well-written editorial entitled "Sex Is Sacred," in which the officers of SWEPT came down hard on any young woman who exploited her night with Elvis for personal gain. It cited hearsay of young women who were trying to blackmail Elvis and it mentioned a rumor about a young woman from Decaturville who was pressuring Elvis to either marry her or face the legal consequences. Here the editorial opined, "Imagine Mary Magdalene dragging Jesus to the altar! Where would we all be today?" The comparison troubled Elvis, but he certainly appreciated the sentiment.

The third and final page of the newsletter was devoted entirely to lists of girl's names under various rubrics, ranging from "Near Misses" (Krafty Plaster was listed prominently here) to "Plans Under Way" and "In Our Dreams," which listed young woman who had experienced "vivid nocturnal reveries and hallucinations" of being deflowered by Elvis. That phrase was undoubtedly the product of one of Manard Frew's rewrites. In the middle of the page, framed in curlicues, was the ultimate list: "Done the Deed!" The first name recorded here was one Jennifer van Duesen, aka "Ann-Margret" van Duesen. Frew had attempted to mimeograph her photograph next to her name, but it came out looking more like one of those connect-the-dot puzzles in the funnies section than any recognizable face. Nonetheless, there was little doubt that Miss Jennifer was the Ann-Margret look-alike of the SWEPT crew. Elvis found this oddly reassuring, not that he ever believed the real Miss Ann-Margret could possibly have any connection to this scandalous organization. What was less than reassuring was the notation next to Miss Jennifer's name: "Five times and still counting!" Elvis did not want even to consider the implications of that—not just yet, at least.

There were three other names listed under Miss Jennifer's:

Carol-Sue Crampton	Nonmember (Once)
Muffy Kent	Nonmember (Once)
Amy Coulter	Charter Member (Once—Nice work, Amy!)

Amy Coulter! Elvis had not recognized the name his first time through the newsletter. Amy was the young woman Frew had photographed in flagrante delicto on the trunk of that Cadillac with his license plate on it. Either Miss Amy had been unaware of SWEPT's no-exploitation policy, or she was unaware that her encounter was a setup for a photo op.

Elvis ran the Amy Coulter connection by Mr. Southern. "That tells us that this Miss Amy was definitely in communication with the SWEPT crew, maybe even on their staff, in a manner of speaking. So there's a good chance that Frew knew Miss Amy as a client for his newsletter business," Elvis said. "And that means there's a good chance he actually got the job taking those photographs of Miss Amy through Miss Amy herself, in which case she knew all about the setup beforehand. In these parts, one degree of separation between two folks almost always means they're in bed with each other in a half dozen ways."

"Sounds right," Southern said. "Which means we should have a little tête-à-tête with Miss Coulter ASAP. Still, my guess is that no Tennessee teenager with sex on the brain is orchestrating a plan to do you harm, either by besmirching your name or blackmailing you or any other damned thing. And I'd bet the farm she's not Frew's murderer either. Teenage girls commit murder for one reason only—jealousy. And I somehow don't think Manard Frew could have inspired jealousy in a woman of any age. No, if Frew was doing this outdoor photography for anybody, it was for your look-alike himself. Or maybe even for some third party. But I've got a hunch Manard Frew came up with the idea of blackmail on his own. The man had an expensive art habit. That Cartier-Bresson alone must have set him back a good thousand dollars. So I bet he decided to make a little more out of his photos than whatever his employer was paying him, which was probably about three dollars and change."

"Slow down, man. First you gotta tell me why you don't think the whole deal was Frew's idea."

"Because he's dead, for starters. He was probably killed to keep him from turning over those photos to Parker, and from telling the story that went with them. So I figure whoever killed

Frew was the person who hired him to take those pictures. When he discovered that Frew had concocted a blackmail plot of his own, he did what any competitive American businessman would do: he sealed Frew's lips by shooting him between the eyes. Otherwise, Frew might have written an entire newsletter revealing this guy's scheme of faking it to look like you are a violator of young girls' virtue."

"You got a whole wheelbarrow full of assumptions in there," Elvis said.

"I like to think of them as hypotheses," Southern replied. "Speaking of which, an obvious one would be that your pal, Colonel Tom, shot Frew."

"Parker wouldn't kill a man for twenty thousand dollars," Elvis said. "Heck, he wouldn't be a genuine suspect until you got up to a million."

Southern laughed.

"But still, your theory ain't even half the story," Elvis said. "I mean, what is this son of a gun after? Sheriff Tip just wanted a tryout for that pimply choir of his, which he's already got, courtesy of the Colonel. So whoever is running this scam is after something more."

Southern nodded in agreement.

"And the sixty-four-dollar question is still the same," Elvis went on. "Who the heck looks and sounds and acts so much like me that teenage girls give up their honor to him in the backseat of a Caddy? And what's *he* after?"

"That boy gets what he's after—those girls," Southern said.

"Heck, he could get that out back of Mildred's Come-And-Get-It without going to all that trouble, far as I can tell. I mean, even *you* got—"

"I get your point."

"This super look-alike must have something else going. Otherwise, he wouldn't be posing for pornographic pictures. But I'll tell you one thing, whoever's cooking this up is preparing a full-course poison supper."

"I like the way you put things, Elvis," Southern said. "You could make a fortune in Hollywood."

"Already did," Elvis said.

It was just after three in the morning when Southern turned onto the interstate that ran down to Decaturville. The plan was for Southern to locate Miss Amy Coulter after he dropped Elvis off, and set up a meeting between her and Elvis for the next night, if that could be effected without spooking her. Meantime, Elvis had an early date with Blount Memorial's Radiology Department.

Theirs was the only car coming or going on the highway. Elvis snapped on the radio, fiddled with the dial. At this hour, stations came bouncing off the moon from every which direction, including a Creole station from someplace deep in Louisiana that was playing wall-to-wall zydeco. A bayou version of "Let the Good Times Roll" segued into a number that Elvis had never heard before: "I'm a Hog for You, Baby." What a hoot! The lyric sure took an honest bead on human appetites.

"As they say in the movies, I think we've got company," Southern murmured, gesturing at the rearview mirror.

A second Cadillac was cruising no more than three car lengths behind them. It was impossible to make out the driver's face or if there was anyone else inside. It was also impossible to tell for certain the Caddy's color. It appeared purple, but Elvis figured that if you subtracted the moon's yellow, that would make it pink. In any event, there was little doubt that the car was following them. Southern tested that theory by speeding up, then slowing down. Throughout, the purple-pink Cadillac stayed right behind them.

Elvis stuck his head out the side window and squinted back at their pursuers. For a fraction of a second, a ray of moonlight beamed on the driver's face. Holy moley! It was one of his look-alikes. And not just any old garden-variety look-alike, but that perfect tintype that Elvis had glimpsed in the back of one of those Studebaker cars cruising Mildred's Come-And-Get-It. Elvis could see the license plate too: Memphis 23.

"Pull over!" Elvis said. "I need to talk to this guy."

Southern started to edge onto the shoulder, when a man on the passenger's side of the car behind them leaned out of his window. He pointed a rifle at them and fired it. The bullet spiraled through the rear window and out the roof just above Southern's head. Mr. Terry Southern pressed the accelerator to the floor.

"Jeez! I can't take two car wrecks in one week!" Elvis hollered.

"Think a bullet through the head is an improvement?" Southern hollered back.

The speedometer hit ninety-five and kept climbing. Southern was now weaving back and forth between lanes. The second rifle shot missed them completely.

"Olé!" Southern cheered. The man was actually smiling.

Surprisingly, Elvis found that he, too, felt more exhilarated than scared. After all the murky second-guessing of the past week, the clarity of a badman firing a rifle was like a ray of sunshine in the eye of a hurricane.

Southern abruptly ripped the steering wheel to the right and, with the benefit of only his two right tires, shot off the highway onto an access road. Behind them, their pursuers overshot the turnoff, screeched to a stop, and were still backing up when Southern took a second right turn doing ninety. They came within a fraction of an inch of smashing into a state park sign that read, "Kentucky Lake—6 Miles."

"Now *this* is verisimilitude!" Mr. Southern shouted.

"This ain't similar to anything," Elvis shouted back. "It's the real thing!"

Only one minute later, the purple-pink Cadillac suddenly reappeared behind them. And the man riding shotgun shot his gun again. This time the bullet completely shattered their rear window, whistled between their heads, and exited through the windshield, leaving a neat twenty-two-millimeter hole. Southern floored it again. They were going downhill to begin with, so they picked up to 110 miles per hour in the blink of an eye.

Later, when Elvis had the time and the inclination to do the arithmetic, he calculated that they must have covered those next six miles in about three minutes flat. Not a whole lot of time in which to make fine steering adjustments while doing 110.

The state park road ended at Kentucky Lake. *Literally*—that is where the water lapped onto the asphalt. Southern hit the brakes, but there was no contest between the Caddy's momentum and its asbestos brake linings—the car kept hurtling forward. Southern yanked the wheel to the right and they careened onto a short wooden pier. At the end of the pier they kept going, flying through the air like a chunky guided missile. Instinctively, Elvis angled across Southern to the electric window panel and pressed every button at once. A car with its windows open does not float for long, especially a two-ton Cadillac. But the car never touched the water.

They landed with a gentle jolt on top of a Mandalay pontoon cruiser that was moored to the pier, ready for another day of fishing and beer drinking. Actually, they first alighted on the boat's sun awning, and in the second or two it took for that to collapse, Southern pulled on the emergency brake. When the tires of Elvis's white Cadillac coupe bounced onto the cruiser's deck—flattening a half dozen deck chairs in the process—the boat lurched forward. Two tons of 110-mile-per-hour forward force would test the strength of a bridge cable; the hemp rope attaching the boat to the pier snapped instantly. Behind them, their purple-pink pursuers plowed window-deep into the lake.

"Precisely as I planned it," Mr. Southern murmured, sweat pouring off his quivering brow.

Thus began Elvis and Mr. Terry Southern's moonlight cruise on Kentucky Lake and down the Tennessee River.

Trembling, neither Elvis nor Southern spoke for a good five minutes. Then Southern snapped off the headlights, lowered all the windows, and shut off the engine. Elvis brushed some shards of window glass out of his hair and off his shoulders, then leaned out the side window and looked around. By golly, somebody up there was looking out for them. An MGM stunt driver could not have landed more squarely on this pontoon rig; the Caddy's winged-victory hood ornament was dead center, pointing straight ahead like a bowsprit.

Elvis opened the passenger door and extended his right leg. His foot made a steady-enough purchase on the deck for him to swing out his other leg and stand up beside the car. If the moon over in Deer Creek had been bright and clear, here it was like a Grand Ole Opry spotlight. Elvis could virtually make out every leaf and needle on the swamp tupelos and loblolly pines that lined the far shore a good five miles away. But it was the air out here that really made his senses thrill. It was "soft as a velvet glove," as his mama used to say—warm on the throat and cool on the brow. There was just enough moisture in it to make his lungs feel like they were being whisked clean by a damp feather duster. And the fragrance— a mix of mustard weeds and floating carp and pine resin—was a tangy whiff of a long-ago happy childhood.

Elvis made his way forward alongside the car, then hefted himself onto the hood, his back against the windscreen. He kicked off his shoes. He took several deep, lung-cleansing breaths. And then Elvis did what he had done since he was a boy when contentment welled up inside him so fast that it had no place to go but out. He sang.

> *"Where are you old moon of Kentucky?*
> *There's somebody lonesome and blue. . . ."*

It was the encore he never got to sing in Deer Creek. Elvis sang with just enough breath to make the melody stick to a whisper.

"Roll along, roll along, Kentucky moon. . . ." The song floated out across the water.

Somewhere in the second verse, Mr. Southern let himself out of the car and then up on the gliding Caddy's hood beside Elvis. Southern joined in on the chorus reprise a full octave below Elvis, his whiskey-cured voice rumbling like a washtub bass fiddle. Hank would have loved it.

"Huck and Jim, together again," Southern murmured after the song had ended.

By now, the high-riding boat had been picked up by the current, steering them south toward where the lake fed into the Tennessee River.

"Why is it that a man never feels so peaceful as when he's between places?" Elvis said, half to himself.

"Because that's the only time we can be ourselves," Southern said. "No expectations. No place to blend into. Or recoil from. Just be."

"Funny, I was just thinking the opposite," Elvis said, still looking straight ahead to where the horizon vanished in a moonlit mist. "That out here, I don't have to be Elvis Presley anymore."

"That might be the same thing," Southern said. "Elvis Presley is so *out there*—not just in the movies and on records, but out there in people's imaginations, that he belongs more to them than to you at this point. That probably makes it hard to be yourself. Except maybe out here."

Elvis looked over at Southern and nodded. This was just about the first time the man had said anything to him that wasn't gilded with irony. Perhaps Mr. Southern was finally being *his* true self out here in the middle of Kentucky Lake.

"I wouldn't mind if we never landed," Elvis said. Some of that mist seemed to be getting into his eyes. "Just roll along. Roll along, roll along, and disappear."

"I hear you," Southern said.

"It's not just because of these troubles, either—Parker in jail and those girls and this crazy fella who's taking advantage of them," Elvis said. "Sure, all that's weighing heavy on me, but I've been wanting to disappear for a while now. I keep thinking I might try it someday—disappear and start all over again as my own self. Seems like the only way I could find my soul again. And my song."

"Amen to that," Mr. Terry Southern said.

Over the next three hours, the King of Rock and Roll and the

Bad Boy of American Cinema drifted down the Tennessee River on the hood of a Cadillac coupe, ducking their heads now and then when the river narrowed and overhanging mistletoe and Spanish moss swept across them. They sang together a few more times, mostly moon songs: "When My Blue Moon Turns to Gold Again," "Dark Moon," "Harbor Lights." Mr. Terry Southern's voice seemed to get deeper and raspier each time around, and by the time they got to "Harbor Lights," he sounded like Johnny Cash reverberating through a foghorn.

Just as the sun began to rise, an eddy spun the pontoons ninety degrees to the right, and their raft floated up and onto the shore as if it were being steered by a Mississippi pilot. Without a word, both men returned to the car. Southern started up the motor, released the brake, and backed onto the loamy bank.

"Tip the deck steward, would you, Elvis?" Southern said.

12

Pop-up Headlights

It was a quarter past eight when they cruised past the Red Walnut Church of Christ just inside the Decaturville city limits. Red Walnut was one of those two-day wonders that came in four parts on the back of a flatbed truck and was put together like a Tinkertoy. The steeple was the dead giveaway: it looked like it had been lifted straight off of a Howard Johnson. Man, the Little Church of the West out in Vegas appeared more spiritual; Red Walnut looked more like a house of detention than a wedding chapel, not that there was all that much difference under the present circumstances.

"Sure hope Miss Sarah can stall them," Elvis said. His X-ray had been scheduled for seven thirty.

Southern took the far entrance into Blount Memorial Hospital so that he could skirt the parking lot on the way to the service entrance in back. But about fifty feet in, he brought the car to a halt. He rolled down his window and pointed at the main entrance.

Miss Sarah Whipple, aka Elvisetta, was seated in a wheelchair under the hospital's portico with a good twenty reporters surrounding her, most shoving microphones up to her face. Standing behind her, with a hand on Elvisetta's shoulder, was Miss Carol-Sue Crampton, all decked out in what appeared to be a Paris, France, chambermaid's uniform, complete with a laced-up bodice that squeezed everything she had up and out like a pair of Sting

Ray pop-up headlights. Beside Carol-Sue was her daddy, who was wearing a seersucker suit, no doubt his first suit of any kind, picked out by his daughter for the occasion. Flashbulbs popped like a disco strobe light, making the principals in this ersatz family portrait look like they were jerking around in a Charlie Chaplin movie. Fact is, the whole crazy scene would not have been out of place in a Chaplin movie.

Elvis and Southern slipped out of the car as quietly as they could, then made their way toward the hospital entrance, ducking behind cars in the parking lot so they would not be seen. About thirty feet in front of the portico, Elvis raised his hand for Southern to stop. From this vantage point, they could view the whole business through car windows and hear most everything that was being said.

What was being said, by a beaming Elvisetta with purple spoke marks decorating her face, was that wedding plans were definitely in the air.

"Oh yes, I've become mighty attached to Miss Carol-Sue here," Elvisetta said. "She stood by me like a real woman while I was out of commission in there, and that means a lot to a man like me. My mama, may her soul rest in peace, used to say that love was silver, but loyalty is pure gold."

She spoke in consummate Elvis tones, but Elvis was doubly aware that Elvisetta's range definitely sounded high tenor compared to his own baritone. That her shoulders were a couple inches narrower than his own also struck Elvis as obvious. Didn't anyone else notice that? Did everyone in Tennessee have vision as fuzzy as Miss Muffy Kent's? Or was Kevin Cote's theory about desire brainwashing eyesight more far-reaching than Elvis would ever have guessed? Heaven knows, every one of those folks under the portico—not just Carol-Sue, but her daddy, and all the reporters—had a heap of desire to believe that they were enjoying a private audience with the King of Rock and Roll.

"Fact is," Elvisetta went on blithely, "the main reason I passed that X-ray exam with flying colors this mornin' is because of Miss

Carol-Sue's healin' hand. I'm here to tell you all that love mends bones."

"Lordy," Elvis muttered. "You'd think an X-ray machine would pick up an ovary or two."

But Southern was just grinning. "Man, she's good," he murmured back. "Hell, if you really do want to take some time off, she could play you in our movie."

"Nobody'd believe it," Elvis said.

"Hell, *they* believe it," Southern said, gesturing toward the newshounds.

"But before I do anything," Elvisetta was saying, "I got some unfinished business back home at Graceland. A little misunderstandin' with a young lady who's been boarding with us while her folks are over in Germany. Just doing them a family favor, don't you know. But seems she's got some strange romantic notions in her head. You know who I'm talkin' about—Miss Priscilla."

That did it! That crossed the line! Time to put an end to this charade before Elvis's entire life unraveled in front of his eyes.

Elvis stood bolt upright. But he remained in that position for only a fraction of a second. Behind him, Southern had popped his kneecaps into the backs of Elvis's knees, causing Elvis to buckle back down.

"Sorry," Southern whispered. "But what we've got here is a golden opportunity. Elvisetta just bought your freedom to take care of business on a full-time basis. And if I'm not mistaken, we do have some pressing business to take care of."

According to information, there was only one Coulter family in all of Madison County, and they lived in the town of Denmark.

"Too bad the river only runs one way," Elvis said. "Guess we'll have to drive there."

But first, there was more pressing business: breakfast. In particular, Mr. Southern insisted that he could be no help at all without his requisite six cups of black coffee to remind his nervous system that a new day had dawned.

Elvis recalled a diner in Huron, where he and Miss Selma DuPres had eaten when they were out driving some five years ago. It was in the colored section of town, so it was probably still in business. And what is more, they could eat in peace because coloreds didn't pester Elvis when they recognized him the way white folks did. Elvis sometimes wondered about that—was it because they were more respectful or because they didn't really think all that much of him? He had once posed the question to his friend, Dr. Billy, adding his persistent worry that black folk might hold it against him for singing their music and making more money out of it than any black singer ever did.

"Some are mad, some are jealous, and a whole bunch others are convinced you're one of us," Billy had answered. "They figure there must be a plantation mammy up in your family tree, otherwise those gospel melodies would step out of your mouth in white buck shoes. That and the way you pop those hips of yours. That's definitely not Anglo-Saxon to our way of thinking."

As far as Elvis knew, none of his ancestors had come anywhere near a plantation, except for a few Mississippi Loves and Smiths who were sharecroppers after the Civil War. Still, the idea of having some black blood surging through his veins pleased him, just the way having some Cherokee and Jewish forebears made him feel like he was a more complete American.

Barbara's Cue looked just as Elvis remembered it. Covering the entire front window was an elaborate hand-painted sign that pictured a pool table on which an entire hog was being barbecued, summing up what Barbara's customers could expect to find inside. For a long moment, Elvis could not compel himself to get out of the car; Selma was visiting his mind again. Sometimes, he could go an entire month without thinking about her—about talking with her into the wee hours and then making tender love to her in her feather bed up in Alamo. But then there she would be again, her fine brown eyes looking out at him from the corners, like the two of them were privy to the biggest private joke in the world. That's what she was doing right now in his mind's eye.

"Let's have ourselves some genuine ribs here," Selma had said as she parked in front of Barbara's Cue those five long years ago. "It's for coloreds, but I'll run interference for you."

"Looks like we're welcome here," Southern was now saying from outside the car as he pointed at a sign on the restaurant's door. It said, "Whites Only."

In Elvis's mind, Selma winked and vanished. Elvis exited the car and followed Southern into Barbara's Cue.

"Well I'll be, if you ain't the first pale faces to come tripping through that door since I put that 'Whites Only' sign out there." The speaker was the proprietor herself, a fiftyish black woman with fright-wig hair, red harlequin glasses, and a smile that could put a condemned man at ease. "The truth being what it is, you are the first vanilla frappes in here since the last time you dropped by, Mr. Presley."

Elvis limped up to the woman and kissed her on the cheek. She, too, had remembered, although the first time around she had not even hinted that she recognized him as Elvis Presley. That had to be respect. Or maybe it was because Elvis had been in the company of a black woman that time, and Miss Barbara had known instinctively how precious their secret relationship was to both of them.

"What *is* that sign all about, Miss Barbara?" Elvis said.

"I found it at the garbage dump. Whole bunch of them there since those four-eyed Yankee vote missionaries came down here stirring folks up. So I hung the sign up here as a little bit of personal commentary on the civil rights movement," Miss Barbara answered.

"For it or agin it?"

"*For* the heart at the center of it, but *agin* how pleased they get with themselves for doing so little."

Mr. Southern regarded Miss Barbara with genuine astonishment. "Madam," he said, "I am nominating you for poet laureate of the United States."

"Whatever you say," Miss Barbara laughed. "Long as I can keep my day job."

While Elvis consumed an entire hog's worth of ribs, Mr. Southern downed his six cups of coffee. He had insisted on Miss Barbara joining them at their booth, and as Elvis chawed, he and Barbara chattered about everything from the politics of Biafra to Little Richard's resemblance to Mickey Rooney. As they were leaving, Elvis saw the two of them exchange addresses and phone numbers.

"You never know where you're going to find a soul mate," Southern murmured as he started up the car again.

The Coulter residence was easily the grandest in all of Denmark, Tennessee, probably in the top ten of all of Madison County. It was one of those mock plantation affairs that rich folks built after World War II, with three-story pillars in front, french doors on the side, and flower boxes under every window. But instead of raising cotton or tobacco, the man of the house was in the bone business. A sign in front said, "Dr. Alexander Coulter, Chiropractor," then in smaller letters below that, "The straighter the spine, the closer to God—Walk-ins Welcome." God was obviously a boon to business in these parts.

"I feel the sudden need for an adjustment," Southern said, getting out of the car. "I'll see what I can find out about the doctor's daughter while I'm on his table."

"Don't bump your head on heaven's gate," Elvis replied.

"Now there's a song title if I ever heard one," Southern said.

After Southern disappeared into the side door that led to Coulter's office, Elvis got out of the car and stretched. By God, he felt a whole lot better than he had any right to. His hips and legs seemed to be in fine working order again, and his head was clear and hopeful. That respite on the Tennessee River had done more healing than any hospital bed could, and topping it off with a full set of ribs had definitely nourished his innards more than Blount Memorial's deluxe chipped beef on toast ever could. What's more, to be perfectly honest about it, the Colonel being locked up where he couldn't wheel and deal with blackmailers meant that

Elvis could go about the business at hand without interference. And on top of that, even if that mouth of Miss Elvisetta's was a treacherous thing, having her out there running decoy for him felt darn right liberating.

But not any one of those things was what was making Elvis's soul sparkle just now, and he knew it. That little mental visit from Miss Selma had ignited that. Elvis felt a sudden stab of remorse: what could he have been thinking when he derided songs about undying love for just one woman? Meat loaf over Selma? God forgive me, he thought. The only possible excuse for that was that he had been protecting himself from longing for her.

Elvis saw a U.S. Mail truck rolling toward him. He slipped back into the car and his hid his face behind a road map. The mail-man stopped at the plantation driveway, stuffed a bundle into the Coulter mailbox, and proceeded on. Elvis waited a minute, then left the car and sauntered to the mailbox. About half the letters were not sealed closed, and the other half—well, what the heck, if you're going to do detective work, you can't be worrying about social niceties.

Judging by one day's mail, the Coulters were a family to be reckoned with in western Tennessee. They received five linen-enveloped invitations to tennis parties and golf club cotillions; two solicitations for contributions, one from the Denmark Downtown Betterment Association and the other from some organization called the League of Southern Gentlemen, a group of college professors who apparently believed that the time was ripe again for seceding from Washington; a letter from Duke University for Mr. Alexander Coulter Jr.; a letter from Miss Krieger's School for Young Ladies marked "personal" for Dr. and Mrs. Coulter; and a large manila envelope addressed to Miss Amy Coulter herself. This last bore the return address of the Shakespeare World Enthusiast Poetry Teachers. Impressive, and definitely not the sort of people Elvis would have expected the naked young woman on the trunk of the pink Caddy to be corresponding with, but when he looked inside, he found the very same edition of *SWEPT* that they had taken from Frew's room. Clever, those SWEPT girls; they knew how meticulously a teenage girl's parents monitored her mail.

The letter from Miss Krieger's School was from Miss Angelica Krieger herself, founder and president of the private girls boarding school in Switch. Miss Krieger went to great pains to express her displeasure with the Coulter's daughter in terms as ladylike as possible. One line in particular tickled Elvis: "Miss Coulter's precocious enthusiasms for adult activities may be entertaining to some of our young women, but they definitely do not correspond to our canon of proper feminine behavior." Apparently, Miss Amy talked dirty right there on Miss Krieger's campus. The letter concluded by stating that unless Miss Amy showed signs of improvement, she would be "invited to leave." Yup, young people today sure were acting rebellious and disrespectful, but at least part of the blame had to fall on the likes of the Miss Kriegers of the world. A smug Old South lady like that made Elvis himself feel like dropping his drawers and letting a full moon shine on the spinster's front window.

From the corner of his eye, Elvis saw Coulter's office door open, then Mr. Southern and a tall salt-and-pepper-haired man in a dapper medical coat—undoubtedly Dr. Coulter—come out, both laughing chummily like they'd just played a round of golf together. Elvis immediately stuffed the mail back into the mailbox—no time to relick and refasten the envelopes—and started off down the road away from them, and away from the car. But not fast enough.

"*Thief!* Stop right there!" Dr. Coulter yelled after him.

Elvis kept going, breaking into a trot. Yes, indeed, hips and legs in fine working order.

"I'll get the bastard!" Southern cried.

Behind him, Elvis heard a car door open and slam shut, the motor rev up, then the wheels whining as it lurched away from the roadside. Elvis kept trotting. Suddenly, his white Caddy passed him on the left, then cut right in front of him and screeched to a stop. Southern bounded out of the driver's seat.

"I'm taking you prisoner!" he said loudly as he came up along-side Elvis. "Citizen's arrest!"

"What are you talking about now, Mr. Southern?" Elvis said.

"For God's sake, just go limp, would you, Elvis?" Southern whispered.

Southern was behind Elvis now, clumsily attempting to put him in a half nelson. To accommodate Southern's maneuver, Elvis lifted his arms away from his sides and ducked his head, then let Southern rassle him into the backseat of the car just as Dr. Coulter jogged up to them. Elvis covered his face with his hands, as if in shame.

"Well done!" Coulter said. It sounded like golf talk.

Southern was already behind the wheel. "I'm taking him in!" he said.

"I'll come with you," Coulter said.

"You better stay here, Doctor," Southern said gravely. "He might have an accomplice."

With that, Southern sped away, leaving the chiropractor in the dust.

"You crack me up, Mr. Southern," Elvis said from the backseat.

"I like it better when you call me Kemosabe," Southern replied.

13

Capitalist Pig–Mobile

est bone cracker I've ever been to," Southern said. "I feel an inch taller."

"That's a start," Elvis said.

Southern had not learned much more about Amy Coulter from her father than Elvis had gleaned from their mail, except that the reason Dr. and Mrs. Coulter had sent her away to boarding school was that she had fallen in with a "bad crowd" at the local public high school.

"She's a very impressionable child. Artistic, like her mother," Alexander Coulter had explained to Southern as he gave his sacrum a good twist.

"Let's hope the mother isn't too artistic," Elvis said when he heard this. "Otherwise, Dr. Coulter is married to a loose woman."

Switch, Tennessee, the home of Miss Krieger's School for Young Ladies, was only forty miles east of Denmark. Southern got there in less than a half hour, parking the car just outside the school's wrought-iron gates.

The folks at the League of Southern Gentlemen would have been thrilled by the Krieger campus. It looked like it had been frozen in time a few years before Lincoln took office—not just the quadrangle of three-story white clapboard antebellum structures surrounding a green-glazed copper fountain, but Miss Krieger's young ladies themselves. They walked in twos and threes along the magnolia-lined paths, their schoolbooks pressed demurely against the starched bosoms of their white shirtwaists, tittering in dulcet, Margaret Mitchell tones. Every skirt reached every ankle, and every lank of long blond hair was combed and beribboned. Needless to mention, there was not a black face in sight. Miss Barbara's little commentary surely had that right: those civil rights folks might be able to force you to throw out your "Whites Only" signs in the town dump, but they couldn't get the Miss Kriegers to open their iron gates to smart young colored girls.

"I thought this might make our job a little easier," Mr. Southern said. He reached inside his shirt and pulled out a scrolled-up photograph. It was of Miss Amy Coulter in full boarding-school attire.

"How the heck did you get that?" Elvis said.

"Snatched it off of the doctor's desk while he was washing up," Southern said. "Fortunately, there was another photo just behind it in the frame. Baby picture of his daughter in a high chair sticking out her tongue. Coulter never noticed the difference."

Elvis studied the photograph. If he had not known that it was the same girl pictured in those pornographic Polaroids, he might not have seen the resemblance between the two. Miss Amy as a southern belle—and, of course, as a supposed virgin—looked like she had just stepped out on the plantation veranda to welcome home her daddy from a strenuous day of whipping. The problem was that in the picture Miss Amy looked an awful lot like every other Miss Krieger girl promenading in front of them.

Mr. Southern got out of the car. "Wait here. I'll nose around," he said.

"You'll stick out like a fox in a henhouse," Elvis said.

"No problem. I have an all-purpose stratagem for situations like this—I tell them I'm scouting locations for a Hollywood movie. And while I'm at it, I'm looking for extras—particularly blond young women."

"You're a dangerous man, Mr. Southern," Elvis said.

"Everybody loves show biz," he replied, and sauntered through the gates of Miss Krieger's School for Young Ladies.

Elvis sat back in his seat and watched Southern approach a trio of the young women.

When he was an awkward, leg-twitchy teenager at Hume High, Elvis used to dream about marrying a girl who looked just like these Krieger belles, all pink and dainty and proper looking. Of course, he had known that they were beyond his reach—a girl like that wouldn't even look at a poor Memphis boy whose greatest ambition was to drive a ten-ton eighteen-wheeler. But now here he was, some kind of superstar, and at least one of these girls was more than eager to forget all about propriety to get her name listed in SWEPT's hall of fame. There should be some kind of satisfaction in that—seeing your fondest boyhood dreams come true—but Elvis felt more bewildered than satisfied. Digby Ferguson, that crazy kid he had met in Vegas, once quoted to him some Arab chestnut that went, "Beware of what you desire, for you will surely get it."

The honest truth was, Elvis still had a hankering for old-fashioned southern girls like these Krieger young ladies—that's pretty much the reason why he wanted Miss Priscilla to be a virgin when he married her. But when it came to his genuine sexual appetite, his tastes ran more to the likes of Miss Ann-Margret, a sassy woman with a saucy laugh who liked to shimmy her hips when she walked down the street just for the sheer glory of it. Elvis had once read in *Time* magazine that he was the biggest sex symbol of the new generation. Wonder what that generation would think if they knew just how confused about sex their sex symbol was?

Southern was now making a beeline for the fountain at the center of the quad. He walked directly up to two young women chatting there. He could not have said more than two or three words to one of them when she suddenly beamed, pivoted around so fast that her long billowy skirt lifted high enough to reveal her kneecaps, and started dashing toward the car. In a trice, Miss Amy Coulter was staring in the window at Elvis.

"What took you so long?" she cooed.

"I was catching up on my blackmail," Elvis replied.

"I had a feeling you'd be coming back for more."

"More what?"

"Southern hospitality," Miss Amy twittered. Her laugh went way beyond saucy into the realm of devilishness. She yanked open the rear door of the car and bounced herself right next to Elvis. She smelled like a honeysuckle rose.

"No offense, miss," Elvis said, scooting to the opposite end of the seat. "But a man needs his breathing room."

"No offense taken," Miss Amy replied. "We remain connected, no matter what obstacles are thrust between us."

"Beg pardon?"

"Poetically speaking, of course," the girl explained.

"Miss Amy, I need to ask you some questions. You know, in plain English," Elvis began, but suddenly he felt another pair of eyes staring in at him from outside the car window. He looked toward them. Elvis did not need a formal introduction. The flinty eyes behind wire-rimmed glasses sitting on a sharp-tipped, narrow nose could belong to no one other than Miss Angelica Krieger herself. Attila the Hun would have withered under that stare. Fact is, no matter what he had been doing, Attila would have felt guilty about it.

Miss Amy turned demurely in her seat and stuck her tongue out at Miss Krieger, obviously an expression that she had been practicing from an early age.

"Get out of there this minute, young lady!" Miss Krieger barked.

Miss Amy leaned back imperiously in her seat, as if she were impatiently waiting for her chauffeur to return so she could continue her rounds of her favorite dress shops.

"Let me explain," Elvis said.

"Sin never requires an explanation," the headmistress replied in a surprisingly even-toned voice.

"This ain't sin, ma'am, it's a misunderstanding," Elvis said. As a gesture of respect to Miss Kriegrer, Elvis leaned over so he could lower the car window between them, but in the process his arm inadvertently brushed against Miss Amy's bosom. Miss Amy rewarded this accidental intimacy with an adoring kiss to Elvis's shoulder. Clumsy is as clumsy does, as Elvis's mama used to say.

"It is not for me to judge you, Mr. Presley," Miss Krieger said. Her voice was somehow soft and clipped at the same time. It gave Elvis the shivers.

"That's true, ma'am, and I know the good Lord will judge me justly," Elvis said. He felt proud of himself; by golly, he could talk scripture talk as well as the best of them, even if he was speaking it from a rather embarrassing position.

"But it is the law of man that will deal with you, sir. And *that* shall come down upon you with a harsh hand." Miss Krieger went on. Her voice had become shriller, now subtly adding the cadences of a hellfire preacher very much like the one Elvis had heard on the radio. "And I am not speaking about the law they issue up there in Gomorrah, D.C."

Elvis had no idea what the headmistress was talking about, but he did not have to wait long to find out.

"Those heathens from the North may have restricted us from meting out true justice to the aborigines who defile our women," Krieger continued, "but fortunately, they are so narrow-minded that they leave us alone when we do what is necessary to white men who violate our young women."

If Elvis was not mistaken, Miss Angelica Krieger was talking about a lynching—one that involved his own neck—right here, deep in Madison County, in a town that probably did not even appear in the FBI's atlas. Had she already phoned the local vigilante linchpin? *Where the heck is Mr. Terry Southern when you need him?*

"I have done nothing wrong and I can prove it," Elvis said. Unfortunately, the words sounded profoundly lame as they came out of his mouth.

Miss Krieger responded by crossing her arms in front of her

chest. For one fleeting, irrelevant moment, Elvis observed that like the teenagers who congregated in back of Mildred's Come-And-Get-It, Miss Angelica Krieger was not wearing a brassiere; in her case, however, the reason was that the apparatus itself would have had more amplitude than anything there was for it to support.

Southern suddenly appeared in front of the car. He took in the dynamics of the situation immediately, and darted toward the driver's seat.

"Help me get this young woman out of here!" Elvis called to him, reaching for the door handle.

"But she'll whip me raw!" Miss Amy cried. She grabbed ahold of Elvis with all her might.

Southern hesitated only a second, then got in behind the wheel, started up the engine, and tore off. Elvis could not help craning his neck to view Miss Krieger receding in their new, open-air rear window. Miss Krieger was bidding him farewell with a ladylike, finger-trilling wave.

"Free at last!" Miss Amy cheered.

"Would she really have whipped you?" Southern asked.

"Fifteen lashes on my bare bum," Amy replied. "Nothing delights Miss Krieger more. The poor woman never had a child of her own to beat."

"How about lynching me?" Elvis said to Miss Amy. "Was Miss Krieger serious about that too?"

"Oh, yes, indeed," Amy said. "Our dear headmistress is well connected in these parts. Her daddy is grand dragon for all of Tennessee *and* Kentucky."

"*Lynching?*" Southern groaned.

Elvis explained.

"God help us, that's one too many," Southern said. "It's bad enough we have that pink Caddy crew following us with a rifle, now we've got the Ku Klux Klan on our tail with a length of rope."

"I know a cave where we could hide," Miss Amy said.

"But we got to keep moving, ma'am," Elvis said. "The clock is ticking."

"What we need is a different car," Southern said. "That'd give us camouflage."

"Now you're talking," Elvis said. "By the way, what the heck took you so long back there?"

"Signing up extras for our movie," Mr. Terry Southern said.

They were tooting along a back road in Beach Bluff when Elvis spotted the campers. At first, he thought they were Indians—all three of them had feathers sprouting from their waist-length hair, and one had red paint on his forehead. Furthermore, two of the three were bare chested—the exception was the one young woman among them, who wore a gauzy peasant blouse—and they were sitting cross-legged under some pines smoking a pipe around an open fire. But the thing is, they looked a whole more *exuberant* than any Indian Elvis had ever seen.

"Love their bus," Southern crooned as he slowed to a stop.

Their bus was one of those Volkswagen rolling boxcars that was painted front to back in Day-Glo colors depicting peace signs and cartoon characters with oversize feet whose captioned motto was "Keep on truckin'," plus an assortment of garish portraits including those of Bob Dylan, Martin Luther King Jr., and Joan Baez. It was parked next to a huge boulder.

Elvis, Southern, and Miss Amy got out of the Caddy and approached the campers.

"Lovely day for a picnic," Southern greeted them.

All three nouveau Injuns gaped up at him quizzically. And then the young woman of the trio burst out laughing. It was not just a polite titter either; she let loose with an exultation so shrill that it made a flock of pinetop starlings take off for cover. Every time it would seem that she was about to simmer down, she would repeat the words "Lovely day for a picnic," and start crowing all over again. Along the way, her two companions joined in, although Elvis got the impression that they did not get the joke any better than he did.

"Must be good stuff," Southern said after the campers had finally gone quiet again and returned to puffing industriously on their pipe.

"Homegrown," the young woman replied. She appeared to be the chieftess of this advanced tribe.

"How lovely," Miss Amy Coulter said. "May I indulge?"

The young man with the red paint on his forehead—it looked like a pitch fork—held the pipe up to her.

"You don't know what might be in there, Miss Amy," Elvis said. He looked courteously at the boy with the outstretched pipe, and added, "No offense implied, of course."

The young woman seemed to be on the very brink of another sky-shattering laugh when she stopped herself and said, "Man, you look like Elvis Presley."

"That's what my mother said," Elvis replied.

"Like, you even have the same car," the youngster with the pitch fork mark said.

"Ah, so you like the car," Miss Amy said. She took three deep inhales on the pipe before returning it to the young man.

"Like, it's a joke—a capitalist pig–mobile," the seated young woman said. She had the unexpected inflection of scorn in her voice. Same tone of scorn that her snooty suburban mama undoubtedly used, Elvis guessed.

"Yup, and this joke's so hip, you don't get it," Southern said. Where *did* he learn to talk like that? Maybe Elvis could become more up to date if he spent some time in New York City.

"Like funny to an accountant, maybe," the girl camper replied sarcastically.

"Lenny drives one," Southern went on. "He says the only way to know the enemy is to walk in his shoes. Which in this case means driving a pig-mobile."

"Lenny?"

"Bruce," Southern said matter-of-factly. "He flops at my pad when he's doing the Apple."

As far as Elvis could tell, Mr. Southern had now lapsed entirely into some kind of pig Latin that was common parlance to these youngsters.

"Bullshit!" the young woman said.

Elvis understood that.

"I don't think you should be talking that way to Mr. Terry Southern," Elvis said. "He happens to be the best movie writer in America."

All three pipe-smokers seemed to get positively bubbly upon hearing the word "movie."

"You really write flicks?" one of the young men asked.

"It pays the rent," Southern replied.

"Like what flick? *Mary Poppins?*" the young woman said.

"Mr. Southern wrote the best movie I've ever seen," Elvis snapped back. "It's called *Dr. Strangelove.*"

With that, the faces of the trio assumed expressions of such innocent awe that they might have been kids at an Elvis concert. But then the chieftess seemed to have some second thoughts.

"What do Communists sap?" she quizzed Southern. She clearly saw it as a trick question.

"Precious bodily fluids," Southern replied in a bored voice. Elvis sensed that the author of the most famous line in that movie had heard it quoted one too many times.

"Man, this is like so weird, meeting the guy who wrote *Dr. Strangelove* in the middle of nowhere," the young woman said. Apparently, she suddenly felt so reverent in Southern's presence that she searched around at her feet for a tie-dyed shawl, which she quickly wrapped around her diaphanous blouse. Elvis's guess was that Southern would have felt more revered if she'd left it off.

"I think I know what Mr. Bruce meant," Elvis said, as guileless sounding as he could muster. "I figure it would do me some good to walk in your all's shoes for a spell. Riding around in that colorful van of yours, I might connect with my own free spirit."

"So why don't we trade, man?" the girl quipped, back to true form again. She clearly saw her proposition as a brazen challenge to capitalist squareness.

"Couldn't do that," Elvis said. "That Caddy cost me almost three thousand dollars." The truth was, he'd given away Cadillacs for nothing on far less provocation.

"Money!" the girl whined, as if she were naming some unspeakable perversion.

"What if you threw in a little of your homegrown tea to even things out?" Miss Amy said cheerily.

Both of the long-haired young men looked expectantly at their leader as she apparently did some intricate mental calculations. It seemed that in spite of herself, she had *some* talent for capitalism.

"Just an ounce," she announced finally.

"It's a deal," Elvis replied.

"Let's smoke on it," one of the chieftess's braves said. He handed the pipe up to Elvis.

Elvis had been dreading that it would come to this. He knew full well what was smoldering in that pipe of theirs. Heaven knows, he was curious about the stuff but he also fretted that one puff of it might send him down the path of no return. The devil's own weed, as Miss Carol-Sue Crampton had called it. But Elvis also knew that if he refused this proxy peace pipe, the car-swapping deal that they had so artfully engineered might go sour real fast. He took a long drag on the pipe and handed it to the boy with the pitchfork on his forehead.

"Hey, that's an upside-down peace symbol you got tattooed there, isn't it, son?" Elvis said to him. He had just now deciphered it.

The boy immediately rolled forward and stood on his head. The upside-down pitch fork instantly became the peace symbol.

"I got me one too," Elvis said, touching his brow. "Except mine's right side up and starting to fade."

The young woman stood, walked right up to Elvis, and carefully inspected the outlines of Elvis's facial contusion.

"This is, like, so magical," she murmured.

"We're reverse twins!" the young man cheered, still standing on his head. He had no idea how spooky that idea sounded to Elvis.

A little later, when they were cruising down a county highway in the Technicolor Volkswagen van, Elvis said to Mr. Southern, "Does Mr. Bruce really drive a Caddy?"

"Actually, I don't think Lenny can drive," Southern replied.

14

Dance Lessons from a Possum

$\mathcal{N}$ow that is a peculiar phenomenon-enon-enon," Miss Amy Coulter warbled. She was now sitting between Elvis and Mr. Southern in the front seat of what Southern had christened their "*anti*-pig-mobile."

"What's that?" Elvis asked.

"You don't *smell* like Elvis," she said.

Elvis grinned. "It's part of my disguise," he said. "Trying to throw off the bloodhounds."

Southern guffawed. "Sniff, sniff," he said, and laughed some more.

In a last-minute side negotiation, Miss Amy had traded her ankle-length Miss Krieger's skirt for the tie-dyed scarf and a tin pipe. The scarf was now tied around her waist, Hawaiian style, and the pipe had been passing between the three of them for the last fifteen minutes. Elvis decided that since he had already taken one puff of the stuff, another two or three or four couldn't make that much of a difference, especially since it barely seemed to affect him anyway. Well, maybe it made him feel a trifle light-headed and tingly, but he sure as heck couldn't figure out what all the fuss was about. *He* didn't see any flying elephants or blue unicorns anywhere. It was probably all in these young people's heads.

"I'm sneer-ious," Miss Amy said.

"*Sneer*-ious?"

"You know what I mean."

"Sneer-ious about what?" Elvis said. Actually, he kind of liked her new word; it kept "serious" from taking itself too seriously.

"Your smell," Miss Amy said. "Last time you smelled more like a train station. This time you smell like a car wash."

"That's because last time you were sniffing some other fella," Elvis said.

"That, and the fact that he recently took a bath at a car wash," Southern said, deadpan.

"What other fella?" Miss Amy asked.

"The one you had your picture took with on the back of that pink Cadillac car," Elvis said.

Miss Amy's open face suddenly clouded up. "If my daddy ever sees those pictures, he'll send me to reform school."

"I thought Miss Krieger's *was* reform school," Elvis said.

Miss Amy giggled, her cloud gone and forgotten as quickly as it had arrived. "I'm sneer-ious," she said, and giggled some more.

There was an important question that Elvis wanted to ask her, but it kept slipping away from him like a greased pig.

"This is the way life should always be!" Miss Amy suddenly declared.

"How's that?" Southern asked.

"Easy," Amy said. "Riding around to nowhere in particular and taking it all in. Just easy riding."

Southern slapped the steering wheel. "Life is a road movie," he proclaimed.

"Now I remember," Elvis said.

"Remember what?" Miss Amy said.

"That greased pig," Elvis said.

"That's no way to talk in front of a lady," Southern said.

"No, listen to me," Elvis said, trying to be as serious as he could, but a silly sneer kept getting in his way. "Those photos we were talking about. Why'd you hire Frew to take them if you thought they could land you in a heap of trouble with your daddy?"

Amy took another long drag on the pipe and said, "Frew who?"

"Gesundheit," Southern said.

"You know, Frew from SWEPT," Elvis said.

"I never slept with him," Miss Amy said.

"SWEPT!" Elvis repeated, more loudly. "Your girls club. Frew did your newsletter."

"He's a nerd," Miss Amy said.

"Watch out for that possum!" Elvis shouted.

Southern hit the breaks and the van shuddered to a stop. Ten feet in front of them, a haggard-looking possum was crossing the road at no more than an inch per minute. The main reason it was taking the varmint so long was because after each step forward, it stopped to execute a little buck-and-wing two-step.

"A man could do worse than take dance lessons from a possum," Elvis said solemnly. Even as he said this, the observation struck him as having untold implications about evolution and world peace. He attempted to make a mental note to remember it.

"Those photographs were Jennifer's idea, not mine," Miss Amy said. "She told me it was a new club rule. *Documentation*. Otherwise, anybody could say they'd done the deed with you. And Jennifer said that would cheapen everything we stood for."

"Gresham's law," Southern said. "Counterfeit money drives genuine currency out of circulation. Applies to people too."

"Jennifer van Duesen?" Elvis said, astonishing himself by pulling the name from a file marked "SWEPT" that had been stuffed haphazardly into a cabinet in his mind's subterranean offices.

"Correct," Miss Amy said. "The one who thinks she's Ann-Margret all over again."

The possum had finally made its way across the road. Southern started up the van again.

"From what I saw, she does bear an awful close resemblance to Miss Ann-Margret," Elvis said.

"So would you if your daddy was the best plastic surgeon in all of Tennessee," Miss Amy said.

Elvis sucked in a lungful of virgin country air and let it out slowly. He looked across Miss Amy at Mr. Southern. "I think Miss Amy just said something that's got some important bearing on . . . on . . . on . . ." The sentence got tangled up with a possum in Elvis's mind, so he had to let it go.

"Me too," Southern replied.

"Remember what she said, would you, Terry?" Elvis said. "'Cuz I need to take a nap now."

When Elvis awoke, the van was parked on a bed of moss by the side of a brook. Through the windshield, he saw Southern and the girl frolicking in the water, Miss Amy in her birthday suit, Mr. Southern in the same chino slacks and short-sleeved blue oxford shirt that he had been wearing for the past few days. No doubt, Southern had remained in his clothes out of modesty—the kind of modesty that seemed to attack lots of men in their forties whose bellies had seen better days.

Two thoughts sprang into Elvis's mind. The first—that possums made good dance teachers—had lost its urgency during Elvis's snooze. But the second—that Miss Jennifer van Duesen had had her face surgically altered by her father so that it would resemble Miss Ann-Margret's—struck Elvis as being jam-packed with clues. Anybody who subscribed to *Movie Screen* magazine was all too aware that Elvis and Miss Ann had had a fling. Heck, anybody who read the *Memphis Commercial Appeal*—like Miss Priscilla, for example—was aware of that. So if you took SWEPT's creepy credo to heart, it would make a certain crazy sense to have a makeover into Elvis's movie-star paramour. On the face of it, it seemed like it would give you an edge in achieving your goal.

Southern and Miss Amy were returning to the van, Miss Amy wriggling into her blouse and panties, Southern trying to shake off some of the brook water like he was a long-haired spaniel.

"So, it's just as I thought . . . or smelled . . . or whichever," Miss Amy said as she got in beside Elvis on the passenger side. "You *aren't* the same Elvis that I surrendered myself to."

"I'm glad you finally realized that," Elvis replied.

"Terry explained it all to me," she said. "Actually, it's rather disappointing. I mean, I think you are a fine person, whoever you are, but I liked *him* better."

For a second, Elvis felt like the movie of his life was racing backward and there he was back in Hume High, odd man out in the ritzy-girl sweepstakes. For that one second, Elvis had renewed sympathy for sorry old Goodyear Bobby.

"For one thing," Miss Amy went on, "he's considerably more passionate about making a girl feel desirable."

"He's a fake, I'm the real Elvis," Elvis explained.

"He certainly felt real to me," Miss Amy countered.

Elvis decided to let it drop for the time being. Mr. Southern squished in wetly on his other side.

"First thing we need to do is drop off Miss Amy," Elvis said, with a surge of clearheaded purposefulness. "Then we should pay a visit to Miss Jennifer and her daddy. Where does she live, child?"

"*Up yours with gauze!*" Miss Amy replied, and she stuck out her tongue yet again.

On second consideration, perhaps Miss Angelica Krieger's finishing-school approach to educating young woman had some merit to it.

"Are you unhappy about something, Miss Amy?" Elvis asked.

"Just where do you think you are going to drop me off?" the young woman said acidly. "If it's down in Denmark, you might as well burn me at the stake right here."

"She has a point," Southern said.

"So what are we supposed to do?" Elvis said. "Cruising around with an underage truant female seems like we're breaking one law too many. Next thing you know, we'll have the police coming after us too. There's getting to be a real long line behind us."

Mr. Southern considered this for a long moment.

"All right, that's it," Miss Amy said, letting herself out of the car. "I'll just wait here for someone to pick me up. Perhaps an escaped convict. Or the police. And I could never lie to the police about how I got here, could I?"

"Gosh almighty!" Elvis roared. "Seems like blackmail's the new national pastime."

"This isn't blackmail," Miss Amy said ingenuously. "It's self-preservation."

"Where do the van Duesens live?" Southern said.

"Medon," Miss Amy said. " 'Melon,' we call it."

"Get in," Elvis said.

Miss Amy did so. "I'll be your tour guide," she said, filling up the tin pipe again.

This time, Elvis declined the stuff—it made him way too sleepy for the task at hand—and he was relieved to see that Mr. Southern passed on it too. On the other hand, Miss Amy did seem a lot more forthcoming and loquacious after a few puffs, so Elvis decided to postpone his lecture to her about the evils of drug taking. He asked her how she had gotten to know Miss Jennifer van Duesen.

"She started a countywide fan club a year or so ago," Miss Amy said, sticking one hand out the side window and flying it in the wind like a paper airplane. "You know, for Elvis."

The way she put it made Elvis think that she was not entirely convinced that she was currently sitting next to Elvis Presley. No reason to dispute that again. Heck, good reasons for *not* being the real Elvis were piling up fast.

"Anyway, all my high school friends were joining up, so I did too," Miss Amy continued.

"Peer pressure," Mr. Southern said.

"Get real!" Miss Amy said. "The reason you wear clothes on a hot day is peer pressure."

Drugged or not, Miss Amy definitely had an original perspective on things.

"Anyway, girls from all over Madison County came to her house once a month for club meetings," she went on. "What a set-up the van Duesens have up there in Melon! It makes my daddy's manse look like the Little House on the Prairie."

Southern laughed. Elvis guessed that he had already decided to put Miss Amy in their movie too. Looked like there was going to be a cast of thousands.

"And get this," Miss Amy continued. "The whole affair was catered. Mint tea and cucumber sandwiches on crustless bread, pecan tarts, the works. As if it was a garden club for old bags instead of a fan club for precocious girls in love with Elvis the Pelvis."

Elvis winced. Yup, reasons for being absolutely anybody but Elvis Presley were mounting by the minute.

"So at one meeting, Jenny stands up—she was kind of the self-appointed president from the get-go—she stands up and says she had the most fascinating dream the night before. And then she describes in erotic detail this whole seduction scene at Graceland. Definitely on the corny side, like when Elvis carries her upstairs on his shoulders, fireman-style, before ravishing her on his silk sheets."

"I don't have silk sheets," Elvis blurted out for no good reason he could think of. Maybe some of that marijuana smoke filling up the van was tampering with his sense.

"And when Jenny finishes up, she looks out at us with a giddy grin on her face and says, 'I had to wash my panties the next morning.' "

Elvis asked Southern to open up the window on his side too. He was suddenly feeling claustrophobic.

"Well, after that, one at a time, just about every girl there stood up and described an Elvis dream she'd had too," Amy continued. "Making passionate love with him on a chaise lounge at poolside in Hollywood. Or in a Pullman. Or on horseback."

"Creative group," Southern said.

"It was a regular game of 'Can you top this?' " Amy said. "I figure most of them were just making them up as they went along. But what the heck, dreams are just made up too."

" 'In dreams begin responsibilities,' " Southern intoned.

"That's about it," the girl said, ignoring his comment. "Once the cat was out of the bag about what was *really* on all our minds, we pretty much dispensed with all the other items on the club agenda. They didn't seem relevant anymore."

"What other stuff?" Elvis asked.

"You know, Elvis's songs and his movies. Garbarge like that."

Elvis felt his insides just about shrivel up and die, right then and there. It was worse—far worse—than he had ever imagined in his worst nightmares. The whole sex symbol business had finally totally eclipsed everything that he was genuinely about. It completely blotted out the music that had made him want to get up there and perform in front of people in the first place. Shiva Ree, his deceiving former girlfriend in Las Vegas, had once told Elvis that you can't tell the dancer from the dance. Well, she had been wrong about that too: the dance was expendable. It was just junk that got in the way of coveting the dancer.

"Had Jennifer had her plastic surgery by then?" Mr. Southern asked.

"No, that came later. After we worked out the details of our *new* organization."

"SWEPT," Elvis said.

Miss Amy giggled. "Stupid name, right?" she said. "Sounds like we're tidy housewives. I wanted to call it FREE, but I was outvoted."

Elvis definitely did not want to know what *that* was an acronym for. He had the sudden need for a little personal affirmation, so he switched on the car radio and spun the dial until he found a station playing one of his songs. It didn't take long. In two seconds flat, their hippie van was drenched with "Wooden Heart."

15

Delusions of Glandeur

*W*ell, Elvis is back in the news again, boys and girls," the radio deejay crooned. The guy didn't have to be on TV for you to know that he was leering.

Elvis's instinct was to snap off the broadcast, but Mr. Southern signaled him to leave it on. Southern was right; it was the only source they had for keeping track of their multiple pursuers.

"Just a couple of hours ago," the deejay went on, "he was seen coming out of the Red Walnut Church of Christ in Decaturville, after a little prenuptial chat with the minister there, Reverend Thomas Wilson, and, of course, with Elvis's teen bride-to-be, Miss Carol-Sue Crampton. The wedding date is now officially set for this Sunday. Mark that on your calendars, boys and girls! Just two days away! . . . Meanwhile, our man at Graceland spotted Miss Priscilla Beaulieu, Mr. Presley's *former* teen bride-to-be, sitting alone in Elvis's garden. She refused to answer any questions, but our man did report that Miss Beaulieu definitely looked like she had been crying her eyes out."

For the first time since all this madness had begun, Elvis seriously considered the option of jumping off a cliff somewhere. The coward's way out seemed like the only honorable way out. But then a little bit of grace descended upon him in the form of a flashback to his rapturous moonlight cruise down the Tennessee River just last night—serene, beatific, anonymous. No, he would be remaining on the high side of any cliffs for a bit longer. He just had to stay strong.

"It gets more delicious," the deejay was now saying. "No more than one hour after that churchyard appearance, Elvis was over in Switch paying a little visit to Miss Krieger's School for Young Ladies. You know the place I'm talking about, boys and girls. Some of you call it Chastity Academy."

"By george, even your *deejays* are more sophisticated down here!" Mr. Southern exclaimed.

"Glad we're making such a good impression," Elvis muttered back.

"According to our sources," the radio man continued, "Mr. Presley and an unnamed accomplice kidnapped one of Miss Krieger's young ladies in Elvis's white Cadillac coupe. Which, by the way, was riddled with bullet holes. The three of them were last spotted cruising around Benton County, painted up like Indians with feathers in their hair."

Both Mr. Southern and Miss Amy howled.

"Redskin herrings!" Southern crowed.

The deejay had taken a short pause before returning to his microphone in tones as subdued as he was capable of. "Personally, I am very worried about Elvis, friends. Some folks think that he's running wild because his handler, Colonel Parker, is in jail and can't keep him under control. But I have a more calamitous theory: I am afraid that car accident of his caused Elvis more brain damage than anyone realized."

With that, the deejay sequed into Patsy Cline singing "Crazy."

Elvis snapped off the radio. "I don't want you putting *that* idiot in our movie, Mr. Southern," he said.

"What movie?" Miss Amy asked.

"This one," Southern said, looking over at Elvis and giving him a quick nod.

Elvis figured that was his cue to finally explain to Miss Amy exactly what their mission was. She seemed to take it all in with equanimity, even when she finally accepted the fact that the young man who had taken her virginity was definitely a fraudulent Elvis, probably in the employ of someone who was out to do some serious damage to the real Elvis, who was, after all, the man who happened to be sitting next to her. When he finished, Miss Amy said, "I should have realized something was screwy when I got that note. The one that said I could get two thousand dollars in cash if I went to the *National Enquirer* with the story about you doing me on the trunk of your car, complete with photographic proof."

"Who sent that note?" Elvis said.

Miss Amy shrugged. "They didn't sign it. Just left a pickup point where I'd get my reward when I did what they said."

"And did you?"

Miss Amy turned in her seat and gave the real Elvis a withering look. "Of course not!" she said. "Whatever anybody says, I *am* a lady."

"And that's the absolute truth, Miss Amy," Elvis told her.

The three of them decided that their best option was to investigate Dr. van Duesen first because his behavior was even more suspicious than his daughter's. Like why would he want to perform a surgery on his daughter that would make her more capable of seducing Elvis Presley? It didn't exactly seem like an appropriate goal for a fine southern daddy to aid and abet, especially if his daughter was only seventeen years old. Still, Elvis was not quite ready to concede that Miss Jennifer was just an innocent, starry-eyed teenager. After all, she had been the one to add the "documentation" requirement to SWEPT's bylaws; she was the one who was ultimately responsible for Manard Frew's back-roads candid camera.

Cruising through Pinson, they spotted a doughnut shop with a "Phone Inside" sign in its window. Southern parked across the street, then left Elvis and the girl in the car and sauntered inside the establishment. Five minutes later, he returned with a tall bag brimming over with doughnuts, plus three paper cups of coffee. Their supper.

"Dr. van Duesen certainly runs an enthusiastic organization," Southern said after downing two doughnuts in quick succession. "His receptionist sounded very accommodating. More like she was making appointments at an escort service than a surgery clinic."

"That's Jennifer's mother," Miss Amy said. "The lady has delusions of grandeur. She actually believes those boobs of hers are a work of nature."

"Delusions of *glandeur*," Southern said.

"Her husband did some work on her?" Elvis said.

"Just on her boobs and buttocks," Miss Amy replied. "What they call a 'T-and-A job.' He didn't touch Mrs. van Duesen's face though. That's her pride and joy. I do have to admit, she *is* one pretty lady."

Mr. Southern said that after some dazzling coaxing on his part, Mrs. van Duesen had squeezed in an appointment with the best plastic surgeon in all of Tennessee at the end of his consultation hours. That gave them fifteen minutes to get to Medon, also known as Melon. Along the way, using the first-aid kit she found in the glove compartment, Miss Amy did an inventive little makeover of Elvis's face. They made it to the clinic with one minute to spare.

"This is the friend I told you about," Mr. Southern announced as he led Elvis into the Van Duesen Clinic's waiting room. They had left Miss Amy in the van a good hundred yards down the street.

The whole set-up looked more Hollywood than Tennessee; in fact, it looked pretty darned close to the back lot of MGM Studios, what with its white stucco outbuildings and connecting pathways lined with potted palm trees. Even the waiting room itself was reminiscent of the waiting room for the studio's casting office.

"What the devil happened to *you*?" Mrs. van Duesen, the receptionist, said to Elvis as she rose from behind her glass-topped desk.

No doubt about it, Mrs. van Duesen was a living advertisement for a T-and-A job. Between her amplified front and backside, she offered enough shelf space to display a dozen bowling trophies. But just as Miss Amy had said, her face—apparently untouched by her husband's scalpel—was movie star gorgeous: big blue eyes, perky little nose, puffy lips that she had painted an indecent shade of pink, and naturally sculpted cheekbones that reminded Elvis of, well, of Ann-Margret's.

On the other hand, Elvis's own face currently looked like it belonged to a bit player in the House of Wax. With his scraggly three-day growth, disheveled, unwashed hair, the remaining discoloration of his spoke-induced contusions, and his fat lip and bruised cheekbones, *plus* the blotches of iodine and Mercurochrome that Miss Amy had artfully applied to his face, Elvis looked like a seriously substandard human being.

"I found myself on the wrong end of a fist," Elvis replied to Mrs. van Duesen, affecting a scratchy voice that came out sounding like Gabby Hayes in a dust storm. "Figured this was as good an excuse as any to finally get that new face I've been promising myself. One that somebody besides my mama could love. Got the cash all saved up for it too."

This last remark seemed to particularly animate Mrs. van Duesen. She approached Elvis and placed a hand on the side of his face. Somehow, the gesture felt more jezebel than nurselike; perhaps that was because at this distance, her front shelf could not help but make contact with Elvis's chest. It felt like being poked by a pair of umbrella tips. You had to wonder what her husband had injected in there.

"You have the bone structure of a matinee idol," Mrs. van Duesen cooed, tracing her fingers from Elvis's cheek to the underside of his chin. "I do believe you are going to come out looking so pretty that women will have to take saltpeter to control themselves around you."

Man, that is precisely what Elvis was sick to death of! For one dizzy moment in which he forgot why he had come here in the first place, Elvis considered marching into the doctor's office and demanding that he give him the face of Bela Lugosi.

At that instant, the good doctor himself, a man about whom it was safe to say that no amount of plastic surgery could transform into a matinee idol, came out into the waiting room. His wife's hand was still smoothly evaluating Elvis's bone structure, but the doctor looked as though this was not the first time he had happened upon his wife in this particular pose. Probably not even the first time this day.

"Mind if my friend comes in with me for moral support?" Elvis said to Dr. van Duesen.

"Why not?" the doctor said in a sprightly, high-register voice. "I'll even give him a free evaluation while I'm at it."

Van Duesen had done up his consultation office to look like a professor's study, or at least a Hollywood version of one—framed diplomas on the walls, walnut bookcases from floor to ceiling, a huge fern in a Victorian planter, and on either side of the velvet-draped window behind his desk, marble pedestals with facsimile classical sculptures standing on them. Elvis recognized them both from Selma's art books: Michelangelo's *David,* and the Venus de Milo. Somehow, that armless Venus did not look like it would inspire confidence in the surgeon. There were several gold frames propped up on the doctor's desk, but from his side, Elvis could not see the pictures inside them.

After filling out some forms—Elvis listed himself as "Joby Baker," the name of the actor who had played his drummer in *Girl Happy*; and under Form of Payment, he wrote "CASH" in all capitals—Elvis followed van Duesen into an alcove. There, the doctor seated him in what looked like a dentist's chair. High-intensity lamps snapped on all around Elvis's head. Dr. van Duesen pulled a magnifying glass attached to a swivel arm in front of Elvis's face. Only then did Elvis observe that Mrs. van Duesen had joined them and was now hovering behind her husband.

"Symmetric contusions extending from lower maxilla to upper malar," Dr. van Duesen reported.

Mrs. van Duesen scratched on her clipboard.

"Recently healed facial lacerations at twelve o'clock, three o'clock, and four o'clock," the doctor continued.

More dutiful scratching by his wife.

"Possible chipping of upper right mandible, but no signs of fracture." Van Duesen glanced at his wife. "We'll double-check that on the X-ray."

Mrs. van Duesen nudged her husband aside and took a long gander through the magnifier.

"Gol-*ly*, I thought so! You know who he looks like underneath all that scum?" she said. "Elvis Presley."

"That's just what my mama says," Elvis said. "But she's prejudiced, of course."

"No offense, but I believe Mr. Presley's head is significantly smaller than yours," the doctor said.

"And I bet you can't make a man's head smaller, can you, Doctor?" Elvis said.

Van Duesen chuckled. "Not without shaving off some of his intellect," he said.

"Don't have that much to spare," Elvis replied, joining in the laugh. If he ever ran into the real Joby Baker again, he would have to quote him that line; Joby would get a real kick out of it.

"Come to think of it, that sure would make your mama happy," Mr. Southern piped up from just outside the examination alcove. "You know, coming home looking more like Elvis than Elvis Presley himself."

Although Elvis could see where Mr. Southern was going with this—and, of course, that it was only playacting—he felt momentarily chagrined by invoking his mama as if she were still alive.

"I think it would be preferable if Mr. Baker was just tweaked a little here and there to become a better version of himself," the doctor said seriously. "That makes for a much less traumatic psychological adjustment."

"But could you if he wanted?" Southern asked.

The doctor looked uncomfortable. "It is highly inadvisable," he said.

"But you made that sweetheart on your desk look just like Ann-Margret," Southern said.

"Isn't she divine?" Mrs. van Duesen said vivaciously. "That's our daughter, Jennifer."

"And she sure was pretty to begin with," Southern went on amiably. "I can see that from her baby pictures."

"Jennifer had an awkward adolescence," Mrs. van Duesen said in what she apparently thought was a suitably motherly tone, but Elvis detected just a hint of glee in it. "Some of those van Duesen genes suddenly asserted themselves and poor Jenny's face started to veer disastrously toward my mother-in-law's."

"That's enough!" Dr. van Duesen said sharply. Elvis could not tell if it was the unflattering reference to his mother or something else that was irritating the doctor.

"But why did she choose Ann-Margret?" Southern said.

Elvis was afraid that Mr. Southern was pressing too hard too fast, but apparently Southern sensed that he had tapped into one of Mrs. van Duesen's favorite subjects. Plus the fact that her husband seemed to have no control over her.

"Actually, many people believe I bear a strong, sisterly resemblance to Miss Ann-Margret," Jennifer's mother said coquettishly. Even with the near-blinding high-intensity lamps shining in his eyes, Elvis could see her execute a miniature shimmy upon saying this. But that surgically altered front porch of hers rocked back and forth more like a two-seater swing than like the Jell-O bowls of the actress she believed she resembled.

"So it was just a way of keeping it in the family," Elvis said. "Your daughter's face, that is."

"Exactly!" Mrs. van Duesen said.

"*Please!* I am running late already," her husband said.

"Of course, being a big fan of Elvis, Jennifer feels a special kinship to Ann-Margret," Mrs. van Duesen went on blithely.

"So you killed two birds with one scalpel," Elvis said.

"Why, Mr. Baker, you *are* a funny man," Mrs. van Duesen laughed, scooting up to Elvis's right side. "And you *do* look like Elvis, no matter what this wearisome old doctor says."

"Does she belong to any of those Elvis clubs?" Elvis asked. By way of establishing a little extra intimacy between the two of them, Elvis edged his right arm off of the armrest so that it nudged Mrs. van Duesen's hip. Shameful what a man had to do to perform conscientious detective work, especially with the lady's husband watching it all through a magnifying glass.

Mrs. van Duesen seemed to eye her husband apprehensively before replying. "Just the local fan club," she said finally.

"That one's called SWEPT, isn't it?" Elvis said.

"*No!*" Mrs. van Duesen snapped. "It's called the Madison County Elvis Presley Fan Club."

Elvis shifted his eyes from Mrs. van Duesen to her husband and back again. It was clear that Jennifer's mother knew full well what the club's new name was—not to mention its scandalous credo—but that Jennifer's father did not. Furthermore, it was pretty obvious that Mrs. van Duesen wanted to keep it that way.

"I can give you only five more minutes, Mr. Baker," Dr. van Duesen announced.

"Sorry, Doctor," Elvis said. "But if I am going get myself made over to look like Mr. Presley, I should probably know what I'm getting into."

"But we've said nothing about making you look like—," the doctor began.

"So, can you or can't you?" Elvis interrupted. He was riding a hunch. "Can you make me look just like Elvis Presley?"

"Definitely not!" the doctor said.

"Of course, you can," his wife said. "For heaven's sake, you've done it once already. And that boy didn't look half as much like Elvis as Mr. Baker here does to begin with."

Bingo!

"Gee, sounds like I've got competition," Elvis drawled, trying to keep it light. But it was too late. Dr. van Duesen snapped off the lamps and scurried back into the main part of the consultation office.

"I believe you need to find yourself another surgeon," he said curtly.

"But what about me, Doctor?" Southern said. "Can you make me look like Pat Boone? Or how about Perry Como?"

"I am going to have to ask you both to leave now," Dr. van Duesen said.

16

A Message for the King

When Elvis and Mr. Southern returned to the van, Miss Amy was lounging on the lawn next to it, lying on her stomach, her bare legs wagging like a teenager's—which, after all, she was, in spite of that precocious mouth of hers. She was reading.

"Get this," she said, barely looking up from a sheaf of papers. "'Known to our young people as Elvis the Pelvis, the so-called entertainer is on an all-expenses-paid mission to defile and corrupt vulnerable Christian children. Do not be fooled by his songs, Legionnaires. The lyrics may sound innocent—"Love Me Tenderly," "Please Do Not Step on My Blue Shoes"—but these are just a cunning diversion from Presley's real message, the one emanating from his hips! Let there be no doubt about it, our children are being visited by the Antichrist.'"

Elvis shook his head. Man, just the year before, he'd had those fanatics out in Vegas who were convinced that he was the Second Coming, and now he had a new bunch of nutcases calling him the Antichrist. *Come on, people, it can't be both!* Or could it? Just how different could the Inner Elvis be from the walking, talking Elvis on the outside? Now that's a question he would like to pose to Dr. Helga—that is, if he survived long enough to see her again.

"Where did you find that?" Mr. Southern said to Miss Amy.

"On their hall table," she replied. "The van Duesens'."

"In their *house*, child?" Elvis said.

"What did you expect me to do while you were gone?" the young woman said. "Just sit around and get stoned?"

"It's what I would have done," Southern said.

"Well, we are all smoked out, for one thing," she said. "And for another, a Miss Krieger's lady always lends her man a helping hand."

Mr. Southern gestured to the papers in Miss Amy's hands. "Those sentences have a familiar ring to them," he said.

"That's for sure," Elvis said. "Lately, I'm hearing this crazy Elvis-is-the-devil talk from every which direction."

"I'm referring to the syntax," Southern said. "If I'm not mistaken, that's a genuine Manard Frew rewrite."

Elvis snatched the papers from Miss Amy's hands—four pages stapled together in the corner, newsletter style. Elvis flipped to the front page. Yes indeed, the Legion of Decency, western Tennessee chapter, had its very own newsletter too. In a box in the upper-right-hand corner was a woodcutty line drawing in the same style as the one in SWEPT's newsletter. In fact, the drawings themselves were similar, but in this one the giant Elvis was not surrounded by pretty young women wielding brooms; no, here the giant was being attacked by a dozen little Davids with slingshots in their hands and crosses on their togas. Manard Frew had taken some license with Bible history for this drawing.

"Mr. Frew certainly had an open mind when it came to business," Elvis said.

"He isn't the first publisher to play both ends against the middle," Mr. Southern said.

"Strange you didn't find this newsletter in Frew's files," Elvis said. "Frew struck me as real persnickety about keeping complete records of his clients."

"Maybe those Ku Kluxers who got there before us swiped it so nobody would find it," Southern said.

Elvis nodded. "If Dr. van Duesen is a dues-paying member of this Decency organization, he is definitely no fan of mine," he said. "Makes you wonder why he would be willing to give an

154

Elvis face to some boy. Not to mention an Ann-Margret face to his daughter, no matter what reasons her mother had."

Man, this was getting to be one of those puzzles that was draped all over with an enigma.

"The person we need to find now is that young man who's been carved up to look like me," Elvis said. "I'll bet you anything he was the one who drove us into that lake. And the same one who compromised you on the trunk of his car, Miss Amy."

"I didn't feel compromised," Miss Amy said, looking innocently up at Elvis. "I felt idolized."

"That's not the way it looked in those pictures, ma'am," Elvis said, as delicately as he could.

"It's all in the eye of the beholder," she retorted.

It seemed Miss Amy *had* absorbed a thing or two besides beatings at Miss Krieger's, after all.

"What we need to do now is get into Dr. van Duesen's files," Elvis said. "And try to find out the name of that boy who's borrowed my face."

"I bet Mrs. van Duesen can help us out with that," Southern said. "She did seem to take a fancy to you."

"No. She's not to be trusted for all kinds of reasons," Elvis said. "One of them being the way she sticks out front and back, like one of those Studebaker cars—you don't know which direction she's going in."

"Maybe I could ask—," Miss Amy began, but she was cut off by the roar of a motorcycle.

It came racing out from behind one of the outbuildings of the Van Duesen Clinic and was headed straight for them, sparks flying from its engine, its twin exhausts shooting flames like a blowtorch. Driving the rig was a bearded man with tattoos covering his bare arms, his T-shirt emblazoned with a swastika.

"Blitzkrieg!" Southern shouted. He jumped into the driver's seat of the VW bus and started her up.

Elvis hesitated at the front passenger door, waiting for Miss Amy to get in, but she motioned for him to get going without her.

Miss Amy was undoubtedly not this Nazi's prime target anyhow, so Elvis vaulted in. He was still pulling the door closed when Southern began burning enough rubber to make a rain slicker. The van finally jerked away from the curb.

The motorcycle was no more than a hundred feet behind them now, and it looked like it was gaining. Through the rearview mirror, Elvis could see that its driver was grasping a cylinder in his right hand. A pistol, no doubt.

"Step on it!" Elvis yelled.

"Doesn't help!" Southern yelled back.

Elvis glanced down at Southern's foot. Sure enough, he'd floored the accelerator, but the hippie mobile was only doing forty. Probably a shrewd safety measure on behalf of the Volkswagen folks, considering that their typical drivers were usually too stoned to go any faster without bumping into a roadside tree or two. However, it did not make Elvis feel particularly safe at this moment, especially now that the motorcyclist was no more than ten feet behind them, brandishing that pistol in his outstretched hand.

Southern took an abrupt left turn that startled Elvis as much as it did their pursuer, who overshot the turn and had to slow way down to circle back around. Elvis grabbed the door handle to keep from careening into Southern's lap. The van was now skittering on top of a narrow pebble road.

Elvis wondered who the heck the hairy Nazi could be working for. Probably Miss Krieger's KKK daddy, although it could just as well be Dr. van Duesen. *Or* his wife. *Or* Elvis's born-again lookalike. *Or* any number of daddies of prematurely deflowered young women—daddies with vengeance in their Christian hearts.

Straight ahead, by the side of the road, stood an antebellum manse reminiscent of Miss Krieger's School for Young Ladies—the van Duesens' nearest neighbors on this posh row. Southern's sharp left had swung the van onto their private driveway. It ended at a stable converted into a four-car garage just fifty feet in front of them. The motorcycle was back behind them, its wheels throwing off pebbles like high-gauge buckshot.

"Jump and run as soon as we stop!" Southern hollered, stomping on the brake pedal.

"*Kee*-rist!" the motorcyclist yelped. His head suddenly jerked to the side, almost touching his right shoulder. A split second later the rest of his body followed suit, veering right while his machine kept hurtling forward without him.

The motorcycle rammed into the back of the just-halted VW, making it lurch forward several feet just as Elvis was leaping out the door. The impact was enough to catapult Elvis into the air. Without even thinking about it, Elvis tucked in his head and swung up his legs. He landed on the gravel in a perfect somersault that absorbed the impact and pivoted him upright onto his feet. Studying those stuntmen on the MGM back lot had just paid off.

To Elvis's right, Mr. Terry Southern was slumped in a heap at the foot of a magnolia tree. He did not appear to be seriously injured. You could surmise that from the fact that he was giggling. "Precisely as I planned it," Southern chortled.

Behind Elvis, the motorcyclist was moaning, both hands pressed to the right side of his head. Elvis approached him cautiously; a man flat on his back could still shoot a gun.

"Help me! *Please!*" the man whimpered. He reminded Elvis of Sheriff Tip—full of piss and vinegar right up until he started oozing out big baby tears.

"Hands above your head," Elvis said.

The man did as instructed. Elvis could now see the wound just above the man's right temple. It looked like he had been shot in the head. But who the hell could have shot him?

Leaning over, Elvis inspected the gash, a raw and bloody half-inch-deep sinkhole in his skull. At the bottom was a single pebble. The man had been shot in the head by a chunk of driveway flung up at him by his front wheel.

It was only then that Elvis saw that the man was still grasping a cylinder in his right hand. Elvis was about to jump back when he realized that it was not a pistol—it was a rolled-up piece of bluish paper.

"A . . . a . . . a message for the . . . the King," the prone man stammered, and he passed out.

While Southern made his way to the plantation house to call an ambulance, Elvis did what he could to make the man comfortable. He removed his cowboy boots, placing one of them under his head as a pillow, and he loosened his belt. And then he removed the scroll of blue paper from his fist.

"Son," it began:

I used up my one phone call days ago. Nobody at G-land knows where the deuce you are. But fortunately, the bearer of this message, my erstwhile cellmate, Mr. Flip Payne, says that he has an inborn talent for finding missing persons. (Flip was released today after serving five days for driving a motorcycle while intoxicated—his seventh imprisonment for the same offense in the past year.)

I find myself in a perplexing situation, son. Captain Rooks of the Bolivar Police Department—I believe you made his acquaintance in your hospital room—along with his good friend, the district attorney, have offered me a proposition. They are willing to drop all charges against me and let me go as if nothing happened. That, of course, would be a major blessing for Mrs. Parker, who is not taking my current incarceration well at all. (In fact, she is having her hyperventilation problems again.)

Naturally, I would have to do something in return. Or, in this case, I would have to promise to do *nothing* in return. That "nothing" would be *not* contesting the authenticity of those Polaroid photographs, if, for example, they were to fall into the hands of the *National Enquirer* or *Silver Screen* magazine. Both of these periodicals apparently have expressed a willingness to make substantial contributions to the Bolivar Police Athletic League, which, by all accounts, is a credit to the community.

Perhaps there is another solution to our dilemma. Who knows? If you can think of a more attractive option, I suggest you pay a visit to Bolivar A.S.A.P. It would be a pleasure to see you again.

> I miss you, son,
> Col. Thomas Parker.

Elvis read the letter a second time, his rage deepening with each sentence. By God, there it was in black and white—or in this case, black and blue—a thinly disguised blackmail threat from the man who liked to call himself Elvis's fairy godfather. Man, only the Colonel could word a blackmail note so that it sounded like a Christmas letter.

On their way back to pick up Miss Amy, Elvis read the Colonel's letter to Mr. Southern.

"You don't think he really did kill Frew, do you?" Southern said.

"No."

"So they won't be able to prove anything. Then why is Parker so desperate to get out of jail before the trial that he'd pull a stunt like this?"

"Probably because of the accommodations," Elvis said. "Parker likes his feather pillow."

"You're saying Parker would sell you out for a feather pillow?"

"I'm also saying that at this particular moment, I could kill him," Elvis said.

"Not in this movie," Southern said. "But what I really don't get is why you keep that son of a bitch as your manager."

Elvis took a deep breath and let it out slowly. "Because we shook on it," he said. "Shook on it right in front of my mama."

"You're crazy, man," Southern said.

"I am who I am," Elvis replied.

* * *

Miss Amy was exactly as they had left her, lying on her stomach, bobby-soxer style, although without any socks or even much of a skirt to speak of—just that tie-dyed scarf bunched up around her waist—she looked more like a picture on a gas station calendar than one you would find in *Look* magazine. She was still reading.

"Timothy Conrad," she said when they pulled up beside her.

"Who's that?" Elvis squinted at her through the open van window.

"The man who would be Elvis," Miss Amy said, smiling up at Elvis. "Actually, I do believe Timmy is my lover. The man who made a woman of me."

"What have you got there, child?"

"Timmy's medical files," she said. "And let me tell you, that boy did not start out looking anything like you. Or at least like you used to look. No, Timothy started out looking a lot more like that guy on *Get Smart*. I sure am glad he had that surgery before we got together. Otherwise it would be mortifying."

"Where did you get that?" Elvis said as he got out of the van.

"Where do you think?" Miss Amy said, winking.

"How did you get into Dr. van Duesen's office?"

"Easy. Jennifer let me in. She has a key." Miss Amy stood and handed a manila folder to Elvis. "And boy was she burned up when she saw this! She would never have guessed in a million years that it wasn't really you who did her. And five times, too."

"I can just imagine," Elvis said. He felt a ripple of shame in his gut that was fast becoming all too familiar.

"And imagine how she felt when she realized it was her very own daddy who made it possible," Miss Amy said. "Sort of perverted, isn't it?"

17

Louisiana Hayride

Elvis perused Timothy G. Conrad's medical file as they headed down to Bolivar. First things first: keep those Polaroids out of the *National Enquirer,* then find the Conrad kid, who happened to live not all that far from Bolivar in Hickory Valley.

Sure enough, the "before" picture of Timmy looked like one of those mule-faced boys you find on just about every page of every high school yearbook—it usually says, "Quiet, but nice" under his photo, which is yearbook code for a real nobody. But the "after" shot was a genuine shocker. It could just as well have been a publicity still of Elvis from *Roustabout;* in fact, Elvis's first reaction was to check the back for MGM's copyright stamp. But there was a second "after" shot that showed the Elvisfied Timothy standing between a white-coated Dr. Van Duesen and Mrs. van Duesen, as if they were his proud parents, which in some peculiar sense they were. Their made-over Timothy Conrad was a feature-perfect reproduction of Elvis, complete with his pitch-black slicked-back hair and bashful smile. He looked a whole lot more like Elvis than Elvisetta ever could, good as she was.

The rest of the file was full of charts, one of which listed every incision of the surgical procedure by length and depth in millimeters—a total of fifteen incisions. There was hardly any personal information about the recipient of these cuts and bone shavings and cartilage shifts except that he was twenty-five, lived somewhere in Hickory Valley, and listed his occupation as "entertainment." On the last page was the bill for five thousand dollars, half again the cost of a new Cadillac car. It had been paid in cash.

"He must be rich," Miss Amy said. "I like that."

"Could be somebody else paid for it," Elvis said.

Mr. Southern punched on the van's radio, and just like that, Elvis's voice filled the air with "I Forgot to Remember to Forget." An oldie but goodie with that good old fifties punch and wit. It was a pleasure to hear it again. But just as it finished up, Mr. Southern's favorite deejay came on, crowing, "News flash, boys and girls! Looks like Elvis hasn't forgotten to forget one little thing. State trooper Mack Edwards tracked down the King's white caddy up in Henry County, parked in front of a Piggly Wiggly. Our man in Henry has the whole scoop."

Our man in Henry had Trooper Edwards right there in front of his roving microphone.

"We waited in our vehicle for the reappearance of the suspects," the policeman said in a monotone. Clearly, Edwards had graduated summa cum laude in trooper-speak from the police academy. "At exactly twenty-hundred plus fifteen, the three suspects emerged from the Piggly Wiggly carrying a large paper bag. Later inspection revealed that the bag in question contained three containers of Mountain Dew pop and twenty Tootsie Rolls, but no firearms. However we did discover a canister of what appeared to be cannabis in the vehicle's glove compartment. The three consisted of one female Caucasian and two male Caucasians, not Injuns, as had been erroneously reported. The apparent cause of that misidentification was their feathers and face paint."

Mr. Southern and Miss Amy started cackling again, but Elvis raised his hand for them to quiet down.

"The three apprehendents turned out not to be the objects of our search for Mr. Presley, his accomplice, and the young woman they kidnapped," Trooper Edwards plodded on. "They identified themselves as Philip Bloom, Patrick Bonavitacola, and Miss

Roberta Russell, all of Passaic, New Jersey, a state that borders New York."

"Now there's a damning geographical detail for you," Southern said.

"Miss Russell claimed that they had traded their Volkswagen vehicle for the white Cadillac vehicle from a man who claimed to be Mr. Presley himself, although Miss Russell contended that on consideration the man might have been someone else, like Presley's much older brother. Our records, however, show that Mr. Presley does not have an older sibling of either gender. The three are currently being held in Henry County Jail, in Homer, pending verification of their allegation and a laboratory analysis of the contents of that canister. In the meantime, our APB has been revised to be on the lookout for a Volkswagen vehicle painted with cartoon pictures of a Mr. Robert Dylan and a Miss Joan Baez, both northern cult figures. Mr. Presley, his unnamed accomplice, and their hostage, Miss Amy Coulter, a minor from Denmark, remain at large."

"Gosh almighty!" Elvis said, but between his companions' laughter and his own sound track rendition of "Trouble" which the smart-aleck deejay had tagged to the end of the report, they did not hear him. Elvis snapped off the radio. "Going to have to change cars again!" he hollered.

"Not cars—*vehicles*!" Southern giggled.

"I'm glad you're having such a grand time, Mr. Southern," Elvis said. "But you may be forgetting that as an accomplice to the kidnapping of an underage female, you are looking at twenty-five years to life."

Southern stopped giggling. "I have an awful feeling that this trade is not going to be as easy as the first one," he said. "We are not exactly offering quality goods this time around."

As it turned out, this car switch was much easier. And it certainly was more efficient. They were no more than five miles south of Medon on a back road when Elvis spotted the rear end of a two-wheeled manure spreader jutting out from a tobacco field. He told Southern to stop, then got out and waded between the eight-foot-high plants until he found what the spreader was hitched to—a four-cylinder New Holland tractor that had so much of its customary cargo caked to its sides, it looked like a sculptor had fashioned the whole rig out of red-dirt clay. Its driver was snoozing underneath the spreader, a straw hat covering his face, and enough flies buzzing around him to wake a dead man. One at a time, Elvis kicked the bottoms of the man's boots. It took five kicks to rouse him.

"Sorry to disturb you," Elvis said.

The man slithered on his back from under the rig, his hat remaining over his face. When he stood, the hat dropped, and he casually caught it in his right hand. He was a black man in his sixties or older, his hair and close-cropped beard white as bleached cotton.

"I know you," he said, smiling.

"Really?"

"That's right. From Doc Billy's clinic up in Alamo," the man said. "Heard you and Billy sing some gospel in the waiting room up there one day."

Elvis smiled. "Doc Billy has the sweetest tenor voice I ever heard," he said.

"You ain't bad yourself, Elvis," the black man said. "Where'd you learn to sing like that?"

"On my own, I guess. Never had a music teacher."

"I mean, where did you learn to sing with soul?" the man said.

"Well, everybody's got one," Elvis said.

"Now that's a soulful thought," the man said, scratching his beard. "But not everybody has the knack for pouring it into their voice."

"You got a point there."

"Ever been to a Pentecostal church? A black one, I'm saying."

"When I was a youngster, every chance I got."

The black man nodded. "Thought so."

Elvis was convinced that the man was thinking that he was the lowest kind of thief—a *soul* thief—when the man extended his hand to him.

"You got a genuine affinity, Elvis," he said. "And that's a blessing for both our peoples."

Elvis shook his hand long and hard.

"Musky," the man said. "That's short for Muskrat, one of those godawful nicknames that stuck since I was too little to fight for something better."

"Be happy to call you something else, if you like," Elvis said.

"Too late. I wouldn't know who you was talking to," the man said, smiling. "Some way I can help you, Elvis? Or did you just wander back here to take a whiz?"

Elvis explained pretty much his whole predicament, including the fact that he was not only trying to dodge the state police, but some Ku Klux Klanners, and who knew who else. Musky took it all in without batting an eyelash.

"I don't have any use for this rig until pickin' time anyhow," he said after Elvis had finished. "And God in heaven knows, the last place in the universe anybody is going to look for Elvis Presley is in the back of a dung flinger."

"But you were using it for *something* today. You got it out of the barn."

"You saw what I was using it for—napping under," the man said. "Smell puts me right to sleep. Take it for as long as you need, Elvis."

"Where will you sleep?"

"Guess I'll just have to give in and sleep with the wife till you get back," Musky laughed. "And listen, in case you was worried, this black man owns this rig, front to back, all paid up."

"I didn't figure you'd be lending me anybody else's," Elvis said. "I am very much obliged, Musky. Hope to be able to return the favor one day."

Minutes later, with the Volkswagen bus hidden in a copse of winged sumac, Mr. Terry Southern got behind the wheel of the

New Holland tractor, sporting Musky's straw hat; Elvis had traded his—or rather, Miss Elvisetta's—lightning-flash belt buckle for it. Miss Amy and Elvis sprawled side by side in the manure spreader on a blanket they had found in the back of the anti-pig-mobile.

"Bolivar, please, driver" Elvis called up to Southern.

"On the double, sir," Southern called back. And off they went, tractor and hitch, sometimes gaining enough momentum to sail along at fifteen miles an hour.

It had been near dusk when they waved good-bye to Musky, and now, as Southern turned onto the county road for Bolivar, he had to switch on the tractor's amber-colored headlights. No doubt about it, that manure odor was definitely on the overwhelming side, but Elvis found an unexpected comfort in it, an airborne connection to Mother Nature. Miss Amy did not seem bothered by the smell either. She started singing:

> *"Well, that's all right, mama*
> *That's all right for you . . ."*

It was just about the perfect song for the occasion, and not only because at that moment everything felt about as all right as could be, but because it had been the song that everybody loved the most when Elvis sang it on the *Louisiana Hayride* in his very first appearance on that radio show back in 1954. And, by golly, that is just what this felt like, an old-fashioned moonlight hayride.

Back in high school, when some of the girls turned sweet sixteen, their fathers would hitch a team to a hay wagon and drive out to the countryside with a dozen or so kids lolling on the straw in pairs, stealing kisses when the old man was not looking—and the old man made it his business not to look much at all. Elvis would be lying next to his steady, Dixie, her hair spread out under her head, just the way he was lying next to Miss Amy now. She might be singing too, like Miss Amy was, and Elvis would reach his arm around her shoulders and—goldang!

Elvis suddenly scooted himself over to the far end of the spreader, putting so much distance between himself and Miss Amy that he was completely off of the blanket and onto ten planting seasons' residue of cow patties. As far as he was concerned, he deserved even worse. That Inner Elvis had no more judgment than, well, a teenager. Miss Amy stopped singing.

By the time they reached the outskirts of Bolivar, it was going on midnight. The authorities were surely back at their homes, smoking on their front porches if they were not already in bed as, undoubtedly, their prize prisoner, Tom Parker, was by now, even without his feather pillow. Mr. Southern turned off the county road onto one that led to the edge of a pond, where he parked under a stand of Virginia pine. The three of them fashioned a bed of pine needles, covered it with the blanket, and stretched out for the night. Elvis made darned sure that Mr. Southern lay down between him and that underage schoolgirl.

It was only when he was drifting off to sleep that Elvis realized that of all the people he had run into lately, only Musky had recognized him right off the bat, no doubts at all. Maybe Musky had that gift for seeing past the five o'clock shadow and contusions and blotches to the essence that made Elvis who he was.

18

Spiritual Growth

Miss Amy was gone.

Elvis trotted all the way up to the county road and back, looking for her, calling out her name, but she was nowhere to be found. He feared the worst—a genuine kidnapping. Or maybe the state police had swooped in in the middle night and grabbed her, and now were assembling an assault team to raid their encampment—taking no prisoners, of course.

When Elvis returned, Mr. Southern was still sleeping, a remarkably nonironic smile on his face. Elvis spotted a sheet of paper flapping from the rear of the manure spreader, the corner wedged under a reflector button. Elvis began to read it right there, grasping the bottom edge to keep it from fluttering. It was Miss Amy Coulter's first-marking-period report card from Miss Krieger's School for Young Ladies. Miss Amy was a straight-A student in American history, French, English literature, and plane geometry. That did not surprise Elvis in the least, certainly not any more than her straight "UU's"—for ultra-unsatisfactory—in deportment, social attitudes and behavior, and—Elvis's favorite—spiritual growth. But none of this told him where the heck she had gone.

When he let go of the report card, it flapped again, and Elvis saw that there was handwriting on the back. He pried the paper from the reflector and took it with him to the edge of the pond, where he sat down to read it:

Dear Elvis and Terry,
If I live to be 102 and roam from here to Madagascar and back, ours will forever be the road trip of my life. I have never felt more alive in all of my seventeen years—not even at Miss Krieger's. HA!

But last night, lying there next to you two and looking up at the stars, I had what they called in English literature an epiphany. And that epiphany told me that the right and decent thing to do would be to get my darling self out of there. I just couldn't stay, knowing that the police and Miss Krieger's KKK daddy were after you two because they thought you had kidnapped me and were doing who knows what to me, when you have both been perfect gentlemen. Damn it! HA!

So I'm going out there to set the record straight. I think whatever my old daddy has in store for me, I can handle. I'm a big girl, you know.

I'll see you in my dreams, guys.

Love, Amy

P.S. Elvis, don't think I didn't notice you wriggling away from me on our hayride last night. I take it as a compliment.

By the time Elvis got to that P.S., tears were slipping down his cheeks so plentifully that he had to hold the paper at arm's length to keep it from getting spotted. *Damn you, Miss Krieger, you wouldn't know an A-plus student in spiritual growth if the Lord himself showed her to you!*

In fact, Miss Amy's departure did simplify Elvis and Mr. Southern's plans. Exactly how to approach the Bolivar police, what with an all points bulletin for their capture buzzing on the airwaves, had presented a dicey problem. But now that the buzzing had stopped, they decided to just drive up to Bolivar headquarters in what Mr. Southern liked to refer to as their "vehicle."

But first, of course, was the question of breakfast, which was answered in just five minutes' time one mile down the county road by Buddy's Pancake Chateau. Mr. Southern rumbled the tractor into Buddy's parking lot and stopped next to a ten-foot billboard that pictured stacks of wheats of varying heights arranged to look like the Notre Dame Cathedral in Paris, France. Pretty darned sophisticated for these parts, even if a cathedral did not exactly qualify as a chateau.

Elvis jumped out of the manure spreader and took a couple of steps toward Buddy's entrance before he stopped. "Maybe it's not too wise for me to be seen in public just yet," he said to Southern.

Southern walked up to Elvis, doffed his straw hat, set it low on Elvis's head, and stepped back to admire his work. He started to laugh.

"The hat is superfluous," Southern said. "Nobody's going to recognize you. But with all those dung blotches on your face, you may have a problem if they refuse to serve lepers."

They walked in and took a booth in the back. When the waitress came over to them—she was a forty-something woman who looked as if she had consumed enough pancakes in her lifetime to build a *full-size* Notre Dame—Elvis noticed that she kept her order pad up in front of her nose to fend off his odor. Well, at least she realized his spots weren't leprosy. Both men ordered Buddy's "Bonanza Breakfast," a meal that included three sunny-side-up eggs, bacon, sweet sausage, spoon bread, grits in redeye gravy, hash brown potatoes, corn muffins and raspberry jam, and, of course, Buddy's pièce de résistance, a ten-decker stack of buttermilk pancakes with pure cane syrup on the side. Elvis pretty much ate both of their portions; he had not had a decent meal since they'd stopped at Miss Barbara's. Anyway, Mr. Southern seemed happy enough just to munch on a muffin while downing his six cups of java.

Elvis was pouring some gravy on his last little hill of grits when Southern abruptly stood up and shouted toward the counter, "Turn that up, would you mind?"

They didn't mind. The voice of Mr. Southern's favorite deejay came blasting out from somewhere in the kitchen, ". . . and first thing she did, before she even went home, is hitch a ride up here to our studios. And now she's sitting right here next to me, boys and girls."

Doesn't that man ever sleep?

"Hi," a young woman's voice said. It was Miss Amy. "I just want all your listeners to know that I am safe and sound. And that Mr. Presley and his friend, Mr. Southern, didn't kidnap me. No, they just helped me escape from a truly unhealthy situation, that situation being Miss Krieger's School for Young Ladies over in Switch, an institution that has a lot more in common with a prisoner-of-war camp than a finishing school."

God bless you, Miss Amy.

Five seconds later, the manic deejay was introducing his second guest of the morning, also a young woman. Her name was Miss Carol-Sue Crampton.

"My, but it is a pleasure to be here on this fine Tennessee morning," Miss Carol-Sue crooned into her microphone.

Man, if that little bucket of trailer trash did not come off sounding like a Miss Krieger's A student in social attitudes and behavior.

With very little prompting, Miss Carol-Sue went on to describe her wedding gown in detail: it was strapless, in a simple A-line style, with crystals across the bust, silver piping on the hem, and a ruched chiffon overlay gathered at the waist, whatever the devil that was. She laughed demurely and then added, "It is a truly flattering dress. Expensive, of course—over fifty dollars—but you only get married once, don't you know?"

Elvis stuffed another spoonful of grits into his mouth just to keep from yowling.

In a tone that was slimy enough to gather mildew, the deejay asked what color the wedding gown would be.

"White, of course," Miss Carol-Sue answered primly. "Elvis wants everything to be traditional and proper."

"But isn't white a symbol for . . . ?" The deejay let his voice trail off into the gutter.

"White will be perfectly appropriate in my case," Miss Carol-Sue responded, with just a hint of reproach in her voice. "That is also a tradition that Elvis and I both believe in deeply."

Mr. Southern burst out cackling, but he wasn't the only one—just about every customer in Buddy's Pancake Chateau was right there with him. If he hadn't had so much else on his mind, Elvis might have found it personally insulting.

"One last question, Miss Carol-Sue," the deejay was saying. "Don't you find it disconcerting that your fiancé has been running all over western Tennessee rescuing damsels in distress and fraternizing with dope fiends just days before your wedding day?"

"Somebody must be mistaken," she replied. "Elvis has been right at my side just about every minute of the day since he got out of the hospital."

Elvis was pretty sure he detected a tremor of uncertainty in Miss Carol-Sue's voice this time. Heaven knows, it had to be confusing enough for the girl to have the man who had deflowered her not only refusing to sleep with her until they were married, but also refusing to allow her to caress his chest—apparently one of Carol-Sue's favorite modes of affection. You had to wonder what in heaven's name Miss Sarah Whipple had planned for their wedding night.

The deejay capped off the interview with Elvis's "You're So Square, I Don't Care."

"You have to admit, that deejay does have a wry sense of humor," Mr. Southern said.

Elvis responded by standing right up and making a beeline for Buddy's kitchen. There, he tipped his hat to the chef, snagged a butcher's knife off of his worktable, tipped his hat again, and dashed into the men's room, where he bolted the door behind him. He took off all his clothes, worked the bar of soap on the sink into a lather, and washed himself from hair to toe three times over, then lathered up his face again, and shaved himself with the butcher's knife with nary a nick. He dressed, ran his fingers through his hair front to back, and returned to the kitchen, where he handed the knife back to the chef.

"Much obliged," Elvis said.

"I was thinking you were going to slit your wrists in there," the chef said. Then he smiled and added, "You have yourself a nice wedding day, Elvis."

Elvis drove the tractor himself this time, letting Mr. Southern ride behind in the dung spreader. Elvis figured that would allow Mr. Southern to soak up a little verisimilitude. The center of Bolivar was just under five miles away, a half-hour trip by their current mode of transportation, and just long enough for Elvis to dry up naturally. There was definitely something to be said for cruising through the countryside at fifteen miles per hour: it allowed a man to have a thought or two about everything he saw before he passed it by.

Elvis and Southern marched through the front door of Bolivar Police Department headquarters and right up to the reception desk.

"Mr. Elvis Presley and Mr. Terence Southern to see Captain Rooks," Elvis said to the young policeman sitting there.

The policeman gaped up at Elvis for almost a full minute before saying, "Well, goddamn. And I mean, *goddamn.*"

"I'm in a bit of a hurry, son," Elvis said. By golly, it sure felt good not to be trying to pass himself off as someone else for a change. It gave him more authority.

Captain Rooks rose to his full six and a half feet when Elvis and Southern were ushered into his office.

"Just heard them talking about you on the radio," Rooks said, sticking out his hand to shake Elvis's. He certainly appeared more welcoming than the last time Elvis had seen him—in the hospital room, where Rooks had wagged his finger at Elvis and accused him of being unchristian. Rooks gestured for his guests to sit down, then began rifling around in the top drawer of his desk. "Might as well do the honors first thing," he said.

Rooks withdrew a five-point gold star from the drawer, then walked around his desk and pinned it on Elvis's chest.

"I heard you collected these," Rooks said, winking. "Glad to have you on board, Deputy."

Elvis mumbled a thank-you. At this particular moment, his little hobby struck him as juvenile, not to mention demeaning, but he could not very well remove the star without seeming ungrateful.

"Mr. Southern here is my attorney," Elvis said, trying to impart a little dignity to the proceedings.

"Should I bring in Colonel Parker so we can get started?" Rooks said.

"No!" Elvis snapped, then added in a more solicitous tone, "That won't be necessary at this point, Captain."

Captain Rooks nodded.

"Parker told me that you have a very active Police Athletic League here in Bolivar," Elvis said. "Unusually active for such a small town."

"We try to keep our young people busy," Rooks said. "Helps keep them out of trouble."

Elvis looked steadily into Rooks's eyes. "Must be the administrative costs that make it so expensive," he said. Lord help him, if Elvis was going to play this crooked game, at least he wanted Rooks to understand that he knew its name.

"Six thousand dollars. In cash," Rooks said, looking just as steadily back into Elvis's eyes.

That probably meant that the *National Enquirer* had offered him five thousand for the photographs. It also probably meant that Elvis had to produce those six thousand dollars awfully fast or Rooks would go ahead and do his business with the *Enquirer*.

Elvis did not have his checkbook with him—he had left that and everything else he usually carried with him back at the hospital. And a trip back to Memphis to get the money meant one more detour before finding Timothy Conrad and getting to the bottom of all this craziness. Not to mention the inevitable run-ins with Miss Priscilla and the press that would be hanging outside Graceland's gates.

"How does ten thousand sound?" Mr. Southern said.

"What's that?" Rooks said, raising his eyebrows. "Why I'd say ten thousand sounds *very* good."

"I imagine you'll make at least that from an Elvis benefit concert right here in Bolivar," Southern said. "Probably bring in folks from all over this state and a few others if you get the word out, say on that radio station that everybody seems to listen to out this way."

Elvis looked from Mr. Southern to Captain Rooks. Truth is, he did not know how he hoped Rooks would react to Southern's proposition. Giving a benefit concert was one thing, but giving a benefit concert to pay blackmail was another. Elvis could barely swallow the idea of paying blackmail in cash; paying it with his God-given talent seemed absolutely heretical. On the other hand, Southern's idea certainly seemed like an efficient way to take care of business under the circumstances.

Captain Rooks looked up at the ceiling for a good minute or two, and then said, "I'd need it in writing."

"Of course," Southern said.

"And I'd want it pretty quick," Rooks said. "Like a week from the day before yesterday."

"No problem," Southern said.

You could see that Rooks was really getting into it now. He was out of his chair, pacing up and down behind his desk, snapping his fingers.

"I just got an idea," he said, looking expectantly at Southern.

"Let's hear it," Southern said, his voice full of enthusiasm.

"We call it—now get this—we call it Elvis's Wedding Party Concert!" Rooks exclaimed. "And we schedule it for the day after the wedding. That's day after tomorrow."

That did it! That crossed the line by a mile! There was no way in hell that Elvis was going to give a benefit concert that celebrated a wedding he was not going to have in order to pay off blackmail on some pornographic pictures that were not of him. He would rather rot in a prison cell for the rest of his life.

"Brilliant!" Southern proclaimed, getting to his feet and extending his hand to Rooks. "Did you even consider a second career in show business, Captain? I'm serious."

Captain Rooks looked about as proud as a ten-year-old who has just passed his first arithmetic test, an event that Elvis seriously doubted had ever happened in Rooks's entire academic career.

"I guess a man never really knows what kind of talent he has until opportunity knocks on his door," Rooks said, grinning as he shook Southern's hand.

Elvis stood up too. Time to put the kibosh on all this madness before it got completely out of hand.

"Well, Elvis and I definitely have our work cut out for us," Mr. Southern was saying. "A whole lot to do to put this concert together on such short notice. And the thing is, we have a little logistical problem, Captain. Our vehicle broke down and we've had to make do with a tractor we borrowed."

"How about I lend you a squad car?" Captain Rooks said. "What the heck? Elvis *is* a deputy now."

"Thanks, partner," Southern said, shaking Rooks's hand once again.

Elvis just stood there, speechless.

Rooks suddenly looked pensive—*guiltily* pensive. "I hope you gentlemen won't take this the wrong way, but we did a little background check on your Colonel Thomas Parker and it turns out he's not who he says he is. He's actually Cornelius something or other from Dutchland."

"Nobody is who they say they are these days," Elvis said, finally breaking his silence.

"Anyway," Rooks went on, "I'd feel a lot more secure about all of this if I kept the Colonel here until the concert day."

"Now that sounds real prudent of you, Captain," Elvis said.

19

Master of the Mount

"Mind if I call you Sergeant?" Southern said.

"Just as long as you don't call me Colonel," Elvis replied.

They were sitting in their Bolivar Police Department squad car, Elvis driving. Both men were wearing official BPD headgear—smart wide-brimmed jobs with a leather strap and brass buckle for hat bands—which Southern had appropriated from Rooks after promising him a major role in their movie.

"As for myself, just call me Inspector," Southern said.

"I'm not real happy about this concert, you know," Elvis said.

"Not to worry," Southern said. "We can always get Elvisetta to do it."

By Ford, Hickory Valley was only a twenty-minute drive from Bolivar. Just inside the town line they stopped at a diner, where Mr. Southern grabbed the directory from the phone booth, brought it to the counter, and sat down next to Elvis. There were three Conrads listed in Hickory Valley, a town that looked to have no more than a hundred people in it. None of those Conrads had the first name Timothy.

"Well, golly day, but if you don't take the cake!" A blond woman in a candy-striped waitress uniform stood across the counter from them with her arms crossed under her substantial bosom.

Mr. Southern gazed at her chest for longer, certainly, than was tactful in Tennessee, but who knew what the time limit was up in New York City? "Inspector Closely," he said.

"Beg pardon?"

"Inspector Closely, on the job," Southern repeated, tipping his police hat to her.

But the waitress ignored him. She was gazing at Elvis. "Two Elvises in one town?" she said. "Now if that don't take the cake, I don't know what does."

"Well, this Elvis is looking for that other one," Elvis said.

"Gonna duke it out?" the waitress said, winking. She leaned forward at the waist, planted her elbows on the counter right in front of Elvis, and then propped her face in her hands, Kewpie-doll style. Some of that bosom was now staring Elvis straight in the eye.

"No, ma'am," Elvis said. "Just need to talk to him."

"You use the same surgeon Timmy did?" the waitress asked, still hovering in Elvis's face.

"No, ma'am," Elvis said. "I used a different fella."

"Well, you sure got your money's worth," the woman said.

"Thank you, ma'am," Elvis said.

"But don't it get in the way of your police work?" she said, flicking her eye at the five-point star on Elvis's shirt.

"Actually, it kinda helps," Elvis answered.

"Well, I bet it does at that," the young woman said. She did a little waggle with her shoulders that set things in motion no more than an inch in front of Elvis's face; then she stood up straight again and said, "What can I get for you fellas?"

"Two coffees," Elvis said. "And maybe a little small talk, if you've got the time."

"Time is the one thing we've got no shortage of in the valley," she said.

She left them for no more than a minute, returning with three cups of coffee. In the cup for herself, she ladled in five teaspoonfuls of sugar.

"One of these days, I am just going to burst out of my uniform," she tittered.

"And I hope to be there to stuff you back in," Mr. Southern said. Elvis glowered at Southern. The man had no manners at all.

"This Timothy Conrad fella must come from one rich family," Elvis said.

The waitress laughed. "Oh, yeah, his daddy made a fortune in mushroom futures," she said.

"That a fact?"

"No, that a joke," the waitress said. "What is your name, by the way, Officer?"

"Sergeant Monroe Peabody," Elvis said. "But my friends call me 'Musky'—that's short for 'Muskrat.' "

"Well, your face sure is prettier than your name, Musky," the waitress said.

"So you're saying Timmy's folks are not rich, is that it?" Elvis said.

"Poor as Job. Every time Adelaide puts together a little butter and egg money, her Reggie takes it all and sinks it into one of his harebrained schemes. Like that mushroom farm of his. He couldn't give those stinkers away."

"So how do you figure Timmy paid for his face job?" Elvis said. "I mean, mine cost me five thousand dollars."

"Well, how'd you pay for yours?" the waitress asked.

"Sold my house," Elvis said.

"How'd your missus take that?"

"Sold her too," Elvis said, winking.

The waitress started laughing so hard she had to set down her coffee cup to keep it from spilling. Elvis figured that at least some of that laughter was prompted by the information that he was single. Yes, indeed, it sure was shameful, the insinuations you had to make in order to do diligent police work.

"Everybody in the valley's got a different theory about how Timmy came up with the money for his face," the waitress said finally. "Most popular one being that he was part of that bank holdup over in De Kalb, but I don't believe that for a Yankee minute."

"You got your own theory?"

The waitress nodded, but did not say a word. Obviously, she wanted Elvis—or Sergeant Peabody, as it were—to pry her theory out of her.

"Ma'am, do you mind if I ask you a personal question?" Elvis said.

"Depends."

"I was just wondering if you ever had the occasion for some cosmetic surgery yourself," Elvis said, as earnestly as he could.

"Now that's a peculiar question," the waitress said, with the faint beginnings of a smile.

"I figure, it was either that, or nature was working overtime," Elvis said.

The candy-striped waitress just stood there glowing for an entire Mississippi minute.

"There's only one person Timmy knows with that kind of money," she said, finally. "And that's Mr. Blantyre, the one he shovels shit for, you should pardon the expression. Timmy's been working for him since he dropped out of school. Cyrus Blantyre's one of those big babies who never worked a day in his life. Just sits around his great-great-granddaddy's plantation thinking up ways to spend the family fortune."

"Even for a rich man, that'd be one heck of a big gift to give your stable boy," Elvis said.

"Unless there was something in it for Blantyre too," she said.

"What could that be?" Elvis said.

The waitress simpered silently. "More coaxing," that smile said.

"When do you get off here, ma'am?" Elvis said.

"After supper. Nine o'clock tonight," she said. "Why do you ask?"

"Personal reasons," Elvis said, looking shyly down at his coffee. *Absolutely shameful.*

"Why don't you come by at about eight thirty? I can show you the sights of Hickory Valley. Just you and me, I mean." She cast a slighting sideways glance in the direction of Mr. Southern.

"Don't worry about me," Mr. Southern said airily. "I've got a hot date with a gymnast."

"Cyrus has family complications, like most of those prodigal sons of bitches," the waitress went on, apparently sufficiently coaxed. "First, that Kraut wife of his runs off on him. And then his daughter takes up that sick hobby of hers and runs off too. Maybe that's what made Blantyre just about adopt Timmy as one of his own. You know, one family member he could control."

"What kind of hobby does his daughter have?"

The waitress folded her arms under her bosom again, wearing an expression of disapproval. Looking up at her, Elvis could see that the woman's good looks did not have more than a year or two left to them, and she knew it. It made him want to hug her right then and there.

"Plaster casting," she said. "Making little statues out of rock-and-roll stars. And not out of their faces, either. Something a little closer to their belt buckles."

Well, how about that? Blantyre was Krafty Plaster's daddy. Elvis asked where Blantyre lived and she said in Bath Springs, not far from Decaturville. Hot damn, if things weren't coming full circle.

Elvis put a dollar bill on the counter and stood up. "I'm looking forward to this evening," he said, feeling every inch a scoundrel.

"I sure am glad you aren't the real Elvis," the waitress said, smiling brightly.

"Why's that, ma'am?"

"'Cause you'd be getting married tomorrow," she said.

Somewhere between Jack's Corner and Scott's Hill, Mr. Southern started fiddling with every button and switch on the squad car's dashboard. Pretty soon, their siren was wailing and their top lights were spinning and flashing. There was not another car on the roadway, so Elvis saw no harm in it. Fact is, he was getting as big a kick out of it as Mr. Southern.

"Festive way to go on an outing," Elvis called over the blare of the siren.

"Every boy's dream," Mr. Southern called back. He switched on the scanner and turned it way up so they could hear it. There was a "domestic situation" in Coble and a runaway mare over in Nunnelly, but those appeared to be the only current emergencies in southwestern Tennessee. A dispatcher came on to repeat that the APB for Elvis Presley and company had been canceled. She then said that because of an anticipated traffic crisis on Thursday, due to Elvis's Wedding Party Concert down in Bolivar, all interested policemen, sheriffs, and deputies were invited to put in for overtime at time and a half starting Wednesday night.

Elvis knocked off the siren. "Man, that didn't take long," he said.

"Heck, I could use the overtime," Inspector Southern said.

The Mount, Blantyre's thousand-acre plantation in Bath Springs, was not difficult to find; it was the only establishment larger than a trailer in the entire town. Elvis let the car idle twenty feet in front of The Mount's main entrance, where an iron gate blocked the way. Next to the gate was a sentry box that looked like a little kid's playhouse, what with its curtained windows and flower boxes on three sides. Elvis and Southern switched seats, Southern taking over the wheel.

"I'm looking for Mr. Blantyre," Southern said gruffly to the gatekeeper as Elvis turned his head away. "Official business."

"Is he expecting you, Officer?" the gatekeeper said.

"How the hell should I know who he's expecting?" Southern snapped back.

The gatekeeper blanched, then opened the gates.

"Oh, the *power* of the uniform!" Southern crooned as they drove in. "I love it! *I love it!*"

"Power corrupts, you know," Elvis said.

"That's the part I like about it," Southern replied.

Cyrus Blantyre had apparently been alerted to their arrival by his sentry. He was waiting for them where the driveway circled under the main building's portico. Blantyre was about the same height as Elvis, but with half again the weight, much of it in a gut that looked like pregnancy with twins. That gut made it impossible for him to close the silk smoking jacket he wore over his green-plaid slacks. His face was not much to look at: a pug nose with so many capillaries visible that it looked like a nest of blue worms; narrow-set, porcine eyes; and a lower lip that looked like it was in permanent pucker for the mouth of a beer bottle. Hard to believe that he was sixth-generation southern aristocracy; Cyrus looked more like a Beverly Hillbilly. There sure was more Hollywood in Tennessee than Elvis had ever been aware of before.

"Good morning to you, Captain," Blantyre said to Mr. Southern as they drove up beside him. Blantyre's diction sounded like the result of a liquid breakfast.

"We need to talk with you about an employee of yours who may be in some trouble," Southern said.

But Blantyre was now staring confoundedly at Elvis. "I hope you aren't who I think you are," he growled.

"Me too," Elvis answered, trying to work up as dumb an expression on his face as on the one facing him.

"I don't want to see you anywhere near here, Elvis!" Blantyre said. "For your own well-being. You hear me?"

"I am not Elvis," Elvis said. "But folks said I sounded so much like him that it would be a shame not have his face too. Had to sell my house to pay for it."

"What in God's name for, boy?" Blantyre said. His tone was obviously meant to strike a note of upper-class disdain, a note which conveyed that even if the Blantyres did not own their workers outright anymore, that did not change the way Cyrus Blantyre related to the little people of the world. But the words came out sounding about as classy as the man looked.

"The look-alike contests," Elvis said. "I got me three blue ribbons and one belt buckle."

"Waste of your money," Cyrus sneered.

"Those ribbons are worth their weight in female pulchritude," Elvis replied, grinning up at Blantyre. Elvis was baiting him. From what Miss Krafty had told Elvisetta, Elvis knew that the man had strong religious convictions on the subject of sex—the kind of religious convictions that loosen screws in the head.

Blantyre squinted his already pig-size eyes. The blue worm's nest on his nose went pink, then red. "Ungodly filth!" he snapped.

"You ought to try it yourself, Cyrus," Elvis said, getting out of the car. "Get yourself an Elvis face like Timmy's and maybe you can finally get some of that sweet young flesh for yourself."

Blantyre was sputtering, little bullets of spit flying from his mouth. "Get off my land!" he hollered.

Mr. Southern was out of the car too, advancing on Blantyre from one side while Elvis strode toward him from the other. The master of The Mount trembled.

"Here's what I don't get, *massa*," Elvis drawled. "You being such a champion of young women's virtue and all. Why'd you give Timmy an Elvis face when you knew he was just going to use it to poke every teenage girl from here to Jackson?"

"I give you five seconds to leave," Blantyre said, trying to sound authoritative, but his voice quavering.

"You and who else?" Southern said. Man, maybe Mr. Southern wrote trendy movies, but when he got excited, he talked like he was in a forties B flick.

"I should inform you that The Mount has its own militia," Blantyre said.

"We are police officers," Elvis said. "I wouldn't do anything foolish if I were you."

Cyrus Blantyre sneered back at him. "The police answer to me in these parts," he said.

"I don't," Elvis said. "I asked you a question, Cyrus. Why did you pay Dr. van Duesen five thousand dollars to give Timmy Conrad an Elvis face? You knew what he'd do with it. Or maybe that was part of your plan too. Except I can't figure why a good Christian father like yourself would set things up so that young girls would be sorely tempted to break the Ten Commandments. And that would include your very own daughter."

"I—I—I will not have you mention her name in my presence," Blantyre stammered, taking a step backward.

"Okay, I'll call her by her nom de goof, Krafty Plaster," Elvis said. "She must be an embarrassment to you, Cyrus. A Blantyre woman should be sewing quilts for a proper hobby."

Elvis was flying by the seat of his pants now, saying his mind as fast as he could put his thoughts together. He wanted to push Blantyre over the edge while he still had him backpedaling. Between the man's panicky fear and his trumped-up aristocratic pride, he just might blurt out his entire sick scheme right here and now, complete with the good Christian rationale behind it.

"But that Krafty, she's got some of her mother in her, don't she?" Elvis continued.

"Captain Montgomery!" Blantyre howled. *"Front! Now!"*

"They're all harlots, aren't they, Cyrus?" Elvis pressed on. "Mrs. Blantyre, your Miss Krafty, all the young girls these days. And we both know whose fault it is, don't we? It's mine. Elvis, the Antichrist."

"Elvis! By God, I knew that was you all along," Blantyre snarled. The sneering confidence was fully back in his voice, and now Elvis could see why.

Jogging toward them from both sides of The Mount were at least a dozen men, every one of them wearing blousy long-sleeved shirts, and smart white riding breeches tucked into knee-high black boots. Those who were not carrying rifles were waving six-shooters above their heads. The Mount's militia was here.

"Stop right there!" Southern shouted. "Or we shoot Blantyre!"

It was another forties movie line, and a valiant try. But it took about two seconds for everyone involved to realize that neither Mr. Southern nor Mr. Presley were armed.

"Run!" Elvis bellowed.

20

The King Is Dead

*I*nside was the only way out.

When Blantyre attempted to block the way through the front door, Elvis knocked the master of The Mount onto his green-plaid bottom. Mr. Southern executed a surprisingly balletic vault over the toppled mound of flesh, following Elvis into the manse's vestibule.

It was Tara redux. Salmon-colored walls covered with huge oil portraits of six generations of Blantyres, some in Confederate army uniforms, one in a KKK robe, and each one more forbidding-looking than the next. Beholding the lot in one ten-second sweep was like viewing a genealogical table that charted the Blantyres' incremental dumping of every good-looking gene they had started out with. Squandered genetic beauty. The sole exceptions were in the most recent generation's family portrait, which pictured Cyrus, his former missus, and Miss Krafty, in what were obviously happier days. Miss Krafty was a delicate but spirited-looking girl who took after her fine-boned mother, at least in this artist's rendering. The mother was a classic beauty; there was something familiar about her face too.

After they had lifted Cyrus onto his feet, the militia got tangled up as a half dozen of them tried to squeeze through the entrance at once. The Keystone Kops in *Ring Those Southern Belles*. But this setback gave Elvis and Mr. Southern only an extra thirty seconds at the most. Elvis calculated his options. On his right, an open archway that led into the parlor; on his left, French doors that led to a glass-domed conservatory; and straight ahead, a hallway that probably led to the kitchen, and to a grand curved stairway that narrowed as it approached The Mount's second floor. Elvis chose the stairs, even if it meant putting twenty feet between him and terra firma. Mr. Southern chugged alongside him.

They had only reached the stair's midpoint landing when over his shoulder Elvis saw a row of Cyrus's resplendently outfitted militiamen at the bottom, each one of them with his rifle raised and aimed at him, a picturesque firing squad. Elvis crouched, then sprang behind a cherrywood sugar chest that sat in the corner of the landing. But Southern froze. Elvis saw the militiamen shift their aim toward him. "*Terry! Look out!*"

Elvis would never be able to say exactly how he and Mr. Southern instantly choreographed and coordinated those next twenty seconds—maybe they had developed some kind of telepathy from keeping such close company the past few days. Elvis grabbed one end of the sugar chest, Southern the other, and they sent it tumbling down the stairs at their would-be assassins. Along the way, the chest's cabinet doors popped open, and a shower of raw sugar sprayed out like a sleet storm. A whole bunch of it shot right into the militiamen's eyes. Sweet revenge.

"Frankly, my dear, I don't give a damn," Southern said. The man simply could not help himself.

They ran the length of the second-floor hallway. Elvis tried a door at the far end, but it was locked. Southern, still revved up from their sugar-chest triumph, took two long steps back from the door, then barreled at it, knocking it clean off its antique hinges. Both men stomped over the door and inside the room.

"Poor Mrs. Haversham," Southern said.

It was a large oval bedroom whose current occupants were an entire insectarium of spiders that had turned the place into an aerial tramway of interconnected webs. More oil portraits hung on the walls, the subjects just discernible through the spider threads, but visible enough for Elvis to make out the former Mrs. Blantyre and what were clearly her progenitors. The men, all bearded, wore sashes covered with medals; the women, all beautiful, wore tiaras atop their gold-red hair. They looked foreign, European. His Kraut wife, the waitress had said. And now Elvis finally recognized the former Mrs. Cyrus Blantyre. She was Dr. Helga Volk.

Feet pounding up the stairs. Men shouting, "Over there, Cyclopse!" and "Prepare to fire, Titan!" "Cyclopse," "Titan"—those were ranks in the Klan. The Blantyre militiamen were obviously Klansmen wearing more fashionable clothes for their day job.

Sunlight flickered through a gap in brown velvet drapes to Elvis's right. He swung them aside. Glass doors. Outside, a weather porch.

"Take no prisoners!" Cyrus Blantyre shouted from somewhere far behind his soldiers. The bravery gene of his Confederate army forebears had clearly been dumped along with their beauty genes.

Elvis flung the glass doors open, stepped out onto the porch, looked down over the iron-filigree balustrade. A pair of bamboo sun umbrellas stood side by side twenty feet below.

"I'll take the right one," Elvis said. He sucked in his breath, then hurdled over the balustrade, drew in his knees like a cliff diver, and landed ass-first on the umbrella—the one on the right, as pledged. The umbrella's bamboo ribs snapped in slow succession, slipping Elvis one gentle foot at a time down to the ground on his feet.

A whoosh and a plop, and Southern was beside him. His umbrella had been less forgiving, collapsing in a single crack on contact, but nonetheless there he was, on his feet also, and grinning like a madman.

"We're going to need a crane shot to do this scene justice," he said.

A gun blast from the second-floor porch tore through what was left of Elvis's umbrella. Elvis and Southern were running again.

They were behind the mansion. A barn straight ahead. A tobacco-drying shed next to it and behind that a granite stable. Beyond it all, a cattle pasture fenced in by electric wire, probably carrying enough current to turn an errant cow into instant pot roast. Not exactly a glut of promising options.

A second shot whistled overhead and lodged itself in the tulip poplar that shaded the entrance to the barn.

"Elvis! *Over here!*" A young man's voice that sounded eerily familiar.

The young man was standing just outside the stable, waving frantically at Elvis with his cowboy hat. He wore denim bib overalls and a khaki work shirt rolled up at the sleeves, but all the rest was as familiar as Elvis's own face. And that is exactly what it was. In the flesh, Timothy Conrad was Elvis's identical twin.

The shock of seeing Miss Sarah Whipple that first time was nothing compared to this. For sure, she came about as close to looking and talking and moving like Elvis as a natural person could, but after a while the differences had reassuringly asserted themselves: the higher register of her voice, the slightness of her build, even the smaller pores on the skin of her face. And all that, of course, *before* she took her shirt off.

But Timmy's voice was in the exact same register as Elvis's, his build and skin were exactly the same too, and, with the benefit of Dr. van Duesen's scalpel, his face was a precise tintype of Elvis's own. Elvis had believed that something more than flawlessly replicated features was needed to perfectly re-create himself, something inside that integrated those features—a genuine feeling for who he was, for his very essence. Well, if that was the case, Timmy Conrad had that in spades.

"Hurry!" Timmy cried. "I'll hide you!"

But just one minute. Timmy was surely the one who had been chasing them in that pink Caddy while his sidekick took pot shots at them. That electric fence was starting to look like the safer bet.

"I know what you're thinking, Elvis," Timmy said. "That shooting at you wasn't my idea. I did my best to keep swerving so that lunatic wouldn't hit you."

A third gunshot ricocheted off of the stable's roof and into the dirt at Elvis's feet. *Choose your poison.* Elvis followed Timmy inside the stable, Southern panting behind him.

Timmy immediately yanked open a stall gate and out pranced a huge Clydesdale stallion. The animal shook its noble head from side to side, then went charging out of the stable.

"Hold your fire!" Elvis heard Cyrus shout from the house. Like any decent gentleman farmer, Blantyre knew a choice stallion's value—considerably greater than that of any run-of-the-mill two-legged animal.

Timmy was now furiously pitching hay off the floor of the emptied stall. Then he was on his knees, brushing away more hay by hand. And finally he was on his feet again, pulling on an iron ring attached to the oakwood floor. A two-foot square of floorboard swung up revealing a dark subterranean cavity, a rope ladder dangling down into it. Timmy gestured to Elvis with a quick tilt of his head. Elvis dropped to his knees, squeezed himself through the opening, caught one foot on a hemp rung, and let himself down. Seconds later, Southern was down too. The square opening slammed shut.

Pitch black. The stench of manure. A cold dampness that made Elvis's skin go goosey.

"Over there!" Timmy was shouting somewhere above them. "They cut through the stable into the pasture!"

Feet thumped overhead. A load of cursing. Then it was Timmy again. "Sorry, Daddy Blantyre. I couldn't stop them. They cut loose Simon Peter to run interference."

Apparently Cyrus Blantyre named his steeds after apostles.

"Don't you worry, son," Elvis heard Cyrus reply just above them. "Those sinners are going to meet their maker ahead of schedule."

More thumping and cursing, and they were gone.

"I think I know where we are," Southern whispered in the dark.

"In bowels of the animal," Elvis whispered back.

"A lot of the old plantations had rooms like this for hiding slaves," Southern said.

"The Underground Railway?"

"No, not for the runaways, for the good-looking ones. The prettiest young African girls. The slave owners hid them in rooms like this so their wives wouldn't know what they used them for. But their wives knew, of course, every time another mulatto baby appeared in the slave nursery."

"That is one ugly piece of history, Mr. Southern," Elvis said.

"There's uglier."

Minutes later, the trapdoor again opened, and a beam of light shined down. Elvis backed against the clammy stone wall.

"Just me," Timmy called down. "Coast is clear. For the time being, at least. They're all out running with the bulls."

With that, Timmy swung down to the rope ladder, closed the door above him, and clambered down with a flashlight tucked under one arm. He walked past Elvis and Southern to a nook in the wall, where he withdrew a box of wooden matches. Then, one at a time, he lit a half dozen hurricane lamps that hung from the beams. The underground room flickered with yellow light.

"Isn't it romantic?" Mr. Southern said.

Elvis gazed around him, dumbfounded. Except for the stone walls that were so sweaty they had moss growing in the crevices, the room was a replica of his den back at Graceland, complete with the cypress-crotch coffee tables, mirrors framed with pheasant feathers, massive pine chairs and couches carved by a chain saw, and, of course, the green shag carpeting on both the floor and the ceiling.

"Makes you feel at home, don't it?" Timmy said pleasantly, sitting down in one of the pine chairs. He gestured for Elvis to sit down opposite him, but Elvis remained on his feet.

"Yes and no," Elvis replied.

"Even got your books in here," Timmy said. "Dr. Norman Vincent Peale, *Diary of a Yogi, The Harvard Vocabulary Builder.* And your favorite, of course, *The Impersonal Life,* by that Mr. Anonymous. I've read it twice, Elvis, and I still don't get it."

"I don't imagine you do," Elvis said.

"Maybe you can explain it to me sometime," Timmy said.

Elvis stared at the young man. Timmy even had his smallest gestures down, like the way he slowly turned his head from side to side while keeping his eyes stuck on you. Elvis had not been aware that he did that himself until Ann-Margret pointed it out to him; she had said it was a look that sent shivers down a girl's spine. Well, when Timmy did it, it sure as heck sent shivers down Elvis's.

"Got your gold records, too," Timmy went on. " 'It's Now or Never' and 'Are You Lonesome Tonight?' Framed and matted same as you. Except I can't keep them on the walls for long or the dampness seeps in. But if you want, I can put them up now. Do ya?"

Elvis shook his head. Mr. Southern had laid himself down on the pine couch. The man knew how to pace himself.

"How about a little something to eat then?" Timmy said cheerily. "You must be hungry after all that running around dodging bullets. I've got a fresh meat loaf straight out of Cook Mary's oven. Now how does that sound?"

Elvis braced himself against the back of the chair. "Cook Mary," he repeated numbly.

"Nobody makes meat loaf like Cook Mary," Timothy Conrad said brightly. "The secret's in the bread crumbs. She soaks them for a day in knuckle fat. That's where all the bass notes in the flavor come from."

"Mary doesn't cook for you!" Elvis cried out much louder than he should have, considering he was trying to keep his whereabouts unknown to twelve men with guns who were no more than a hundred yards away. But, damn it, that was one blasphemy Elvis was not going to let just pass by. "She only cooks for me, boy!"

"Same difference," Timmy said, grinning.

Elvis sucked in a long breath of manure-scented air, let it out slowly, and finally sat down. Oh yes, Timmy Conrad had a feeling for Elvis's essence, all right. Timmy had studied him like one of those method actors that Marlon Brando had told Elvis about in the MGM commissary. Timmy had immersed himself in Elvis's world and soaked up every little thing that had meaning for Elvis, right down to the bread crumbs in his favorite meat loaf.

"Why did Blantyre pay for your face?" Elvis said, looking straight at Timmy. "Just to make you happy?"

"Cyrus?" Timmy said, shrugging. "He's crazy, Elvis. Comes from all that inbreeding. Same reason some purebred Shetlands come out of their mamas with one eye in the middle of their forehead and a pecker hanging out of their ear. If Cyrus hadn't bred with some new blood, Kathy wouldn't have come out so pretty, that's for sure."

"Kathy? The one who calls herself Miss Krafty Plaster?"

"Well, I guess she's a little crazy too," Timmy said. It was difficult to tell in the yellow lamplight, but the young man appeared to blush. "But she surely is one beautiful child. Always was."

"I don't think Blantyre paid for your operation simply because he's crazy," Elvis said.

"Oh, he had his reasons," Timmy said. "But *they* were crazy."

"Name 'em," Elvis said. From the corner of his eye, Elvis saw Southern sit up straight.

"He thinks we're the devil, you know," Timmy said.

"He thinks that *I* am the devil, you mean," Elvis corrected.

"Same difference. He writes all that Legion stuff about your hips. That they hypnotize good Christian girls and lure them into becoming the devil's disciples. Harlots of the Antichrist." Timmy paused a second, smiling to himself before he went on. "Of course, he's not completely off his rocker in that department. I mean, I can't hardly count all the sweet young virgins who come just begging me for it. A whip of the hips and they're all mine."

"That is an unholy thing you do," Elvis said.

Timmy laughed. "You sound just like Daddy Blantyre," he said.

"So why did he give you the equipment to do it?" Elvis said.

"Oh, I had *some* of the equipment to start with," Timmy said with a sneer that went way past any genuine Elvis smirk. "But

Cyrus needed me to make a public example. One that would get daddies all over Tennessee angry enough to raise Cain and then some. And he needed documentation."

"So he hired Manard Frew to take those photos of you and Miss Amy on the back of that car," Elvis said.

"Miss Amy?" Timmy said raising his eyebrows in a mocking gesture. "You know, it's hard to keep track of all their names. I mean, it's gotten to the point where all that sweet young flesh just kinda merges and blurs. You know what I'm saying, don't you, Elvis?"

"No, I don't!" Elvis retorted. "But what about Frew? Cyrus knew him from his Legion of Decency newsletter, right? So he hired him to take those photographs."

"Yup, that's what I understand," Timmy said airily. "Although it turns out he got paid double for the job—Miss Amy wanted a memento too."

"And then when Frew tried to blackmail me, he murdered him."

"Probably didn't do it himself," Timmy said. "Daddy Blantyre hardly does one thing himself. He's got employees for every little job." Like his fellow Klansmen.

"This doesn't make sense," Elvis said. "Cyrus gets you to seduce underage girls saying you're me so he can prove the world that I'm doing the devil's work, but—"

"*To bring you crashing down, Elvis!* That's the point!" Timmy interrupted. "Just like Jerry Lee Lewis, but worse. Much worse."

"But in the meantime, he's aiding and abetting the very thing he hates the most—soiling young Christian girls," Elvis went on. "It makes no sense at all."

"Oh, it makes sense, Elvis," Mr. Southern said from his couch. "The sinister ends justify the perverted means."

Timmy smiled at Southern. "I knew you'd understand. You're that New York writer fella, aren't you? The one who wrote *Dr. Strangelove.*"

"That's right."

"I really liked that scene of the general with his girlfriend in her underwear," Timmy said. "You know, the one where he kinda dithers over what's more urgent, saving the world from blowing up or doing his girl one more time. Made me laugh. Actually, I think you coulda gotten more yuks out of that if you had played it up more. Had him get in and out of bed with her a few more times. Know what I'm saying?"

Elvis's world was exploding, and this kid was doing script criticism. Of course, on Dr. van Duesen's intake form, Timmy had listed his occupation as entertainment.

"Meantime, you had yourself a whole bunch of perverted fun, didn't you, Timmy?" Elvis said to his perfect look-alike.

"Beats shoveling horseshit," Timmy said. "Of course, after a while, it's all in a day's work. Gets kinda tedious, don't you know, driving all around and doing one girl here and one girl there. But you know, Elvis, it makes a man long for a little quiet time at home, just eating some meat loaf, picking his nose, and catching up on his reading. When you come down to it, those are the truly important things in a man's life."

Holy Jehoshaphat, if that didn't sound exactly like Elvis's own thinking only a few days back. Heck, he had already been writing songs in praise of those very same everyday pleasures. And a movie too. Was it really that easy to immerse yourself in another person's mind and think his thoughts? Not just think them, *steal* them! This kid was guilty of cerebral breaking and entering. Well, maybe that would make it easier for Elvis to sink his own mind inside of Timmy's.

"You don't really give a rat's bottom for Blantyre's virtue crusade, do you, boy?" Elvis said, staring hard into Timmy's eyes.

Timmy shrugged coyly. There was something girlish in that shrug that gave Elvis the fantods. Elvis did not shrug like that himself, did he?

"But you've got bigger plans, don't you, Timmy? A whole lot more ambitious than some dumb mushroom farm. Or anything that idiot Cyrus could ever think of. Not that Daddy Blantyre wasn't real helpful without realizing it, giving you that face and Cadillac car and all."

Oh yes, Elvis was walking around inside Timmy's brain with a torch and a magnifying glass. But on the outside, Elvis started to slide slowly forward in his chair. He shot his eyes to Mr. Southern's, then flicked them to the rope ladder that hung down from the ceiling about halfway between them. Almost imperceptibly, Southern nodded back.

"Nothing wrong with ambition, is there, Elvis?" Timmy was saying, still sitting back comfortably in the chain-saw chair. "It's the American way. I mean, we're the same that way too, when you think about it—we both come from real humble beginnings. No silver spoons stuck in our kissers, not like Blantyre. There's not a kid in all of Tennessee who doesn't want to be a one-of-a-kind celebrity, but you're the only one who did it, Elvis. So far, at least. But now, of course, we're two of a kind."

"But there's still only one true me," Elvis said. He was at the edge of his seat now.

"To go from rags to riches, you need to seize opportunity the minute it strikes," Timmy went on blithely. "I learned that from studying your Colonel Parker. That man is a genius at seizing opportunity while other folks just dither. And that's how he made you into the man you are today, Elvis." Timmy winked at Elvis. "Or actually, the man you *were*."

Elvis pushed off from his chair and charged for the rope ladder, his hands up and ready to chop Timmy if he stood in his way. Southern was already bounding toward the ladder from the other side.

"Now you were brought up better than to leave in a hurry like that," Timmy said lazily from his chair.

Elvis was halfway up the ladder when the canister landed just below him, blue smoke gushing out of it. He had just enough time to turn his head and see Timmy still sitting cozily in his chair. He appeared to be smiling, but it was hard to tell with that gas mask on his face.

Elvis's limbs went numb. He fell backward, his head bouncing on the green shag carpet. Before his brain shut down completely, Elvis saw Mr. Southern drop to his knees, twist to his side, and topple over completely. Then he saw Timothy Conrad slowly rise, step over Southern, climb up the rope ladder and out the hinged door at the top. There, Timmy stuck his head smack in the middle of that square of sunlight and smiled down at Elvis. That smile—it was Elvis's very own.

"The King is dead!" Timmy said. "Long live the King!"

The light went out in Elvis's brain.

21

God Laughed

God said, "We are all one thing, Elvis. One thing, indivisible."

"Then how come I feel like just me, sir," Elvis said. "I mean, if you'll pardon my asking."

God smiled. And what a smile it was—as if all the gladness in the universe were summed up in it. "Because you are that one thing, Elvis. We all are."

"You too?"

"Yes, me too, Elvis."

"You're saying you feel like *me*, God?"

That smile again—fatherly, but no judgment in it. "Yes," God said. "That me we feel is life itself. And when we feel it deeply, it is love itself."

Elvis had to look away for a moment. It was kind of overwhelming to look on God's face without a little break now and then.

"I'm confused," Elvis said. "I mean, each one of us has a personal responsibility, right? To do the just thing by you. To be the best individual person we can be. So how can we all be the same thing then?"

"It is confusing, son," God said. "It defies human logic. But it makes perfect sense in my mind. That is why you need faith to understand me."

Elvis nodded. "I'm working on my faith, sir," he said.

"I know you are, Elvis."

Elvis considered everything that God had said for a long minute. Then he said, "But what about my face, sir? Is that just mine?"

God laughed. It was a big, joyful, Santa Clausy laugh, and Elvis could not help but join in, even though he was not entirely sure what the joke was. Elvis laughed so hard that his eyes squinched up and teared.

"Ha! Ha! Ha!" God laughed.

Elvis opened his eyes. God's face looked different. Not so pretty anymore, and sort of ironic around the eyes. It said, "I'm glad you think it's funny."

"But since we are all one thing, God, if *you* think it's funny, then I should think it's—"

"It's a friggin' miracle. That's what I think, Elvis."

"Mr. Southern?"

"The one and only," the ironic face hovering over Elvis said.

"I thought you were God," Elvis said.

"It's a common mistake," Mr. Southern said.

"What happened?"

"Nitrous oxide happened. Laughing gas. Enough to put a small army asleep for eternity."

"I sure did sleep long," Elvis said.

"We both did," Southern said. "In fact, we slept right through the explosion."

Elvis sat upright, opened his eyes wide. A column of mote-filled sunlight streamed down from a small circular hole in the ceiling. The antique beam which had once supported that section of the ceiling was cracked in two, its broken ends now burrowed in the green shag rug like a pair of haphazard pillars.

"One of the hurricane lamps must have ignited it," Southern said. "The miracle part is that it exploded *up* and not *down*."

Elvis rubbed his eyes. His head was clearing. "But the folks in the big house must have heard it," he said.

"You'd think so," Southern said. "Maybe they came by, took a look down the hole, and figured we were dead. I'm sure we didn't look very lively lying here in all this wreckage. Blantyre is undoubtedly having himself a celebratory postmortem cocktail in his conservatory right about now."

Elvis stood up. "We should probably get a move on, Mr. Southern," he said.

"My very thought," Southern replied.

The rope ladder, of course, was gone, either fried or buried in the debris. Elvis did a rapid survey of the surviving furniture— one of the chain-saw pine chairs appeared still to be intact, as did a pair of cypress-crotch coffee tables by the wall. Elvis and Southern piled the two tables on top of one another, then the chair at the top. The whole setup looked about as steady as a pyramid of milk bottles at the bean-bag throw at the county fair.

Elvis went first. He had gotten as far as planting one foot on the seat of the chair when it all came tumbling down, Elvis landing painfully on one shoulder.

"Plan B," Elvis said. "We try it with just the tables."

The stacked tables got Elvis up to within an arm's length below the hole in the ceiling, but from there he could see that he was far too broad shouldered to pull himself up through that hole. And if Elvis was too broad shouldered, Southern was way too broad in the beam. A hacksaw sure would be handy for hacking off a couple of the stable floorboards to widen the hole, but a saw did not seem a likely item to be found in Timmy's lair. What the situation called for was a karate chop, the kind with which Elvis's karate teacher, Kang Rhee, could split open a solid oak door. But that was chopping *down,* and Elvis needed to chop *up*—and while balancing atop a tower of tippy tables at that. Elvis formed his right fist into *nukite*—"spear hand." (Strange how using a Japanese term made it feel more feasible.) Then he thrust upward with a *yoko uraken uchi*—"horizontal backfist strike." Overhead, two floorboards instantly detached and came sailing down on each side of Elvis.

"You're a handy fellow to have around," Southern said.

"Follow me and I'll boost you through," Elvis said.

Both Southern and Elvis balanced on top of the second table, and then Southern clambered onto Elvis's back, caught the rim of the hole, and hoisted himself up and through. Southern then sprawled on the stable floor and hung down one hand for Elvis to grab hold of. Seconds later, Elvis was topside too.

That telepathy thing clicked in again. There were only two horses left inside the stable, both Clydesdales—the others must have been evacuated to the barn after the explosion—but all the saddles and bridles were still hanging neatly in the tack room. Without a word spoken between them, the two men dressed the steeds and mounted, quick as rodeo champions.

The stable's back door had been blown wide by the blast; it opened onto the pasture. Elvis led, slowly easing his stallion over burned straw and charred bits of wood. Then, out in the open air, he slacked the reins and dug his heels into the animal's ribs. It burst into a gallop.

Mr. Southern was right behind him. "Hi-yo, Silver!" he cheered.

No, the man simply could not help himself.

They had been riding hard for close to an hour, putting as much distance as they could between themselves and Bath Springs, when Elvis finally slowed to a trot and tried to reckon their bearings. Judging by the sun, they were headed west and it was midafternoon—but midafternoon of which day, the sun was not telling.

So far, they had managed to stay in open fields, only occasionally coming up on a low stone wall or rail fence. On those occasions, the Clydesdales took charge, not shying for an instant, but leaping over the barriers like show horses half their weight. It was only slightly more thrilling than it was frightening. Elvis had not seen a single house or barn or car or truck in all that time.

But now he heard a car horn blaring on his left, then another. He signaled Mr. Southern to halt. Both men dismounted, tied their steeds to a wild rosebush, and headed on foot in the direction of the horns. Just beyond a copse of pines lay a county highway jam-packed with cars and pickups, even one yellow school bus, all in the west lane, while the east lane was all but empty. Several of the vehicles had hand-drawn signs pasted to their side and rear windows. Elvis shaded his eyes with his hand and squinted. The first sign he could make out said, "Lonely No More!" The next, "Happily Ever After!" And the next, "Congratulations Carol-Sue and Elvis!"

"Looks like you're a married man at last," Southern said.

"Funny, I don't feel married," Elvis said.

"It takes a while to set in," Southern said.

"I think we must've slept through a whole day, Mr. Southern," Elvis said. "These folks are on their way to Bolivar for that wedding concert."

"Starring Timothy Conrad, if I'm not mistaken," Southern said. "He thinks he killed you, so now he can take your place without anybody knowing. This is going to be his virgin concert as Elvis himself. The King is dead, long live the King."

"Except I don't feel any more dead than I feel married," Elvis said.

"Pardner, it looks like there's gonna be a showdown in Bolivar city," Southern drawled in his rendition of a southern drawl.

While they were remounting their horses, a jet plane soared by overhead. Mr. Southern watched it, smiling. "We're the last cowboys," he said.

Elvis and Southern managed to run their horses over fields and through patches of woods all the way to Hornsby. They paced the animals the best they could, galloping a piece, then slowing to a trot, then galloping again. They stopped twice at streams, where all four of them gulped fresh water. Elvis could not remember the last time he had ridden horseback for so long a stretch—certainly not in any of his movies, where every five minutes he would have to dismount so that they could freshen up his makeup. He could not remember the last time he had felt so exhilarated either. Free as the wind. And free of any thought or worry that stood still. No, there was nothing in the world like flying through the countryside on a stallion's back.

But in Hornsby, they ran out of grass and shrubbery. Two roads lay ahead of them, one gravel, the other macadam, both going to Bolivar. They chose the gravel; it would be better on the horses' hooves, and, as Southern put it, "It was the road less traveled." In fact, they encountered only three vehicles between Hornsby and Bolivar, all of them rickety farm trucks loaded with fresh-cut tobacco leaves. While galloping past these trucks, Elvis tucked in his chin by way of personal camouflage, but not one of the drivers even looked his way—they probably thought that Elvis and Southern in their soot-soaked gear were just a pair of rich executives down from Jackson for a few days to play cowboy.

The sun had dropped behind the Laconia Hills by the time they reached the outskirts of Bolivar. Elvis could hear the whine of an amplifier's feedback somewhere to the right of them. Under that, he heard a rumble that sounded like distant thunder, but he immediately recognized it for what it really was: the clamor of a crowd of fans waiting for their idol to appear.

"It's magic time," Mr. Southern said.

22

The Man Who Elvis Called Himself

ood evening, ladies and germs."

Captain Rooks had certainly chosen a stunning venue for his first foray into show business. Following their ears, Elvis and Mr. Southern had ridden up to the edge of a bluff overlooking an abandoned pink limestone quarry. Below, enclosed on three sides by Tennessee marble cliffs, was a grand wooden platform illuminated by expert-looking flood- and spotlights. Facing the stage were easily five thousand eager fans, come to pay their respects—not to mention their entrance fees—to the King of Rock and Roll. And it looked like a good five thousand more were still streaming in. About the only aspect of the whole picture that appeared less than professional was Captain Rooks himself, who was now standing center stage under a spotlight, wearing a horrendous shiny pink tuxedo that he must have sent for up in Jackson. But God only knew where in the world Rooks had sent for his concert-opening comedy material.

"We are here to celebrate Elvis's wedding," Rooks was saying as he crouched over in front of a microphone. "You know what that means, folks. Getting married is like going to a restaurant with friends. You order what you want, and when you see what the other fellow has, you wish you had ordered that."

There may have been a few scattered laughs in the crowd, but it was hard to tell over the general din they were making, not that

Rooks would have noticed. He was far too busy amusing the heck out of himself.

"As for myself, I never knew what happiness was until I got married . . . and then it was too late!"

Elvis and Southern dismounted, then led their horses along a narrow path that zigzagged down the side of the bluff like a five-story fire escape. In a few minutes they reached the bottom, about fifty feet behind the stage and catty-corner from a pup tent that looked like it served as the performers' dressing room. Without any lights playing this far back, no one could possibly see them.

Rooks had finally garnered the audience's attention with some "but seriously folks" talk about his personal relationship with Elvis. "I can't tell you how thrilling it was to finally meet the greatest man ever to come out of the state of Tennessee," Rooks said. "When he walked into my office here in Bolivar, you could have knocked me over with a barbecued chicken wing. There is nobody in the entire universe like Elvis, people. As my daddy used to say, 'Before they made Elvis, they broke the mold.' "

At least Mr. Southern thought that line was funny. He chuckled and said, "The man is growing on me."

"You ought to see a skin doctor," Elvis replied.

Rooks was explaining to the audience how Elvis had taken a deep interest in Bolivar's Police Athletic League and its mission of keeping young people busy with healthy pursuits, and how the idea of a benefit concert for the PAL to coincide with his wedding had grown directly out of that. The crowd was listening to every word now, breaking into sustained applause every time Elvis's name was mentioned. God love them, they accepted the whole package like it was true and earnest, and not the ten-decker sham that Elvis knew it to be. It made his heart go out to them. It also made him worry what an unprincipled politician might do if he ever figured out how easy it was to fool tenderhearted people.

"And now I would like to introduce another great man who I have come to know closely these past few days," Rooks went on. "I am talking about the man who helped Elvis achieve greatness by making one personal sacrifice after another on that young man's behalf. I am talking about an individual who I, personally, misjudged, making the most atrocious mistake of my entire professional life. Thank goodness that's all over now. Ladies and gentlemen, put your hands together for Colonel Tom Parker!"

The quarry reverberated with applause, and out came the Colonel in an orchid-colored Hawaiian shirt, a cigar danging from his lower lip, the moon reflecting off his bald dome.

"Well, Colonel, looks like you shaved too high again," Rooks quipped. "Why, I'd like to put my finger in your ear and go bowling!"

Parker ignored him. He stepped right in front of Rooks, grabbed the microphone stand with one hand, and removed his cigar from his mouth with the other. He looked sincerely out at the crowd. "I am a happy man today, my friends," he said. "All I can say is that two days ago, I had the best godson a person could wish for. But today, I have the best goddaughter-in-law in the world too!"

Another echoing eruption of applause, during which Elvis had to swallow hard to keep his stomach down where it belonged.

"One way Elvis tries to help young people," Parker went on, "is by giving talented youngsters the kind of opportunities that he had—with a little help from his friends, of course."

This got a ripple of laughter that Elvis did not much appreciate. One of the spotlight operators did a slow zigzag through the crowd, and Elvis recognized some familiar faces out there. Definitely that candy-stripe waitress he had flirted with down in Hickory Valley. And not far from her was Kevin Cote, all dressed up in tails and a high hat—no doubt rented from the same formal-wear emporium where Captain Rooks did business. From the way he was jumping around, it definitely looked as if Kevin was still working on the "neck thing." Elvis thought he caught a glimpse of Mrs. Agnes Rule too, the boardinghouse lady who made him sing to all of Deer Creek that moonlit night. And over on the edge of the crowd, wasn't that Musky himself, the man who lent him his dung spreader? And up near the front, if it wasn't Miss Amy herself, wearing a neat white blouse and an ankle-length skirt. Man, if she wasn't in full Miss Krieger's uniform. Standing next to her was her daddy, the bone cracker, and next to him a matronly woman—no doubt Mrs. Coulter. It gave Elvis a sting of regret to see that: to save Elvis's and Southern's necks, Miss Amy had crawled back home to do her parents' bidding. Now *that* was an awesome sacrifice indeed.

"Ladies and gentlemen, to open for Elvis tonight," the Colonel said, "I give you the King's very own discovery, the pride of Sheriff Tip Oliphant—the Waynesboro Five Minus Two!"

As the crowd roared, Elvis could not keep from chuckling to himself. Say what you would about the Colonel, but that man could kill more birds with one stone than a duck hunter shooting buckshot. Of course, the biggest laugh was yet to come—when the Waynesboro boys opened their insufferable mouths.

And here they were, trotting out onstage with their Gibsons in hand, wearing identical midnight blue, four-button Edwardian suits and solid ties, completing their Beatles mimicry with fresh Dutch boy haircuts. The thought crossed Elvis's mind that if he really were out scouting for new opening acts, he sure as heck would not pick any Beatle look-alikes, not even if they had voices like angels.

"We'd like to start off with the very first song we ever played for Elvis," their front man, Jarvis Oliphant, said into the microphone. Sheriff and Mrs. Oliphant's pride and joy had clearly piled on several layers of foundation in an effort to cover up his acne, but the spotlights were already baking so hot that the makeup was popping up in miniature volcanos all over Jarvis's forehead and cheeks. It did not enhance his looks.

Such Vicious Minds

The Waynesboro Five Minus Two sang:

> *"Love is like love*
> *Even more like love*
> *Than love is*
> *Ya, ya, ya*
> *Even more like love*
> *Than love is . . ."*

Elvis got back up on his horse, the better to study the audience's reaction. At first, most folks seemed to listen politely, out of respect to himself, Elvis figured; after all, they did believe that he had hand-picked the group for their special consideration. But as the Waynesboro Five Minus Two sang on, Elvis saw a number of faces in the audience scrunch up in grimaces of bewilderment—although Elvis had to admit that those were mostly middle-aged faces. Then again, it probably took some maturity to straightaway recognize gibberish when you heard it. But by the time the boys got around to their first reprise of "Love is like love is like *you!*" Elvis saw groups of young people here and there dancing the Frog or whatever they called it, and seeming to have themselves a pretty good time. Not just a few groups of kids either, but several of them. Half the audience, actually.

It was just about then that a strangely soothing thought descended upon Elvis: *He could ride back up the side of that bluff right now and never look back.* Just disappear the way he had fantasized when he and Mr. Southern were rolling down the Tennessee River. Disappear and start all over again as someone else, which is to say, as his own true self. Why *not* let Timothy Conrad carry on as Elvis Aron Presley? In a way, Timmy would just be doing what Elvis himself had been doing since he had returned from the army—impersonating the man who lived in the public's imagination, but who bore less and less of a resemblance to the man who Elvis called himself.

"Elvis! *Look!*" Southern was aboard his Clydesdale again too and he was pointing into the audience.

It took a minute before the roving spotlight zigzagged over the spot where Southern was pointing, and then it only illuminated the faces there for a fraction of a second. But that was enough for Elvis to make out Priscilla's woebegone face as she stood motionless right in front of the stage. It was enough to make Elvis's heart break in two. *Priscilla*. Did he want to disappear from her too?

Onstage, the Waynesboro boys had just finished their second and final number, "Twist and Shout," an imitation of the Beatles' cover of the Isley Brothers' hit. When you got that far removed from the original, you would think the flattery would get pretty insincere. But that did not stop the crowd from cheering and stomping their feet. God love them, the Waynesboro Five Minus Two were on their way to stardom.

"And now, without further ado—just a couple of 'I do's,' actually—the man of the hour, the blushing groom, *Mr. Elvis Presley!*" the Colonel hollered into the microphone.

The whole audience—young, middle-aged, even a few white-haired folk—broke into thunderous cheers and whistles that bounced around the walls of the quarry, piling echo on top of echo until it sounded like every voice in the entire world was clamoring for Elvis Presley. For a few seconds, Elvis's heart swelled with gladness and pride.

"Let's grab him," Mr. Southern whispered, gesturing toward the pup tent.

Emerging from the tent was Timmy Conrad, resplendent in a gold lamé tuxedo, a ruffled silvery white shirt under it, a big gold five-point star on one lapel, and a gold band on his ring finger. In spite of himself, Elvis could not help but admire Timmy's getup. The kid definitely had sound show business instincts—or had the Colonel picked out that outfit for him?

"No, let him get on with it," Elvis said to Southern.

"Why wait?"

"I need to see this," Elvis said.

It did not seem possible, but the volume of the crowd's roar seemed to double and triple as Timmy stepped up onto the platform and, waving shyly, made his way to the microphone at center stage. That wave, the rolling gait, the tilt of his head, the slow, lopsided smile appearing on his lips—they all belonged to Elvis, and there was not a reason in the world why anyone, front row to the back, would doubt that that was who Timmy was.

"Thank you. Thank you very much," the performer said. "I feel like a new man today. And I guess you know the reason why."

A huge laugh, followed by another long round of applause. Timmy took this opportunity to take his guitar from a stagehand and slip the strap over his shoulder. He strummed a few chords and then went back to the microphone.

"You know, some songs—they take on new meanings as you get a little older. They kinda resonate with the stuff that happens in your life. And one of those songs was a favorite of mine already, but then along came my bride, and suddenly that song was newer than new."

Man, Timmy could even talk that new talk and still sound like Elvis talking. The plain fact was he was an updated version of Elvis—some folks might even say an *improved* version. Could it be that the Colonel knew Timmy was a fake, but he liked it that way? Parker sure had been talking a lot this past year about the danger of Elvis slipping behind the curve.

Timmy broke into a heartrending rendition of "It's Now or Never," one of Elvis's all-time favorites. It had an authentic tune—taken from some Italian opera—and the lyrics spoke the plain and simple truth about love. "It's now or never; my heart won't wait."

A pink Cadillac coupe was circling the edge of the crowd, folks jumping out of its way. It crawled toward the platform as the performer swooped into the heartbreaking finale, "Let your arms invite me, For who knows when we'll meet again this way." The crowd went wild.

"Now this here is a special moment for me," the performer said when the din had died down. "You know, most songs I can sing for all of you out there, and that's the way it should be. But there's this one song that I need to sing to just one single person. That song is 'Love Me Tender.' And that person is—" He paused, looking soulfully out at the crowd. All you could hear were the tree frogs. "That person is my wife, Mrs. Elvis Presley! Come on out here, little darlin'!"

There was a collective sucking-in of air that sounded like an airplane taking off right there in the quarry canyon.

"Here comes the bride," Mr. Southern whispered.

From out of the pup tent, a Bolivar policeman on each side of her, came a vision of feminine loveliness in a white chiffon wedding gown, the kind you see on magazine covers—simple, elegant, and in the way it clung to her voluptuous body, incredibly sexy. In every sense of the word, Elvis knew that body. He knew that shimmy of her hips. And he knew that bouncy red hair too. Elvis got so dizzy that he had to hold on to the saddle's pommel with both hands to keep from toppling off of his horse.

"Dr. van Duesen's other masterpiece," Mr. Southern said. "Miss Jennifer, his daughter."

"Jeez, for a second there I thought it was—"

"You and everybody else," Southern said. "But why would Elvis marry trash when he could have the most beautiful woman in Hollywood?"

Elvis drew in as much air as his lungs could hold, a desperate gasp against unconsciousness. Miss Jennifer van Duesen, the perfect likeness of Miss Ann-Margret, was up on the stage, sashaying toward Timmy with saucy steps that made Elvis break into a cold sweat. In that single moment, Elvis knew that if he did not hop on the next plane to Los Angeles and race to the real Miss Ann-Margret's door with a ring in his hand, he would be making a mistake that he would regret for the rest of his natural life.

Timmy took Miss Jennifer into his arms and kissed her like it was now or never. Some people in the audience looked perplexed; they had seen photographs of Elvis's intended, Miss Carol-Sue, in the newspapers, and wondered what in heck was going on up there. But they let go of that contradiction in a single sigh. If this was Elvis's *true* love, so be it. Anybody who read *Silver Screen* magazine knew about that romance. Yes, indeed, these folks were bearing witness to the happiest of happy endings.

Reflexively, Elvis searched the crowd and found Priscilla's face again. Was it just the light out here, or had her face drained to a ghastly white? Elvis mouthed the words "Forgive me" to her, but of course she could not see him.

Not far from Priscilla, Elvis spied a pair of familiar faces that he had not seen before: those of Dr. and Mrs. van Duesen, the parents of the bride. The missus looked like she was about to burst out of her blouse with excitement, but the best plastic surgeon in all of western Tennessee looked all frozen up with misery. Maybe he was a genius at duplicating people, but it sure looked like he was not pleased to see his daughter paired off with a facsimile, even if she was one herself. *But just one minute*—they both probably thought that was the *real* Elvis up there kissing their daughter. Why not? Everybody else believed that. That would make Jennifer's mother happy, all right. And her father livid.

"Love me tender, Love me sweet, Never let me go." Timmy was down on his knees, singing up to his bride with all of his heart.

The pink Caddy had reached the far edge of the platform and now looped around behind it, coming to a halt no more than twenty yards in front of Elvis and Mr. Southern.

"Holy shit!" Mr. Southern said. "Welcome to the Twilight Zone."

Out of the driver's seat jumped Miss Sarah Whipple—*Elvisetta*—and she was wearing a gold lamé tux too. There must have been a run on them up in Jackson. Her shirt was ruffled too, but it was blue—blue silk, with a smart red ascot tied around her neck. Between the padding in her coat's shoulders and the ascot covering her slender neck, Miss Sarah appeared more genuinely Elvis-sized than Elvis had ever seen her. The fact was that at least from this distance she looked as much like Elvis as Timmy did, except maybe a tiny bit younger and more innocent-looking. If Timmy was the new, improved Elvis, then Miss Sarah was the boyish Elvis at the height of his fifties fame.

Miss Sarah was now opening the passenger door of the Caddy and out stepped Miss Carol-Sue, wearing the strapless, A-line wedding gown with sparkles across the bust that she had described on the radio. She gave Elvisetta a big, wet, openmouthed kiss that sent shivers down Elvis's spine. Then Miss Carol-Sue waved around in every which direction, displaying her quarter-sized diamond ring. But everybody's eyes remained glued to the stage.

Miss Carol-Sue took in the whole scene in a single sweep of her sultry eyes. Then she grabbed Elvisetta by the hand and headed straight for the stage steps. It was not until that moment that Captain Rooks spotted the pair. He immediately charged toward them, one hand automatically reaching for his holster, but of course he was not wearing a holster on his shiny pink tux.

Elvis shot a glance at Mr. Southern. It was telepathy time again. *This needs to play out, right, Terry? This show must go on.* Southern dug his heels into his horse's ribs. In two seconds flat, he was in front of Rooks, cutting him off and blocking his way to the stage. Rooks gaped up at Southern, dumbfounded. The show went on.

Onstage, Timmy abruptly stopped singing. He rose from his knees just as Elvisetta strode up to him. All four of them—the two Elvises and their two brides—froze as they stared at one another. The ten thousand strong who filled the limestone canyon went dead quiet. Gazing out at the crowd, Elvis saw that virtually every pair of eyes was fixed on Carol-Sue. *She* was the bride they had been expecting. *She* was the bride that these local folk had been rooting for in their hearts all along.

Suddenly, Mr. Southern was onstage too, the wire from a hand microphone twisting behind him. Southern thrust the mike into Elvisetta's hands and scurried off the stage.

Elvisetta hesitated for only a fraction of a second, and then began to sing: "Love me tender, Love me sweet, Never let me . . ."

Talk about channeling—it could have been the original *Love Me Tender* movie sound track issuing from Miss Sarah's lips. It was not simply the timbre of her voice or her intonation that was pitch perfect, it was the very breath that propelled it and sailed out along with it like a whispery descant. Anybody who listened could surely tell the difference between Miss Sarah's definitive Elvis voice and Timmy's near miss.

Timothy Conrad, apparently, was not one of those people. He planted his feet wide, brought his own mike to his mouth, and sang: "You have made my life complete, And I love you so . . ."

Elvisetta immediately dropped out, letting Timmy take the lines solo, but when the next verse began, she turned to Carol-Sue, took both her hands in her own, and sang with a soulful voice: "Love me tender, Love me true, All my dreams fulfilled."

At first, Timmy kept singing too, turning to Miss Jennifer with one hand on his heart and pumping up his volume, apparently trying to drown Elvisetta out. But the audience made sounds of disapproval, many stamping their feet on the stone floor of the canyon amphitheater. By golly, in two minutes' time this crowd had gone from a mass of utter confusion to a mass of rabid zealots, hungry for a showdown between these dueling Elvises. They had come out here for entertainment, and by George, they were going to get it, one way or another.

Timothy finally got the message and let Elvisetta take the rest of the verse solo, but then he picked up with the next verse: "Love me tender, Love me long, Take me to your heart . . ." Elvisetta let him own that one.

Mr. Southern was on his horse back alongside Elvis. "Will the real Elvis please stand up?" he said, smirking.

"Not yet," Elvis murmured, his eyes on Miss Carol-Sue.

Heaven only knows what had transpired on the young woman's wedding night to Miss Sarah. It boggled the mind to think that Carol-Sue possessed so much desire to believe she was married to the real Elvis that she could overlook every piece of evidence to the contrary, including the fact that her husband would not make love to her. It reminded Elvis of the Colonel's favorite joke about a man who came home to find his best friend in bed with his wife. The friend in bed looks up at the man and says, "Before you say anything, what are you going to believe—*me* or *your eyes?*"

But maybe Carol-Sue *did* know that Elvisetta was not the real McCoy—or, at least, maybe she half knew. For Carol-Sue Crampton of Decaturville, Tennessee, the choice was most likely between marrying a local boy who worked at the canning factory and spending the remainder of her days in a tin-roofed two-room cabin on Tinker Street next to her daddy's, or marrying a glamorous singer who adored her—a glamorous singer who was somewhat lacking in the sex department and maybe was Elvis Presley or maybe wasn't, but what the hell, *he wasn't another deadbeat Decaturville boy*. Whatever else could be said about Carol-Sue, that girl had a genuine appetite for a larger life than the one she had been born to. And right about now, satisfying that appetite looked like it was worth fighting for.

Carol-Sue was glaring hard at Miss Jennifer, who maybe was Miss Ann-Margret or maybe wasn't, but whoever she was, she was standing in the way of her dream.

"Where'd you get those titties from, girl—Sears and Roebuck?" Miss Carol-Sue hissed.

Elvisetta's microphone picked up Carol-Sue's verbal assault and sent the words careening around the canyon. Half the crowd laughed and the other half gasped. The singing stopped. Miss Jennifer's plump bosom was heaving. Her eyes burned into Miss Carol-Sue's. Jennifer pulled back one arm like she was about to pop Carol-Sue in the kisser, but when she thrust her hand forward, it went straight for the front of Elvisetta's ruffled silk shirt. Jennifer grabbed ahold of that shirt and yanked it open, revealing the wraparound bandage on Miss Elvisetta's chest. It also revealed about an inch of cleavage squeezing out from the top of that bandage.

Only folks in the first couple of rows could have spotted that telltale inch, but the way that crowd communication works, folks out in the last row knew all about it in ten seconds' time. Some folks laughed, some screamed, and here and there red-faced good ol' boys started to stalk toward the stage with vengeance in their eyes. *No sirree, this perverse duplicity will not go unpunished.*

Elvis dug in his heels and raced his horse to the front of the stage. He flung his right leg over the animal's back directly onto the wood platform. In two long steps, he was between Elvisetta and Miss Jennifer. Timmy and Miss Carol-Sue backed away to the rear of the stage. Elvis took the microphone from Elvisetta's hand. Only then did he turn to face the crowd.

"Good evening, folks," he said. "My name is Elvis Presley."

Not a sound. Even the tree frogs seemed stunned into silence. The rednecks stopped in their tracks. Everyone in Bolivar Quarry was staring slack-jawed at Elvis.

But who in God's name did they think they were beholding? A thirty-year-old man in burned and tattered clothes, his face covered with scrapes and soot and trail dust, his filthy hair shooting off every which way to Sunday. A man whose natural sweet voice had accumulated enough gravel in these past few days to pave a highway.

They knew exactly who it was.

And they burst into a deafening cheer. "Sing, Elvis!" someone called from the front row. "Sing for us!" came another. Then another and another, voices echoing the echoes off of the limestone walls.

Elvis held up his open palm, signaling them to quiet down. In a minute, only whispers could be heard.

"Everybody else has his gal up here," Elvis said into the microphone. "So before I sing, I think I'll get mine up here too." He pointed directly out at Miss Priscilla. "Come on up here, darlin'!"

The spotlight swung to Priscilla. The look of joy and surprise and pure love on that little face made Elvis's heart feel surer than it ever had.

" 'Love Me Tender' happens to be *our* song—mine and Miss Priscilla's," Elvis said into the mike. "But you know—it's really *everybody's* song, isn't it, friends?"

A pair of burly young men grasped Priscilla at the waist and hoisted her up onto the stage. She began to walk slowly toward Elvis, a vision of young innocence. Among the whispers, Elvis heard a few sniffles.

"Hey there,'Cilla," Elvis said in a whisper that wailed through the loudspeakers. "It's been a long time, babe."

"Hey, Elvis," Priscilla replied as she took his outstretched hand.

"This one's for you, sweetheart," Elvis said. And then, a cappella, he sang.

"Love me tender . . ."

In the canyon, bliss erupted. Good ol' boys with ironclad hearts wept like mama's boys. And a fair dozen women of various ages had to be braced by their shoulders, lest they fall to the rocky floor in perilous swoons.

"For my darlin' I love you" . . .

"Elvis is dead!" A scream. Elvis turned his head. Charging at him with a drawn knife was the man who would be king, Timothy Conrad. Elvis planted his feet, then raised his right hand, ready to administer a *soto yoko* chop to the boy's outstretched hand. Timmy's face was burning red, his eyes brilliant with rage.

Timmy was only a foot away from Elvis when the bullet pierced Timmy's forehead just above his right eye. The boy took one more step and then dropped at Elvis's feet, his misshapen face running with blood and brains.

Shrieks and howls. Some people running for the exit, but most dropping to the ground and covering their heads. Elvis saw a silvery flash in the zigzagging spotlight.

Elvis's horse was still standing where he had left him. He ran for him, leaped on. The stallion took off at a gallop, charging into the crowd. Screams echoed from every side.

Elvis's horse reared up directly in front of the shooter. The man turned the tip of his rifle toward Elvis's head. Elvis leaped out of his stirrups and over the animal's neck. In midair, he slapped the rifle's barrel to the side, then came crashing down, knees first, onto the shooter's head, smacking it hard against a rock. The man went out cold instantly.

"Daddy?"

Elvis struggled to his feet. Sheriff Tip was already beside him, his service pistol drawn and aimed at the unconscious man.

"Daddy?"

Elvis looked to his right. A teenage girl in a tight-fitting T-shirt and jeans was stumbling toward the man on the ground. She stopped, reached into her jeans pocket, and pulled out a pair of glasses, which she fitted carefully on her face before continuing toward the man she called Daddy. Those glasses were as thick as hubcaps.

"Miss Muffy?" Elvis said, gently.

"Yes?" She looked at Elvis, her magnified eyes full of sorrow. "Who are *you*?"

23

Last Analysis

*J*ust say whatever comes into your head," Dr. Volk said.

"Don't know where to start," Elvis said. It sure felt peculiar to be lying on your back, facing away from the person you were talking to. Seemed kind of rude.

"Well, what are you thinking about right *now*?"

"Miss Sarah."

"Miss Sarah who?"

"Elvisetta. That one who dresses herself up to look like me, except underneath she's all female."

"And how does that make you feel?"

"It's how it makes Miss Carol-Sue Crampton feel that's on my mind. She married Miss Sarah and is staying married to her, even now that she knows she's married to a woman."

"Love is blind, they say," Dr. Volk said.

"Sex too?"

Elvis heard the psychiatrist laugh softly. "Oh, yes, especially sex," she said. "But I must say, Miss Carol-Sue's blindness may have set a new standard for sexual delusion. In any event, love usually trumps sex anyhow. That is the secret to a long marriage."

Elvis was not sure what Dr. Volk meant. Actually, he was not sure if he *wanted* to know what she meant. But one part of it did seem pretty clear: the doctor surely did not believe that love and sex were the same thing.

"What are you thinking about now?" the doctor said.

"Miss—" Elvis hesitated. He did not know just how personal he wanted to get in here. But Volk had promised him that anything he said would never go beyond the walls of her office. "Miss Priscilla."

"Go on."

"I don't know," Elvis said. "This whole business has been kind of hard on her, you know. Even after I explained how little I had to do with everything."

"I imagine she wants you to prove your love to her once and for all," Dr. Volk said. "And for a girl like that, that can only mean one thing—marriage. Sooner rather than later."

"Actually, much sooner," Elvis said.

"And how do you feel about that?"

"I don't know. How do *you* feel about it, Doctor?" Elvis snapped.

"You sound hostile, Elvis."

The doctor certainly had that right. "Well, what did you mean by a girl like that'?" Elvis said.

"Just that she is a normal young American woman," Volk replied.

"Seems you got married young and you're not American," Elvis said.

"We are not here to talk about me."

"I thought I was here to talk about everything on my mind," Elvis said. "And that includes you. And your former husband. And your daughter."

There was a long silence, during which Elvis sat up on the couch and craned his head around to look at Dr. Volk. The doctor had cupped her fine forehead in one slender-fingered hand. She looked lost. Her ex, Cyrus Blantyre, was behind bars in Bolivar now, awaiting his trial for aiding and abetting the murder of Manard Frew, plus aiding and abetting the late Timothy Conrad's statutory rapes. But Elvis had no idea what had become of her daughter, Kathy, the plaster caster.

"It's so classic, it's banal," Dr. Volk said, finally. "I married

Cyrus because he was a duplicate of my father. Cold, obsessed, and, of course, deeply repressed."

"Doesn't sound real romantic," Elvis said, back down on the couch again.

"The peculiar thing is that it felt that way at the time," the doctor said. "Romantic, I mean. There is an American lady poet who wrote, 'Every woman loves a fascist.' Soon afterward, that poet committed suicide. I just got divorced."

"He sure had it in for me, didn't he? Took me awful personal for someone who never met me," Elvis said.

"The first time I ever heard your name was from Cyrus," Dr. Volk said. "You are everything he hates. A dirt-poor Tennessee nothing who became richer and more powerful than any Blantyre ever was or could be. You were the *new* southern gentleman, and Cyrus could never forgive you for that. Especially because you got to where you are by singing black people's music. That made him sick to his stomach."

"It bothers some black folks too, but for a different reason," Elvis said. "But what about your daughter?"

"I am very proud of Kathy."

"Really?"

"She is her own person," Dr. Volk said. "That is quite an achievement for a young woman today."

"Her hobby doesn't bother you?"

"It's an art form," Dr. Volk said.

"That's not the way some folks would describe it."

"Some folks, as you say, do not describe rock and roll as authentic music," Volk said.

"Sometimes I think they're right," Elvis said.

"You have a generous mind, Elvis."

"I don't feel a hundred percent about marrying Miss Priscilla," Elvis suddenly blurted out. He had not planned to say that.

"That must make it difficult for you," Dr. Volk said. For the first time, her voice sounded genuinely sympathetic.

"It does indeed, ma'am."

"I can just tell you one thing, Elvis," the doctor said. "Far too many people get married out of guilt. It does not make for happiness."

Elvis closed his eyes. For a moment that seemed to last an eternity, he was again sailing down the Tennessee River beside Mr. Southern. Just rolling past the countryside going nowhere in particular.

"It's peculiar, Doctor," Elvis said at last, "but when Timmy got shot, it felt like something inside me died too. I guess it was that inner fella that I told you about in the hospital. The one with the messy impulses."

"Do you miss him?"

"More than I ever thought I would," Elvis said. Elvis had no idea where that had come from, but by God, it surely felt good to admit it to himself. In some way that he would never fully understand, it made him feel free.

For what must have been a good two or three minutes, neither the doctor nor her patient spoke. Then Dr. Volk said, "I don't think there is anything more I can do for you, Elvis."

"Yes, ma'am. I understand."

At the office door, Elvis hugged the doctor. "Thank you," he said.

Elvis had taken a couple of steps when Dr. Volk called to him. "If you don't mind my asking, I'm curious about that colorful friend of yours. Are you two still working on that film script together?"

"Mr. Southern? No, he had to leave in a hurry. He got himself a job working on a movie for Mr. Fonda. Peter, not Henry. Mr. Southern just couldn't turn it down. It's a road movie."